THE FIRE TREE
Book 2
THE GIRL WITH GOLDEN EYES

by **Ken Kirk**

Dedicated to the memory of Pamela Lang,
Cydara Verrier, Margaret Beatrice Kirk & Cecilia Reynolds.

CHAPTER 1

"You're a curious little girl, Wild Flower, and there is no doubt about it," laughed The Laird Grant, grinning from ear to ear.

The little girl smiled a shy smile and flapped her hand in front of her face, as if the breeze from it might help to cool her blushing.

"I am me, Your Lairdship," she replied, "With all of my flaws and all of my failings."

"If you have flaws or failings, they must be well hidden, for I am yet to encounter any of them," he laughed, "Your amiable disposition and your good humour have made this house a happier place since you have been here."

Wild Flower gave him one of her elegant curtsies.

"I thank you, Sir, for your kind words."

Wild Flower mused over her new name and gave a little smile. She had begun to like it. It had only been her name for a short while. It had been given to her only a week ago by The Laird Grant. Her name, from birth, had been Greesha, but – by all normal calendars – a total of 829 years had elapsed since then.

Last week, in the year 793, she had set out to stroll across a nearby meadow. By the time she had reached the other side of it, the year had somehow become 1622. This strange event was something she had simply accepted, for she had become all too familiar with bizarre happenings!

Her experience with strange events had started with her having incredibly vivid dreams. The dreams were so much like the feeling of being awake that they seemed to be just like reality. Slowly, she had realised that those vivid dreams actually *were* reality. To her shock and horror, the things that happened in those dreams turned out to happen in real life.

"Your past, as you have revealed it," The Laird Grant declared, frowning and looking troubled, "Has not been free from hardship. This makes me sad. I promise you that, during your service here as my granddaughter's companion, I will try to make your life as enjoyable as possible."

"I am grateful."

There was a silence as The Laird Grant appeared to formulate his next words.

"This house has been no stranger to sadness," he confided.

Wild Flower closed her eyes for a moment and the history of the building flooded into her mind.

"You're doing it again!" her employer laughed, "You are closing your eyes and concentrating for a second or two. It is what you often do just before you say something extraordinary!"

Wild Flower pulled a silly face and they both laughed.

"I don't even realise that I'm doing it," she confessed.

"Well, whatever astonishing inspiration you may draw upon or whatever shockingly accurate insight it may deliver, I can promise you that nobody, here, will try to burn you as a witch."

Although she didn't feel the least bit upset, her face – without her wishing it – adopted a harrowed expression. She promptly accompanied it with a weak and dismal smile.

"I'm sorry! I'm sorry!" exclaimed The Laird, "That was a callous and thoughtless thing for me to say! I apologise!"

"You apologise?" she asked.

"Yes. I do. I *can* apologise. I know how to do it," he declared, "Though it is not something I have been particularly famous for doing."

Wild Flower's sad smile now vanished as her intelligent grey-blue eyes lit up with glee.

"You are reformed!" she quipped.

"You are a good influence on me."

"You are too kind."

"No, it is the truth. I now find it a chore to be…"

"Sour and gloomy?" she suggested, brightly.

"Yes, sour and gloomy!" The Laird guffawed.

A young girl with long, dark hair – who had just peered cautiously around the door – now appeared from behind it and dropped into a perfect curtsey.

"Your Lairdship," said the new arrival.

The Laird Grant scoffed.

"Logan," he berated, amiably, "You do not have to use my title. You are my granddaughter."

"But when you are with company..." she offered, inclining her head towards Wild Flower.

"She is not company, sweetheart," her grandfather replied, "She is..."

Logan raised her eyebrows enquiringly as The Laird searched for the word he wanted.

"She," he decided, with a grin, "Is family."

Logan's eyebrows rose even further. Wild Flower, for her part, blushed crimson and looked embarrassed.

"Whatever you say, grandfather," Logan assured him.

As The Laird Grant rose from his chair to crane his neck in the direction of the window, Logan took the opportunity to cast Wild Flower a withering look.

"There is a messenger arriving," The Laird announced, "I want to see what news they bring."

The Laird immediately hurried past them both and through the doorway.

Logan adopted a belligerent stance – arms folded across her chest and chin stuck out – as she surveyed Wild Flower with a look that flickered between haughty distaste and feigned disinterest. Wild Flower returned her gaze impassively, excluding any hint of a reaction. Then, after casting her eyes idly around The Laird Grant's apartment for a long moment, Wild Flower suddenly addressed her.

"Your grandfather adores you."

Logan jolted, having been taken off-guard. She quickly recovering herself and threw back a barbed reply.

"And *you* would know?"

"It is clear to anybody. He makes no attempt to hide it."

Logan seemed to be riled by this observation.

"His favourite is no longer me," she snapped.

Wild Flower looked puzzled, for she was genuinely at a loss to understand her meaning.

"Then who?"

"Who?" Logan sneered, "His favourite is stood in front of me, right now!"

"Me?" asked Wild Flower, her face a picture of astonishment.

Logan contorted her face and produced a whiney voice from the roof of her mouth.

"Me? Surely not. How could that be?" she mocked.

Wild Flower abruptly sat down on the floor. Logan looked at her blankly.

"What are you doing?" she demanded.

"I'm sitting on the floor."

"I can see that!"

"Then why ask me what I am doing?"

"Because," Logan scoffed, haughtily, "I wanted to know *why* you are sitting on the floor."

"Then you should have asked me why I was doing it, instead of what I was doing."

Logan pursed her lips in annoyance and glared at Wild Flower.

"When I asked you," she growled, "I expected you to understand my meaning."

"But, instead?"

"But instead you are being stupid!"

"Yes, I am. I am being stupid."

Logan blinked in surprise, "You admit it?"

"Yes. I am being stupid and I admit it."

Logan gave a weary groan, but said no more. Several long seconds dragged by before Wild Flower broke the uncomfortable silence.

"Logan, I know when I am being stupid, but it doesn't always prevent me from acting that way. I knew it was a stupid thing to do when I sat on the floor. It hasn't stopped being a stupid thing to do, but I am still doing it. Clearly, knowing I'm being stupid has had no effect on my behaviour."

Logan raised her head to look straight forward and gazed sternly across the room, into the distance, completely ignoring Wild Flower on the floor and pretending that she wasn't there. Wild Flower sat quietly and made no noise. Logan continued to stand as still as a statue, defiantly aloof and unconcerned.

"Imagine, Logan, here I am, at my age, acting stupidly and being fully aware of it," said Wild Flower, at last, "And there are you, at your age, at least four years my senior, acting stupidly and being blissfully unaware of it."

Logan, outraged by the jibe, whirled to face Wild Flower and immediately burst out laughing. Wild Flower was sat with a thumb in either ear, waggling her hands either side of her head, her palms splayed like a pair of huge ears sticking out on stalks. Once Logan's amusement had faded, she became stern again.

"It was my grandfather who invited you here. It was most certainly not me."

"If you want me to disappear," offered Wild Flower, sweetly, "Then I can disappear."

"That would make me happy, but I am not sure that it would please my grandfather."

"I don't think it's fair that you should be forced to have me around, so I can disappear anytime you wish."

"You mean go and hide?"

"No, I mean disappear."

"You don't mean disappear."

"Yes I do."

"What?" Logan asked, screwing up her face, "Nobody can disappear."

"I can."

"No you can't!"

"Yes, I can."

"No you can't!" she snapped.

"Yes, honestly, I can," Wild Flower insisted.

Logan made a face as if she were enduring a particularly nasty taste in her mouth.

"That's impossible," she declared.

"It should be impossible."

"It *is* impossible."

Logan placed the palm of her hand on the top of her own head, as if it might aid her in the process of thinking, and looked mystified.

"You mean," she challenged, "You can vanish?"

"Yes."

"No," Logan assured her, "You cannot."

"I most definitely can."

"You most definitely cannot."

They were interrupted by a soft knock on the door.

"That will be cakes and scones," Logan advised, "To stop our stomachs rumbling before the midday meal."

With this she raised her voice to address the servant at the door, "Come in," she called.

The door opened but instead of one of the servants, it was the housekeeper, Mrs McConnell. She entered by pushing the door open with the large tray she was carrying. On her way across to the table, she paused and looked at Logan quizzically. Logan returned the look.

"Who were you talking to?" asked Mrs McConnell.

Logan turned her head to nod in the direction of Wild Flower and was surprised to find that she was not there. She looked back to Mrs McConnell and then back to the empty space where Wild Flower had been sitting. Her face was blank.

"I'm sure I don't know," Logan replied, bewildered.

Mrs McConnell looked at her with only vaguely disguised unease. Logan's eyes flicked back and forth between the housekeeper and the vacant space on the floor, as her mouth –

a little way ahead of her mind – silently experimented with a few alternative explanations. She settled for one at random.

"If I were to explain it to you, Mrs McConnell, it would sound very strange, but let me say that I am playing an unusual kind of game…"

"Oh! A game? I see," said Mrs McConnell, sounding very much reassured.

The housekeeper placed the tray down and unloaded its contents onto the table. Then, she departed with the tray. As she reached the door, she turned to speak.

"There is enough, of course, for both the master and your friend."

"My friend?" Logan snapped.

Picking up on the thinly disguised contempt, Mrs McConnell rephrased herself.

"There is enough for the master, for you and for your…" She began, pausing as the right level of tact evaded her, "For the other young lady."

Logan blew out a puff of air to show disinterest. Mrs McConnell gave an awkward smile and left.

CHAPTER 2

Logan forced an extended sigh from her nose that took a long time to finish. Wild Flower adopted her most innocent expression and stood patiently.

"So," said Logan, "You are no longer sitting on the floor?"

"No. I am standing."

Logan took a step forward, slapping her foot hard on the ground and widening her eyes, threateningly. There was no mistaking that she did not want to return to their earlier verbal sparring.

"I'm in the same place, though," said Wild Flower, helpfully.

"You disappeared."

It was clearly an accusation. Wild Flower tilted her head, mimicking a pause for contemplation before replying.

"I thought we agreed that that was impossible?"

Logan hooted with laughter. Wild Flower laughed, too. Just as it had before, the tension returned within a few seconds and they were enemies, again. Wild Flower closed her eyes and thought for a moment.

"I'm sorry about your mother," she said, softly.

Logan, who had just sat down at the table, sprang to her feet.

"My mother!" Logan began.

Wild Flower knew that a vicious torrent of anger was about to gush from Logan's mouth.

"Your mother," Wild Flower declared, interrupting her companion on whom she had been forced, "Was, in all respects, the most wonderful, the most gentle, the most kind and loving person that could ever be imagined."

Logan's mouth froze open, unable to persuade any further words from it.

"Your mother's passing, Logan, was such a blow to your father that he rushed off to war in order to deliberately place himself in danger. He fought at the front line, even when he did not need to do so, in order to maximise his risk of death. When he was killed, he was grateful to die. He genuinely did not want to live without her."

Tears rolled down Logan's cheeks.

"They told me that he had received papers," she objected, "They said that he had been called up to serve."

"No, he volunteered."

"You say this truly?"

"I say it truly."

"How do you know these things?"

"How? I don't know," admitted Wild Flower, holding her head in her hands, "But my life was simpler and less troubled when I knew nothing more than anyone else."

Logan paused for a long while.

"You do know that I still hate you, don't you?" she asked.

Wild Flower looked at her passively.

"You don't hate me," she said.

"Yes, I do."

"You would *like* to hate me."

"I *do* hate you."

"You set your heart on hating me."

"And hating you is what I am doing."

"If hating me could make you feel better, then I would want you to hate me more than anybody in the world has ever been hated."

"I can assure you..." began Logan, before faltering, then stopping, as she saw the expression on Wild Flower's face.

"Logan, if your life were in danger and the only way I could save it were to give up my own, then I would not hesitate to do it."

Logan gasped and clasped a hand to her mouth to stifle a sob.

"I would be proud to die for you, Logan. I would feel honoured and privileged, because when you grow to be a woman, you will be exactly like your mother. I promise you:

Your mother will never be dead so long as there is one single breath left in your body."

Logan pressed her hand harder still over her mouth, but it did not hold back more tears.

"Everybody who loves me ends up leaving me," she protested.

"I will never leave you."

"You will."

"I will not. I guarantee it."

"You *can't* guarantee it!" Logan said in a choked whisper.

"Strangely enough," laughed Wild Flower, "I actually can!"

Logan made a strangled sound that came out as half laughing and half crying. Wild Flower approached her slowly, not wanting to provoke her physical resistance. With only one step separating them, Logan's resolve melted and she slumped into Wild Flower's open arms.

"You won't die on me, will you?" she demanded.

"Never!"

"You're sure?"

Wild Flower closed her eyes for a moment, "I'm sure," she confirmed, "And, make no mistake, I *can* be sure."

Logan took Wild Flower by the shoulders and repositioned her so that they were face to face. There, she looked at Wild Flower long and hard. It seemed like she was trying to come to some sort of decision.

Wild Flower looked back at her, but – in actual fact – she was looking into her. Wild Flower could tell that, despite her play-acting, Logan was absolutely not a bad person and was certainly not the hateful one she was trying to portray. As for Logan's pretence at being jealous of the affection that The Laird Grant had shown for Wild Flower, that was – for the most part – a sham, too. Logan had actually resolved to feel nothing what-so-ever for the new arrival.

"Logan," said Wild Flower, in her most grown up voice, "If I ever have to go away, I promise you upon soul, that I will come back for you."

"You will?"

"I will."

"You won't forget?"

"I won't forget."

There followed a comfortable silence, broken only when a spark of curiosity prompted Logan to ask a question.

"Wild Flower? That isn't your proper name, is it?"

Wild Flower made herself jolt and put on a horrified look.

"Logan! You have powers, too?"

Her new friend roared with laughter. Just then, there were loud footsteps in the hall. A moment later, the door sprang open and The Laird Grant entered, looking worried.

"What is it?" asked Logan.

The Laird looked to Wild Flower.

"Tell me the answer," he asked her.

Wild Flower closed her eyes and spoke without opening them.

"One of the local Clans has called together its flag bearers."

Logan looked puzzled, "Flag bearers?"

"Yes," replied her grandfather, "They are people in each Clan who, when required, are in charge of gathering an army from the local men of fighting age."

"There's going to be a war?" Logan asked.

"Perhaps a battle rather than a war, I hope, but they might be making plans for some kind of conflict," he soothed, "Their Laird may, instead, be trying to prevent a war by taking steps to appear strong and prepared."

"A battle with whom?"

The Laird Grant looked to Wild Flower, who shrugged her shoulders and gave an apologetic frown.

"Seeing the future," Wild Flower explained, "Is like having a metal bucket on my head with twenty or thirty holes in it. Sometimes the holes don't line up with anything. Sometimes I can see only a little through a hole and, sometimes, I can see most or everything through it."

"And on this occasion?" asked The Laird Grant.

Wild Flower gave a weak smile, "I can see only what I have told you."

"My scouts," The Laird confessed, "Have little more information for me than that!"

Wild Flower held up her hand and knotted her brow. The Laird looked anxious.

"This," she cautioned, "Is not about what the scouts have seen, but it is somehow connected to it."

The Laird and his granddaughter looked to her, eagerly.

"I can see a woman with hair that is like the morning sun," she revealed, "She is wearing a crown and she is riding a white horse."

"That is the Queen of the West," The Laird grumbled, "She is no friend of mine."

Wild Flower deliberately kept her face totally blank and free of any emotion. This did not escape Logan's notice and it prompted a curious look from her. The Laird Grant, however, was distracted and had begun pacing up and down in front of the fireplace.

Logan mouthed the words *Not a good sign'* to Wild Flower and flicked her eyes to secretively indicate her grandfather. Wild Flower read both the words on her lips and heard them spoken in her head.

"Girls," The Laird called over his shoulder, striding to the door, "I need to speak to some people urgently."

CHAPTER 3

Logan and Wild Flower stood side by side in the vast library, gazing out through the window.

"In a moment," said Logan in a hushed tone, her nose almost touching the glass of the window, "You will see it."

Wild Flower instantly knew what she meant, but didn't say anything. It would be best, she decided, not to scare her friend with any indication of the depth of her insight into certain things. Logan's ability to casually accept her vanishing into the air, like a spark from a fire, had impressed her, but she didn't want to risk testing the full extent of her ability to embrace strange happenings.

"Not long now," whispered Logan.

Wild Flower allowed her eyes to wander over the scene before them. Across the garden, at the foot of a short slope, were scattered trees of varying sizes. Down the middle of them ran a narrow path. This scene was in complete contrast to the front of the stronghouse, where the formal lawns, broad drive and carefully curved paths followed courses that were meticulously precise and exact. Wild Flower imagined teams of gardeners and stonemasons clambering around on planks of wood, pegging out lengths of twine and laying down lines of perfect symmetry with bags of powdered chalk.

"There!" said Logan urgently, her eyes widening.

Wild Flower watched as a dark, hooded figure emerged from the shadows and hurried along the path. They wore black from head to foot. Over their shoulder was slung what looked to be a large canvas satchel. They exuded an air of determination. They had the manner of somebody going about an important task.

Logan leaned closer, "It's a woman," she whispered.

Wild Flower nodded. It was clear from the person's gait that they were female.

"Watch," Logan directed, "As they reach the sundial."

The person they were watching seemed not to have seen the sun dial in their way and they were not slowing their pace.

Wild Flower cringed as she waited for them to painfully collide with the object. Instead, to her surprise, they passed straight through it as if it were not there.

"A ghost!" said Logan, triumphantly.

"Yes, it has to be," Wild Flower agreed.

The dark figure continued along the path, passing effortlessly through a hedge where no gap existed, and escaped from view.

"Now that she has appeared once," Logan noted, "She will usually appear again, presently. If we go upstairs to the uppermost rooms, you will see something that will shock you."

Wild Flower held back from connecting with her inner self, again, instead allowing only her normal senses to prevail. She did not want to steal any of the mystery from what Logan was showing her and confiding in her.

"You had best lead the way, then," Wild Flower urged, "For I would most definitely like to see more!"

Logan looked pleased and, reaching for the lantern that she had set aside on the floor, she slid open the vertical slot in its sleeve so that there was enough light for them to make their way back to the door. Treading quietly and with exaggeratedly careful steps, they made their way along the hall to the grand stairs. There, they climbed three floors to the spacious attics.

The fortifications at the rear of the property were less intrusive than those at the front and sides. This stronghouse, Wild Flower knew, had resisted countless assaults over the centuries, but few of them had ever been made through the tangle of gnarled trees, vicious thorn bushes and dense brambles that bordered the garden, in the spacious grounds that lay beyond them.

"The servants' quarters are up here, on this floor, but we'll be fine if we go into the old blue room," advised her guide, pointing down the hall, "Nobody wants to sleep in there."

"Why not?" enquired Wild Flower, instantly regretting the question, "Please don't answer," she urged, holding up a hand to ward off a reply.

Logan gave her a grim smile that was almost a smirk.

"I thought you might be able to tell."

"I'm trying my best to hold back anything like that," Wild Flower replied, making a face.

"You can stop yourself?"

"No, not stop exactly. It's like winding down the wick of a lamp so that the flame goes really low. I can leave just a glimmer, but I can't make it go away completely."

Logan nodded, slowly. She was clearly fascinated.

"If I put the lamp out," Wild Flower explained, "I might put us in danger, but – to say it truly – I think there is something up here that I am not meant to know about."

"What do you think it might be?"

Wild Flower adopted the expression of a witless fool and Logan only just managed to stop herself from laughing.

"Logan, if I think about it, it would be no use me trying not to think about it."

Her guide pulled her neck in and hunched her shoulders up to her ears to signify embarrassment. Taking pity on her, Wild Flower grasped her elbow and propelled her forward, avoiding her gaze.

As they crept down the corridor, Logan halted outside a particular room and reached to place her hand on the large, ornate doorknob. Wild Flower promptly felt a wave of apprehension, but vigorously pushed it deep down inside her.

Logan slowly pushed open the door, then – closing it behind them – pressed down a lever on the base of the lantern. This caused the shutters on all sides to rise. She turned a knurled wheel, raising the wick, and the room flooded with light.

Wild Flower, with her eyes wide open in amazement, watched as Logan walked straight through the corpses of the two girls who hung by ropes around their necks that were tied to the rafters above them. Wild Flower clenched her teeth and attempted to do the same but – just as Logan turned around to look at her – she stepped aside and dodged around them. Logan halted and gave her peculiar look.

"Why did you do that?" she asked, entirely unaware of the two dead girls.

"I don't know," replied Wild Flower, giving her a weak smile and shaking her head.

Logan was unconvinced and stood gazing in the direction of the dead pair for a few moments, without apparently seeing them. Soon, she shrugged and continued to walk to the window.

Wild Flower looked with undisguised concern at the lantern in Logan's hand and at the bright pool of light it was casting across the inside of the window.

"Don't worry," Logan grinned, "The guards won't say a word if they see the light. They think this room is haunted. Two girls hung themselves here, once, or so it is said."

Wild Flower couldn't stop herself from glancing across at the two girls in question. Following the direction of her eyes, Logan gave a tiny shriek as a sudden wave of cold air hit her. To the relief of them both, most of the noise was muffled by Logan's hand, which had flown to her own mouth.

"You can see them, can't you?" Logan accused.

"Are you *unable* to see them?"

"Yes, I'm glad to say, but I get a terrible feeling when I look."

"I wish that I couldn't see them! They did not enjoy a swift end. They died slowly. Their faces are bloated, they have bulging eyes and their faces are turning purple."

Logan shuddered and looked traumatised.

"Can you make them go away?" she asked.

"I thought you couldn't see them?"

"I can't... but, even still... the idea of them... can you make them leave?"

"I don't know," said Wild Flower, the idea never having occurred to her.

She held out her hand and waved it, vaguely, from side to side as if tentatively trying to polish a pane of glass. The two cadavers obligingly dissolved into nothing."

"They have gone," she declared.

"Are you sure?"

Wild Flower looked back to check, "Yes, truly, they have gone."

Wild Flower suppressed a wry smile. She found it amusing. Logan couldn't see either of the two dead girls, irrespective of who else could see them. Despite this, now that *nobody* could see them, she still sought reassurance that what she couldn't see could not be seen at all.

Wild Flower's train of thought came to an abrupt stop.

'Why could Logan see the ghost in the garden,' she asked herself, *'But she couldn't see the ghosts inside?'*

Her quandary must have shown on her face, she decided, because Logan became curious.

"Is there something wrong?" The Laird's granddaughter asked.

"My mind is just scampering around in my head. I cannot grasp my thoughts, sometimes."

"They *are* gone, aren't they?" Logan enquired, her voice full of concern.

"Yes. They are gone, there is no doubt about it, but..."

"But what?"

"But why could you not see them?"

Logan pursed her lips, evidently not amused.

"Perhaps the better question would be why it is that I am able to see the woman in the gardens?" she suggested, before adding: "If we don't hurry we are going to miss her."

As Logan obligingly closed the shutters on her lamp, Wild Flower hurried to join her at the window. There, they stood in comradely silence as they waited to see what would happen.

They had been waiting for scarcely three minutes before the lady clad all in black appeared, again. From their new vantage point, they could see further across the gardens towards the far wall, and they saw her walk to a horse and mount it.

"Is the horse a ghost, too?" asked Logan in a breathless whisper.

"It is an echo of the past, I think, a kind of visible trace of something that once happened. I can't really explain it. I just get the idea that it is something like that."

They watched as the lady in black urged her horse forward and steered it towards the gate.

"She will get most of the way to the gate," Logan revealed, "Then she will fade away and disappear."

The two watched as the rider made their way down the long garden, staying mainly under the trees for cover. It was clear that she did not want to be seen.

"Wait! Stop!" exclaimed Logan, excitedly, "Every time I see her, she has always vanished before this point."

Suddenly, the rider's body spasmed and her arms, holding the reins, jerked stiffly before she fell forward onto the horse's neck and, then, rolled to the ground. She lay face down in a crumpled heap, an axe buried in the back of her neck.

CHAPTER 4

Slowly, like rain sinking into the soil, the ghostly body of the slain rider, and the weapon that had despatched it, diminished into nothingness.

Logan and Wild Flower exchanged horrified looks.

"I have never seen her reach further than half way to the gate before," Logan confided, "And nothing has ever happened to her like that!"

Wild Flower nodded, thoughtfully, as she struggled to hold back the inspiration that was trying to flood into her mind. In the end, she gave in to it.

"She is the Lady Elise Grant," said Wild Flower in hushed tones, "She is your grandfather's grandmother."

"She has been murdered!"

"A long time ago."

"Yes, but it is still a murder."

"We must speak nothing of this, Logan."

"What?!" she exclaimed, "You cannot be serious!"

Wild Flower donned her most sombre expression, "This is not the time."

"Not the time?!"

"This must remain a secret."

"Wild Flower, I *must* tell my grandfather."

"No. You mustn't tell him. You mustn't."

"I *have* to tell him."

"This isn't what it seems to be."

"A woman has just been slain by an axe!" beseeched Logan, "How can it *not* be what it seems?"

"This isn't what it seems to be," Wild Flower repeated, "What we saw is only part of what happened."

Logan threw up her hands in exasperation.

"So what happened?" she asked.

"I don't know."

"Then how can you…" Logan began, before her voice trailed away to nothing.

"I just know," Wild Flower assured her.

"Yes, I realised."

"Thank you for showing me this, Logan."

"If I hadn't shown somebody, I would have burst!"

"Oh!" said Wild Flower, pretending to be offended, "So, I just happened to be around?"

"No! You *deserved* to see it. You were *worthy* of seeing it."

Wild Flower's grin told her that she was being teased and she burst out laughing before clapping a hand to her mouth and opening her eyes wide in panic. Shaking her head with mock sadness, Wild Flower reached and took away her hand.

"I think we have very likely already woken the servants in the rooms to either side of us," Wild Flower whispered, "They are probably frightened witless and hiding under their covers with a pillow clasped over their head."

Logan gave her a mischievous look.

"Maybe we should start moaning and groaning," she suggested, "And, perhaps, do a little bit of screeching?"

"I think they have already suffered enough!"

Logan's smile made it clear that she had been joking. As they crept out of the door, closing it behind them with great care, Logan whispered in Wild Flower's ear.

"I thank everything holy that I cannot see anything of the things that are said to have gone on in parts of this building."

"But outside?"

"Yes, I see things outside."

"Bad things?"

"Sometimes bad."

"And the other things?"

"Mostly strange… unusual… puzzling things."

"I'm sure there must be a reason for it, Logan."

"Do things *have* to have a reason?"

"I would like to think so."

They walked in silence to the top of the stairs and in silence all the way to the bottom. Then Logan asked something that seemed to have been on her mind for a while.

"My grandfather has never said anything much about how the two of you came across each other. In fact, he has avoided the subject whenever it has arisen."

"It is a complicated story to tell."

Logan snorted at this, "You sound just like him!"

Wild Flower threw up her hands in mock consternation, but then gave a wink as she started to explain.

"Your grandfather was stood in the meadow beyond the gnarled blackthorn trees. It was almost as if he had been waiting for something."

"He had definitely been waiting for something."

"Really?"

"Yes. It's his favourite place," Logan advised, "Did he have a basket with food in it?"

"Yes."

"Sweet foods? Like cakes and scones?"

"Yes."

"May I confide in you?"

"Of course."

"My grandfather is convinced that he has a destiny. He believes that the future has something remarkable set aside for him. He has it set in his mind that he will bring such glory to our Clan that it will extinguish our shame."

Wild Flower thought about it for a moment, "He will. He is right."

"You know this? You know it for certain?" Logan begged.

"I do. It is the truth."

"What it will be? Can you tell?"

"No. I am not intended to know, therefore I cannot know."

Logan gave a forlorn sigh. The sadness in it tugged at Wild Flower's heart so much that, before she knew what she was doing, she found herself apologising.

"I'm sorry, but there's nothing I can do. Some things are just not meant for me to know."

"But he will have his glory?"

"Oh yes!" Wild Flower enthused, "Oh yes! They will sing songs about it."

"They will? Oh please say that this is true!" Logan beseeched, on the verge of tears.

"You have my word."

Logan was so happy that it seemed for all the world as if, at any moment, she might take off and hover in the air like a humming bird. Wild Flower spontaneously started to clap her hands for joy, then halted with her hands frozen in the air.

"I think the servants have been woken up enough times, already," she whispered.

All the way back to her room, Logan seemed to be in the highest possible spirits. It was as if a weight had been lifted from her shoulders. It was a weight that was not rightfully her own, but it was one that she had stubbornly borne, none-the-less.

Logan insisted that Wild Flower join her in her personal study for supper. Once inside, she went across to the fireplace where she opened a small door set into the wall beside it. There, inside, was a tiny shaft with a bell the size of an adult fist suspended in it. Taking hold of the rope attached to its clapper, she rang the bell with two sharp jerks. Wild Flower heard an answering two rings from somewhere far below. Seeing Wild Flower's expression of curiosity, Logan smiled.

"The bell," she explained, "Is set in its own little chimney that runs from the basement to the top floor. There are two marks on the rim of this bell, so I ring it twice when I want to call a servant, so they know where to come."

Wild Flower gave her a half-hearted smile.

Logan furrowed her brows, "You have rung a bell of some kind, before, to summon a servant, have you not?"

"I have never had any servants. I grew up in just one single room. It was home to my mother, my father, my sister and my four brothers. It was divided off at night by a curtain that gave my parents privacy as they slept."

Logan fought to control her face, but lost. She looked appalled. She was having trouble absorbing this information. The idea of it seemed utterly dreadful to her.

"Oh. I see," she said, blankly.

There was a gentle knock on the door and a servant entered. The two girls placed their orders for their meal and the servant departed.

Logan bowed her head, "I have lived a life of privilege."

"If that is the only life you have known, then you cannot be blamed. You would have never imagined that a life such as mine existed, any more than I would have ever imagined yours."

Logan nodded miserably. She could have been forgiven by the whole world, but she would still hold herself to be at fault.

Suddenly she perked up, "The Queen of the West!", she chirped.

Wild Flower looked baffled.

"She dresses plainly," Logan enthused, "Shunning any kind of finery and wearing only a copper crown, bracelets of plain metal and wooden beads."

"Yes, she does."

"She seldom eats her fill and, any time she does, she orders her servants to send extra food to the poor in the local neighbourhood."

"She feels for the poor."

"I want to feel for the poor!" Logan announced.

"And how will you do that?"

"You will help me!"

Wild Flower smiled at her enthusiasm.

CHAPTER 5

Logan cleared away their things from their meal, neatly arranging the plates, bowls, cutlery and napkins onto a tray. She wiped clean the little table and placed the tray in the hall outside her door.

Wildflower placed a hand on her friend's arm, "Something tells me that you didn't have to do that."

"No, I didn't, but I always do."

"Why?"

"Why? Because the servants have enough to do, already."

"Why do *you* care how hard they work?"

"Because I *do*."

Wild Flower laughed, "You would have broken into pieces, Logan, after a few days of pretending to be a girl who was bad, mean, nasty and aloof."

"I was doing well enough at it, though, wasn't I?"

"Only a little well. The real you kept intruding."

"Did it?"

"Yes."

"How?"

"Well, for one thing, you kept laughing at things that were funny."

"Oh. Yes. I did, didn't I?"

"That's not how a bad girl behaves."

"Maybe I just needed more experience!"

"Tell me, Logan, if you were to ride with a highwayman for a month or two, robbing travellers at the end of a pistol, would you be happy to do that, too, after you had gathered enough experience?"

Logan gave a wicked grin, "I could certainly try!"

They both laughed. They laughed so much that they ended up laughing at each other laughing, rather than laughing at the thing that had set them off!

Wild Flower stood rock still for a moment and closed her eyes, seeming to relish some sort of sensation.

Her friend could not contain her curiosity, "What is it?"

"It's a sudden wave of... joy... happiness... love," said Wild Flower, her eyes looking up to the ceiling, "Your mother is so very, *very* proud of you."

"No! No!" said Logan, holding up the flat palm of her hand, "I protest. Not now. Not yet. Let her be as proud as that later, when I have lived a kind and charitable life."

"She cannot wait and nor can I!"

"You shall have to. Both of you."

Wild Flower lofted her hands to show her frustration and made a funny groaning sound. Logan would have none of it and spun on her heels, showing her friend her back.

"Wait I say and wait you must!" she proclaimed, "I am going to be a far better person, yet."

Wild Flower smirked, *'You have no idea just how much!',* she thought to herself.

There was a tap at the door.

"Yes?" called Logan.

"A message for you Ma'am," said a little boy's voice.

"The hour is late!"

"I am sorry Ma'am, but it is urgent."

"What can be this urgent?"

"It is your grandfather, Ma'am, he has been taken ill."

Logan made it to the door in two strides and had it flung open in a second. She ran into the corridor.

"Which way?" she demanded of the page boy.

"This way, he is in his study," he replied sprinting off.

Logan, employing her long legs to the task, had overtaken him within a few strides. At the end of the corridor she deliberately charged against the wall, bracing herself with her hands to absorb her momentum, before pushing away and turning right to race along to her grandfather's study. By this time, Wild Flower was only a second behind her. As Logan reached the door to the study, she shouldered her way through it while reaching out behind her and grabbing Wild Flower's arm to pull her through behind her.

The Laird Grant was slumped half on and half off a couch, panting heavily while contorting in pain.

"It happened as you said," The Laird told Wild Flower, "I heard the sound and I did as you told me, I grabbed my throat with both hands. The dart hit me on the ball of my thumb. Now my arm is numb as far as my elbow and it pains me like somebody is jumping up and down on it."

Logan looked at Wild Flower wide-eyed, willing for things to make sense.

"Don't worry, Your Lairdship, all will be well," Wild Flower assured him, reaching for something hung around her neck.

Wild Flower's hand met only bare flesh.

"I'm not wearing it!" she groaned, "I'm not wearing it!"

"Wearing what?" asked Logan.

"I'm not wearing it!" Wild Flower repeated, again, oblivious to the question.

Logan gestured for her to explain, but Wild Flower's face had frozen in a look of horror.

"Don't look!" Wild Flower barked, "Turn away! Turn your back! Quickly!"

Picking up on her sense of urgency, without challenge, Logan did as she was instructed. Once her friend was behind her, she noticed that a nearby mirror on the wall was at an angle to catch her friend's reflection. She tried to look away, but her eyes seemed to be irresistibly drawn to the mirror. In a heartbeat, Wild Flower had disappeared. A few seconds later, she was back. She was now four years older.

"I have it!" Wild Flower announced, grasping a hollow pendant on a cord around her neck.

Presuming that her exclusion had expired, Logan began to turn back around. Wild Flower didn't object, so she turned fully. Wild Flower took the pendant from her neck, placed it against her grandfather's lips and emptied the contents of it into his mouth. After a minute, his breathing slowed and he stopped writhing.

When Wild Flower looked up, she found that Logan had her fixed with the most extraordinary look on her face. It was half puzzlement and half cold scrutiny. Wild Flower gave her a crumpled look of forlorn dejection. Logan's expression did not change.

Slowly, Wild Flower got to her feet and walked over to where Logan stood. Reaching up, she slowly and gently placed a finger on each of the other's eyelids. There was no resistance and she was allowed to press them closed.

Logan felt the pressure on her eyes remain for a couple of seconds before it released. She paused, wondering if she should now open them, but – before she could decide – the pressure returned. The touch that had held them closed, now attempted to push them open. Logan blinked to clear her vision and found, stood before her, a six-year-old Wild Flower where – moments earlier – had stood a ten-year-old version of her.

Logan raised her eyebrows in question. In reply, her friend became sheepish and uncomfortable.

"I presume," Logan sighed, "That, no matter how fiercely my curiosity burns, it's best for me not to ask you too many questions about what just happened?"

"If you ask me no questions at all, you will have my eternal gratitude."

A rather groggy and disorientated Laird Grant lifted his head from the pillows that propped it, then slumped back down. Without opening his eyes, he addressed them both.

"What just happened, you ask? Yes, please, what was it?"

Logan gave Wild Flower a sour look which yielded, involuntarily, to a smile.

"It was a trick of the light," she told him, "An illusion."

The Laird either didn't hear the reply or decided he hadn't the energy to pursue it. Instead, he returned to his earlier topic.

"It happened just how you said it would," he announced, "Somebody fired a dart at me from a sling. I heard the *woosh* as it was sent at me. It hit my hand, missing my neck. If it had hit me there – I am in no doubt – the paralysis that froze my arm would, instead, have killed me."

The look from Logan was definitely a *'thank you'* and Wild Flower touched her fingers to her cheek to acknowledge it. The Laird, who had placed a hand over his eyes, apparently troubled by the lamplight, now removed it to look at Wild Flower. Her silence roused his curiosity.

"What?" he asked.

"I was waiting for you to ask me something, Your Lairdship."

"I'm not sure how comfortable I am with you calling me that."

"It feels like the right thing to call you."

"You can call me by my name."

"No," said Wild Flower, a little more curtly than she had intended.

"Then choose something."

"I will call you Sir."

"If you insist."

"Please," Logan interjected, "There is no need to be so formal."

"I am an intruder here, Logan."

"No you are not!" Logan insisted, "You are a welcome and much loved guest."

The Laird Grant, who had returned his hand to covering his eyes, now removed it again, and dragged himself up onto an elbow.

"What is this, Logan? That is a dramatic change of heart, isn't it?"

"I honestly don't know what you mean," she replied, employing a clownish pretence at innocence.

"Is that so?" her grandfather grinned, failing to restrain a chuckle.

Logan squirmed theatrically and feigned embarrassment.

"Tell me," he asked, directing his question at Wild Flower, "Could I have died?"

"I cannot change history, except under the most extreme of circumstances, so I believe I was always meant to be here and my intervention was always meant to save you."

"And so?" he prompted.

"And so 'Yes', you might very well have died, but 'No', in the end you were never intended to die."

"But you knew it was going to happen?"

"Yes, I did, somehow."

"What if you had said nothing to me about it?"

"But I did say something to you."

"Yes, you did, but what if you hadn't?"

"Then you would not have been laid there asking me this question."

He groaned with frustration, then shook his head in something like bemusement.

"Tell me, Wild Flower," he urged, "What if you had not had an antidote available?"

"But I did have an antidote and I was meant to have an antidote."

"An antidote?" asked Logan, "What is that?"

"It is a cure for a poison," her grandfather answered.

"And you knew that word?" Logan asked, looking at her friend.

Wild Flower opened her mouth, failed to find the right words, and closed it. She then repeated the same sequence, twice more.

"She is lost for words," Logan announced, triumphantly, to her grandfather.

The Laird swung his legs down to place his feet on the floor, leaned forward enthusiastically, and made an elaborate play of gasping and slapping his head in bewilderment.

"That is simply unbelievable!" he gasped in a purposely shrill voice.

Wild Flower gave him a very adult, very sarcastic and very disgusted look.

"Someone is feeling better, I see!" she told The Laird in a barbed tone.

"Sir, you mean!" he quipped.

"Sir!" she agreed.

They all laughed and laughed. When they had all recovered, he doggedly returned to his previous question.

"What if you had not had the antidote?"

"I was always going to have the antidote."

"You can't be sure of that."

"It is not my place to be sure, Sir. There are forces at work that are far greater than mortal beings can understand. They are more powerful than anything that can be imagined. Our tawdry lives are nothing but a speck of dust in the vast ocean of existence."

Logan looked stunned, "Tawdry?" she asked, giving Wild Flower a meaningful look.

Wild Flower raised her palms in a helpless gesture, "What am I to say? I am inspired, today."

This was rewarded with smiles and chortles. As these died away, The Laird Grant gave a sigh and, leaning back against his pillows, gave a long groan.

"I am suddenly feeling very tired," he declared.

Logan shot Wild Flower a look of panic. Wild Flower smiled and reassured her friend, "Don't worry, he is no longer in any risk of dying."

Logan looked extremely relieved.

A man had somehow appeared in the doorway without them noticing. He gently cleared his throat to draw their attention. All eyes turned to him. He was The Laird Grant's physician.

"He will need to rest," the man announced, "I will strike the bell and supervise the footmen carrying him to his bed."

Understanding that they had just been dismissed, Logan and Wild Flower kissed The Laird on his forehead and moved to the door. The physician held up a hand as they approached.

"I understand you gave him a potion."

Wild Flower glanced at the page boy who was peering around the physician's leg and he jolted in alarm and looked terrified. She gave him her weakest smile. He relaxed.

"I had something with me," replied Wild Flower, looking to see the boy's reaction.

The boy looked attentive, but no longer nervous. From this she deduced that he hadn't been there when she had temporarily disappeared.

"You're a little girl," said the physician, making it sound like an accusation.

"Most of the time," interrupted The Laird, looking stern.

The physician grunted and, at a nod of The Laird's head, stood aside to let the girls leave.

CHAPTER 6

Back in her personal chamber, Logan appeared to have something awkward on her mind.

"It seems to me, Wild Flower, that just as I get used to one level of strangeness, you introduce me to another," she said, doing her best impression of being irritated.

Wild Flower mustered her driest tone for her reply, "I'm not sure if I know what you mean."

They both laughed at this.

"Do you…?" asked Logan, hesitantly, "Do you…?"

Wild Flower waited for Logan to find her words.

"Do you feel," Logan resumed "That there is something very odd happening?"

Wild Flower blinked at her, "Goodness! Are you starting to absorb some of my gifts?"

Logan tried to laugh, but couldn't force herself to do it and gave up, "I keep having the feeling that there are events unfolding around us that don't make much sense."

"That is because they don't."

"And, yet, we're safe."

Wild Flower screwed up her face for a moment, closing one eye and flicking the other towards the ceiling, "Safe isn't the word that I would use."

"If we are not entirely safe, we are not in any real danger?"

Wild Flower gave her a crooked smile at this, "Nothing threatens us directly, just yet."

"But it might?"

"Our safety, and the safety of those we love, is almost certain."

"But not guaranteed?"

"If this were a hand in a game of cards, nobody would be betting against it."

Logan sat down heavily in a chair, placed an elbow on the table and rested her chin in her hand. It was clear that she was unsettled.

"Logan," whispered Wild Flower, taking the seat next to her, "What is it that you really want to know?"

"You knew my grandfather was in danger?"

"Yes."

"He said that you told him what to do."

"I had a vision."

"A vision of somebody killing him?"

"A vision of somebody *trying* to kill him."

"You told him how to thwart them."

"I saw how to thwart them."

Logan frowned and looked to be contemplating something, at length. Eventually, she spoke.

"Do you ever see me in danger, like that, Wild Flower?"

"I don't honestly know how this works."

"You didn't answer my question."

"That is because I have no answer to it."

"Do you ever see blood and death and danger around me?"

"No, I have seen no such thing, so far."

"So far?"

"At this time. Right now."

"But in the future?"

"In the future, maybe. Would you like me to look?"

"No."

"Then I won't."

Logan sighed a protracted sigh and stared at the table. Before long, she resumed her questions with a renewed vigour.

"Do you have nightmares, Wild Flower?"

"No, I don't. Do you?"

Logan didn't reply and Wild Flower didn't use her mind to pry.

"Do you already know if I have nightmares?"

"The ability to know is like hearing a muffled conversation in another room – one that is too hushed to make out – and knowing that I could press my ear to the wall if I wanted."

Logan cocked her head, "And?"

"I try to keep my ear away from the wall."

Logan folded her arms across her chest and jutted her chin. It was clear that she wanted her answer. Wild Flower endured it for almost a minute before giving in.

"I don't know if you have nightmares or what they contain, Logan," she replied, "But I *could* know, if that is what you wished."

"A problem shared, is a problem lessened."

Wild Flower closed her eyes and allowed her mind to absorb the knowledge that seemed to be floating in the air between them like a cloud of flies. When she opened them, the look in them had distinctly changed.

"I gather you saw my nightmares?"

"Yes."

"All that is in them?"

"Yes."

"The things that happen in them and the things that I do?"

"Yes."

"I am a woman in those dreams."

"Yes."

"A woman. Not a man."

"Yes."

"Then those things are stupid, aren't they? They are impossible."

"Why are they impossible?"

"Because I'm a woman!" Logan snapped, "Women don't do those kinds of things!"

"Are you sure?"

"Of course I'm sure!"

"There are women in history who have done things like that."

"Aren't they just…."

"Stories?" Wild Flower interjected.

"Yes, just stories."

"No, they are not."

Logan looked puzzled at this and crumpled her brow in thought, biting the corner of her lip as she did so. Half a minute passed before she responded.

"I am from a good family. A noble family."

Wild Flower guffawed at this and, in deliberate provocation, clapped her hands in delight. She knew that Logan would need to be pushed if she were going to be share her true feelings.

"Don't laugh at me like that!" snarled Logan.

"Why? What will you do, you silly girl. Will you scold me?"

Logan's nostrils flared and she glared menacingly.

Wild Flower gave a derisive laugh, "You are pathetic," she sneered, "You silly little dolt!"

"Don't talk to me like that!" Logan hissed.

"Why? Will you tell me off if I do?"

Logan was visibly fuming, but Wild Flower had not done with her taunting, yet.

"Wait… What, if I insulted your mother? What if I said that she…"

"Don't!" Logan cautioned, stepping closer and drawing back a fist to the side of her head.

Wild Flower flashed her a disarmingly pleasant smile and began to mime the action of gently applauding her, "Now that is more like the reaction I wanted!" she beamed.

Logan was completely taken aback, the abrupt change of Wild Flower's manner throwing her awry.

"Look at your hand," Wild Flower invited, nodding towards it, still hovering in the air.

Logan left her hand where it was and looked up at it, as she was bid.

"You weren't merely going to slap me," Wild Flower congratulated, "You were going to punch me!"

Logan's face was filled with consternation.

"Such behaviour," Wild Flower teased, "And from a fine lady like yourself."

Logan lowered her hand, still clenched in a fist, and looked at it disapprovingly, as if it were guilty of some ugly betrayal.

"Your mother, Logan, was a truly wonderful woman, but her pride in you – which is overwhelming – isn't for your kind and generous attitude towards the poor."

"Then for what?"

Wild Flower held up her hand, entreating a pause in that topic, before changing to another.

"How much do you know of Annis, Queen of the West?"

"Not much. A little."

"You come from a good, noble family, Logan, but *she* is from a line of royalty, a queen."

"Yes, that is likely the reason she wears a crown," sneered Logan, sarcastically.

Wild Flower gave her another round of applause before continuing, "She wears a crown and she carries a sword."

"Yes."

"The sword isn't simply for decoration."

"No, I hear not."

"She wields it in battle."

"Yes."

"She uses it to kill people who wish to kill her."

At this, Logan, gave a grimace, seeming to find the concept somehow distasteful.

"Do you own a sewing basket, Logan?"

"Yes, I do."

"It belongs to you?"

"Yes, it does. Of course it does."

"Do you own an apron?"

"I own several aprons."

"They are your own?"

"Yes."

"Do you own a necklace?"

"I have three. One from my grandfather, one that was my mother's and one a gift from my uncle."

"You feel no shame in these things being your property?"

"Why, no, of course not."

"But in your nightmares, when you recollect them, you feel ashamed that you own..."

Wild Flower left the sentence incomplete, hanging in the air.

"A sword," Logan finished, lowering her head as if she had just uttered a dirty word.

Wild Flower reached out and, placing her fingertips under the embarrassed girl's chin, lifted her face back up.

"Annis is a shining inspiration for little girls and for grown women, alike, right across this land and across neighbouring lands, too. She is courageous. She is bold. She is daring."

Logan shrugged her shoulders, not disputing these words, but not endearing to them.

"You have never seen her, have you Logan?"

"No, only drawings of her. A painting, once."

"She is feminine. She is elegant. She is charming. She is deliciously lovely," Wild Flower revealed.

Logan lifted her chin, enquiringly.

"But, she is deadly," Wild Flower enticed, "She is as quick and as lethal as a scorpion!"

"A scorpion?" Logan frowned, looking puzzled.

Wild Flower touched the tip of her finger to the tip of her tongue, then reached out to Logan and lightly touched the fingertip to the middle of her forehead.

"Oh!" said Logan, seeing the very creature in her mind, "A scorpion! Like a crab, but with a tail. A tail that has a vicious sting. A poisonous sting!"

"Annis will not be Queen of the West forever. There will come a time when she needs to go away. Far away."

Logan nodded, uncertainly, not quite sure where her friend's words were leading.

"When the new queen comes to the throne, she will be betrayed. People who pretend to be loyal to her will betray her. Her life will be in danger."

Logan nodded, a little more positively.

"But those who betray her will be in danger themselves. They will be in mortal danger."

"They will?"

"Yes, for they will fall prey to an assassin. A deadly assassin. A skilled and stealthy assassin."

"Intriguing! Tell me more."

"The assassin will be so accomplished with a sword that they will be able to cut the buttons from the front of a person's shirt or blouse while they are wearing it or, with little or no apparent effort, plunge their weapon into their heart."

This time, it was Logan who mimed applause.

"This skilled assassin," Wild Flower continued, "Will have an otherwise-name by which they are known. Their real identity remaining – forever and always – a secret."

"What will they call themselves?"

"*The Flashing Blade.*"

"The Flashing Blade? I would dearly love to meet him, if it were ever possible."

"Did I say it was a man?"

"What?!" gasped Logan, incredulously.

"That's right. You heard me."

"A woman?"

"A woman."

"I would dearly like to meet *her*, then!"

"You shall."

"You say it truly?"

"I say it truly."

"When? When shall I meet her? When I am a grown adult?"

"Why not now?"

"Now?!" Logan squealed.

"Yes, now. Come with me!"

Wild Flower grabbed her hand and marched her towards the door. Logan almost shivered with delight at the prospect.

"Is she a guest?" asked Logan, breathlessly, "A lady already here? Is she in the guest wing? I did not know that anyone was there. My grandfather made no announcement."

As they neared the door, Wild Flower tugged Logan to go ahead of her but, not sooner had she reached for the doorknob, than Wild Flower placed her arms firmly around her hips and, with some sudden burst of strength, lifted her to the side before planting her back on the floor.

"Behold!" cried Wild Flower, flinging her arm in a sweeping gesture.

Logan gave a little shriek and her hand flew to her mouth. There, right in front of her, was the Flashing Blade, making the exact same motion and appearing to be no less shocked. The two women gazed at each other, utterly speechless. It would have been impossible to determine which of them was the most stunned.

Cautiously, Logan reached out to touch the other's cheek. The other woman held her head still to allow it. Half way across the distance between them, Logan's fingers came to a stop. They could go no further. The other woman's eyes widened, sharing her mutual amazement. They both gasped. Then, they both gave a perfectly coordinated little whimper.

Slowly and with infinite care, Logan stroked her fingers down the glass of the mirror, caressing the others cheek in disbelief. Her reflected image, exactly synchronised, did the same.

CHAPTER 7

"Am I asleep?" asked Logan, "Is this a dream?"

"It is no dream," Wild Flower assured her.

"I am the Flashing Blade?"

"Yes, one day, you are the Flashing Blade and that is the source of your mother's enormous pride in you."

Logan squealed with delight, "How can this be? How do I become The Blade?"

"Only time will tell."

"You don't know?"

"No – and this may come as a surprise to you – but while I know lots of things, I don't know everything."

"Could you know everything, if you wanted?"

"I very likely could, as long as it is not something that I must *not* know."

"There are such things?"

"Yes, there are. Do you know about 'The Quickening'?"

"The Quickening?" Logan pondered, "My grandfather has made mention of it, but he is reluctant to go into any detail."

Wild Flower suddenly broke into a massive grin that stretched from one ear to the other.

"What is it?" Logan asked, a little worried.

"When you become the Blade," she said, enthusiastically, and with no small amount of awe, "Then you will most certainly be a member of a very special and trusted circle."

"I will?"

"Yes, you will," she confirmed, rubbing her hands with glee, "The Quickening is a belief of a very special order. A group of people who live or die by their ability to remain hidden."

"What do they believe?"

"They believe that when the time comes for the will of *The Creator of All Things* to be brought about, then all that is required to be done will be done and all those who are required to achieve it will find themselves gathered together."

"What else do they believe?"

"They believe that there is a power beyond our world, that sent a potent force into it, to bring about all that it wills to be."

"I can understand their thinking. I feel that I agree with it."

"They believe that when that force wishes to draw our attention or make itself known to us, it will appear in a particular form."

"What is that form?"

"As a flame. A single, most glorious flame. Like a candle flame, but if the candle were lit by an angel."

"I love flames!" Logan cooed, "There is something so beautiful and so enchanting about them! When my grandfather has a fire outside, and we gather around it, I feel that there is something about the flames that is almost magical!"

"You are right," Wild Flower agreed.

"All those flames, so glorious and wonderful, but... That single flame you describe... Perhaps, all by itself, even more magical, still!"

Suddenly, as if her own words had stung her, Logan's face dropped.

"What is it?" asked Wild Flower.

"It is that I am a Grant. Such a thing is surely beyond me."

"Beyond you?"

"Beyond my deserving. Beyond my worthiness."

"I am not so sure of that, Logan, and for several reasons."

"What reasons are they? I am of Clan Grant. Surely, with everything that you know, you cannot pretend to be unaware of our shame?"

"The glorious Grants."

"Do you jest with me?" Logan demanded, bitterly, "Is this jibe for wicked amusement?"

"No. That is how your people will be known, one day."

"Surely not! Do you not mean the treacherous Grants?"

"I mean no such thing."

"What of the stain that is upon my family name?"

Wild Flower felt her heart breaking as she watched her friend's lip tremble and tears brim in her eyes.

"Logan, your clan will redeem itself. Fully and for all time."

"This is not a trick you are playing on me?"

"I speak not one word of a lie."

"You say this truly?" she asked, her voice faltering.

"I say it truly."

Logan fell silent, her face animated by some terrible thing that seemed to be troubling her. Without having intended to do it, Wild Flower picked up on a fleeting flash of her thoughts.

"Oh dear!" said Wild Flower.

Logan looked at her with raised eyebrows.

"Logan, you are familiar with what your clan did, all those years ago."

"Yes, I am."

"How did you find out?"

"I heard my grandfather talking about it to an old friend of his from his army days. They were in the garden. I had climbed up a tree and, without knowing that I was there, they came and sat right below me. They drew up a pair of lawn chairs and talked in hushed tones for a long time."

Wild Flower nodded, taking in every word.

"As they talked, they constantly looked around to check that they could not be overheard. They looked in every direction but up. If they had, they would have seen me."

Wild Flower nodded, again.

"I considered making a noise to attract their attention and deliberately give myself away. They were clearly intending to talk in secret. The longer I struggled with what to do, the more awkward and embarrassing my situation became. In the end, I resolved to sit still and silent."

"What did they say?"

"They said that, long ago, my ancestors had been saved from the Vikings by Kiffan the Defiant. They said that she and her army had ridden to their rescue and that the Vikings had withdrawn and marched to join a siege of Aberdeen, instead."

"What else did they say?"

"They said that, late the next day, the Vikings returned, having failed to take Aberdeen. They surrounded our Stronghouse, again, and my ancestors were forced to agree to pay an annual tribute of silver, cattle and crops, in order to be spared."

"And then?"

"And then the Vikings took several servants to sell as slaves and marched off, victorious."

"But the story doesn't end there, does it?"

"No," replied Logan, looking completely grief struck, "They came across the trail of Kiffan the Defiant, who was heading home. She was travelling slowly, because she was burdened by many wounded soldiers. My ancestors had sent out scouts and they returned to report that Kiffan was in grave danger."

"And what did The Laird Grant, of that day, do?"

"He pretended to send out an army to save Kiffan, but he told his troops to go only a little distance before camping overnight and returning the next morning."

"Leaving Kiffan to her fate?"

"Yes, she was captured and taken away to stand before their king in chains. This was not before they killed all of Kiffan's wounded and took the rest prisoner."

"Those must have been hard things for you to hear," Wild Flower sympathised, "It must have been a terrible ordeal for you."

"Yes, it was."

"You must have..." Wild Flower began, before suddenly stopping, "Wait... You were up a tree?"

Logan grinned, "Yes, not a really ladylike thing to be doing?"

They both laughed.

"If the housekeeper or my matron had found me up a tree, they would have scolded me and told me that I was acting like a boy."

"I hope there will be a day when girls and women can do what they want without being judged and criticised for being inappropriate."

Logan gave her a mischievous grin, "The Queen of the West doesn't always act the way a lady is meant to act."

"No, she doesn't," Wild Flower agreed, "But she is often holding a sword when she behaves like that, so it would take a brave man to find fault with her!"

They laughed and exchanged smiles, but their mood soon became serious, again.

"When my grandfather and his friend had left, I waited for a very long time before I dared to climb down out of the tree. When I did, I went straight back to the house and into my room."

Wild Flower watched her as she seemed to be on the brink of formulating some kind of confession.

"My grandfather remained in blissful ignorance of my knowledge. Whenever we had any kind of discussion of history – which he and I had from time to time – I made as little reference to Kiffan the Defiant as I could. He did, however, detect a change in my disposition. It was one that troubled him. As a result, I had to endure some grim interrogations by both the housekeeper and my matron. At his direction, they both sought insights into my state of mind, how I was feeling and how I might be cheered up. My cheering up was, apparently, deemed to be necessary."

"Who is your matron?"

"Why don't you tell me who she is?"

Wild Flower closed her eyes for a few moments, "She was your nanny when you were younger and, later, she became the very best substitute that could be arrived at for a friendship in your life."

"The very best substitute that could be arrived at?" chuckled Logan, "You have a wonderful turn of phrase for a six-year-old!"

Wild Flower dropped a quick curtsey, holding out an imaginary dress that was much larger than the one she wore. As she did so, she bobbed as if a ballerina on a stage, then looked expectantly, causing the word *"And?"* to float invisibly in the air between them.

"And my grandfather's solution, in the end, was you."

CHAPTER 8

The sun rose in a clear blue sky, to the apparent delight of all the local birds, who sang at the top of their voices in the trees around The Laird Grant's favourite meadow. Fully recovered from his ordeal of the previous day, he enthusiastically supervised as his staff unpacked and laid out the lavish breakfast they had brought to eat outdoors. The food and beverages were arranged on a centrally placed tablecloth with cushions and blankets arranged around it to act as seating.

The staff retired to the corner of the field to sit around a generous breakfast of their own. This had been the idea of Logan and Wild Flower and the suggestion had met with absolutely no resistance from The Laird. A week previously, before the arrival of Wild Flower, it was certain that he would have never entertained any such thing.

"Does this take you back, Wild Flower?" asked The Laird Grant.

"It does, indeed," she replied, with a broad smile.

Logan looked curiously at her friend, "And you just appeared? From nowhere?"

Wild Flower laughed as if this were absurd.

"Yes!" The Laird interjected, joining in the laughter, "She just appeared. Out of the air itself!"

As Logan looked across the field towards the hill, beyond the road that bordered it, he exchanged a conspiratorial glance with Wild Flower, for the two of them knew that he had meant it quite literally and not as a turn of phrase. When his granddaughter turned back, her reply wiped the smile clean off his face.

"I know," she said.

The Laird's smile disappeared like the rain from an April Shower that had landed on the baking hot flagstone.

"What?" he gasped.

"I know," she repeated, flatly.

"You know?" he asked, distinctly worried.

"Yes," she said, emphatically, "I know."

The Laird Grant looked at Wild Flower in a state of agitation. She looked back reassuringly, but the reassurance was insufficient to steady him.

"You know? You know what, exactly?" he beseeched.

"Well," Logan revealed, looking at her friend with a smirk, "Let me put it this way: You need to keep an eye on her."

"I do?"

"Yes!" Logan snorted.

"Why?"

"Well, I myself like to always keep at least half an eye on her," Logan said, aiming a broad grin at Wild Flower, "Because she's here one moment, and..."

She left her words unfinished, but their meaning slapped her grandfather in the face and he gaped at her with his jaw open. Logan matched his astonishment and, then, surpassed it.

"You *don't* actually know, do you?!" she marvelled.

"I... I... I..." he stammered, "I suspected, but..."

"You thought it to have been possible and, so, regarded it as being quite amusing," Logan chortled, "But didn't *know!*"

The Laird gazed at Wild Flower with a look of utter incredulity, his eyes wide.

Wild Flower shrugged her shoulders and offered up her open palms in apology, "There was no deception," she insisted, "I just made light of it and allowed you to come to your own conclusion."

"She has done it right in front of me," attested Logan, jumping to her feet, "She has appeared from nowhere, like a genie. Well, right next to me – in actual point of fact – for it was while I had my back turned, but that was every bit as good as in front of me."

His Lairdship looked worriedly at his staff, who were gathered in a circle on the grass at the far corner of the field, eating and drinking contentedly. His expression of relief confirmed him to be satisfied that they had heard nothing of their strange conversation.

"It was *you*," he said, aghast.

"Me?" asked a startled Wild Flower.

"Yes! You."

"What do you mean?"

"It was *you* that my ancestor saw from the hill over yonder!"

"Guilty!" cried Logan, pointing at the time traveller.

Wild Flower gave her a worried look and her friend, dropping to her knees, wrapped her in a hug and shook her from side to side, as a dog might tousle a rag, "Guilty! Guilty! Guilty!" she repeated, this time cheerfully, much more quietly, and with undisguised pride.

"Goodness me!" The Laird declared, "This is extraordinary!"

"Great credit to you, grandfather, for suspecting this but not giving me the slightest hint of it."

He smiled, warmly, before looking back across to his staff to reassure himself they remained unheard.

"That's not the only extraordinary thing that has happened!" cooed Logan, rubbing her hands together as she relished the moment, "We saw the ghost of a woman as she was being slain in our gardens!"

The Laird Grant's head whirled around as if he had been prodded by the tip of a sword.

"What?!" he cried, now even more astonished than before, "What is this you say?!"

Wild Flower cringed as if she had just been caught with her hand in the treat drawer, "It wasn't me who first saw her," she protested, defensively.

"She was slain with an axe," Logan observed, neatly deflecting the conversation to avoid any accusations.

The Laird Grant did not appear to hear what she said, or – if he did – he failed to process her words. Instead, he had fallen into deep concentration and was staring at nothing in particular on the heavy cotton cloth before them. Logan and

Wild Flower traded pensive looks. Eventually, The Laird Grant looked up.

"I would be grateful, Logan, if you spoke nothing of this to anyone."

Logan nodded her agreement.

"The same goes for you, Wild Flower," he added.

Wild Flower nodded, too.

Several further minutes of silence passed, during which the two girls helped themselves to more food and drink from the spread before them, trying to ignore the hovering air of tension.

"Our house," said His Lairdship at last, "Has not always been built up and fortified like it is now."

His return to conversation was so sudden that both of his breakfast companions jolted in surprise. He noticed and gave a little laugh.

"The house started off with a lot less stonework around it. The walls were not as thick and the surrounding perimeter walls were far smaller. It was my grandfather's grandfather who built it up to be as it is now. That was because he feared that our clan had become outcasts."

The girls listened and nodded.

"Alexander Grant was the man who started off our feud with the Campbells. A feud that has continued since. They brought cannon and fired on the house. They did quite a bit of damage before they were fended off. The very next day, he began converting the building into what has become known as a 'stronghouse'."

The girls nodded, again.

"There was a darkness about this place. A darkness that was sombre and gloomy at best. At its worst it was threatening. No, more than that, it was menacing."

"Was?" asked Wild Flower.

"Was," The Laird confirmed, "Until you came here."

Logan thought for a moment and then tapped her knuckles against the side of her head, as if it were a door she wished to be opened.

"Yes, of course," she said, "How is it even possible that I could have forgotten? I often felt it. There were many times that I felt so uneasy that I could not sleep."

"It is the reason that you have your quarters on the ground floor," her grandfather pointed out, "Because you did not feel comfortable on the upper floors."

"Just so. I have always felt safe in my new rooms."

"That", chirped Wild Flower, "Is because they were your great grandmother's rooms."

Two pairs of eyes turned to her in unison with the same question in them: *"How do you know that?"*

"I just knew," came the reply.

Her listeners both shrugged at this, accepting it as if it were an entirely sensible and logical explanation.

Taking advantage of where she was stood, Logan turned to her friend and, without her grandfather being able to see her face, she gave her a long, enquiring look. Wild Flower gazed back steadily, calmly and without emotion, giving nothing away. Almost as if her expressions spoke words, Logan understood her to be saying: *"Let's not mention that we know that it was his grandmother's ghost we saw being killed".*

The Laird Grant stood in silence for a while, then seemed to come to some sort of conclusion.

"The top floor of the house," he began, suddenly, "Is said to be haunted. The first talk of it was a long, long time ago. If you looked very carefully at the west side of the building, you might see a series of small round holes in the stonework. These, it is believed, were made over the course of weeks, months or even the best part of a year, by corrupt stonemasons who were bribed by our enemies to do it, under the guise of making repairs. One night, when the house was mostly empty, it was broken into by a band of marauders who used that series of holes to mount ladders to climb up and in through a window."

The girls looked shocked.

"They had chosen their moment carefully. The Laird and almost all of his guests had taken themselves away to spend the night in tents, out on the moor, during the two days of the Grand

Hunt. This left only a limited number of household staff behind and two young girls, daughters of an honoured guest, who refused to take any part in the hunting activities."

His audience looked dismayed.

"The bandits tied up the staff and looted the house of its finest silverware and works of art. They appeared to know exactly what was of greatest value and left behind anything of lesser quality. Although they had done their best to hide, the two girls were discovered. They were brought downstairs and paraded around before the leader of the burglars, who – according to a maid who was present – took a salacious interest in them."

Logan immediately looked at Wild Flower.

"Base, lustful or carnal," she replied.

"I am no wiser," said Logan.

"The kind of interest that you would absolutely not want a man to take in you if you were a young girl," Wild Flower amended.

"Oh!" said Logan in a disgusted tone, now clearly understanding.

"The girls were forced to wear the very flimsiest of clothing that could be found. According to the maid, the leader of the bandits was most excited to see the girls dressed like that. He pulled at their clothing so that it would reveal even more of their flesh and, then, with great delight, despatched a messenger to bring his master to see them."

Logan's expression was one of dread. Wild Flower's was one of concentration. She was trying hard not to allow any swirling knowledge of that event to come seeping into her mind.

"The girls were taken back upstairs. They were sobbing, weeping and shaking with fear. The maid, in a state of trauma, confirmed for the girls the kind of ordeal that awaited both she and them. She also told them that once the master of the gang, who had been summoned, had finished with them, he would doubtless allow the other men to take turns at doing whatever they wished with them."

Both Logan and Wild Flower looked anguished.

"The maid gave them whatever comfort she was able and then, taking a long, thin stiletto blade with her, went back downstairs. A footman, who was interviewed later, recounted a conversation with the maid when she came down. She told him that the two girls were back upstairs, aware of their doom and in a terrible state, and she showed him the weapon she was carrying. He said that she rushed at one of the marauders and stabbed him to death, but that she had scarcely taken another step before she, herself, was killed."

Logan's grey eyes fixed her grandfather with a calm and steady gaze as she said: "The two girls hung themselves from the rafters."

"Yes!" The Laird gasped, "How did you know that?"

"Because," she replied, "Wild Flower saw them."

CHAPTER 9

The Laird Grant had been fascinated by the revelations of Logan and Wild Flower. He had listened with great interest to every detail about the ghosts of the two girls in the attic rooms. Once their accounts had been exhausted, he rushed from the meadow, back to the house, where he went straight to the great library to consult his shelves of ancient reference books.

The two friends were left to finish breakfast alone, which they did while discussing the ghosts and their annoyance at the tragic historical wrong done to them. Their annoyance grew into anger. Their anger grew into fury.

"I would like to kill them both," Logan snarled, "The man who led the intruders and the man who was behind it all."

Wild Flower shut her eyes to consult the power within her. When she opened them, she gave a very pleased smile.

"One day, Logan, you will strike fear into such men."

"I will?"

"Yes."

"How is that possible?"

"It is your destiny."

"I am ten years old."

"You will not always be ten years old, Logan."

Logan looked mystified, but this did not last for long. In just a few seconds, she seized upon the answer.

"This has to do with me being The Flashing Blade, hasn't it?"

"Yes, it has."

"And this is despite me being ten years old?"

"Yes, this has to do with you being twenty years old."

"How so?"

"Because you and I were always going to be born and you and I were always going to do the things that we are going to do."

"I think I like having a destiny, Wild Flower!"

"Yes, so do I."

"I am ten and I am a nobody, but one day…"

"But one day everyone will know you!"

"I will truly be famous?"

"Yes, you will truly be famous," smirked Wild Flower, "But nobody will know you."

Logan looked puzzled, "Famous *and* unknown?"

"Yes! Famous, but very careful to make sure that nobody knows your true identity."

Logan's face lit up at this, "In that case, famous *and* unknown is entirely acceptable!"

Wild Flower applauded her.

"Whoa! Stop! Wait!" Logan protested, "You said that I would kill men like the ones who caused the death of those two girls?"

"Yes, I did."

"But, before that, you said that The Blade would slay the enemies of the successor to Queen Annis?"

"Yes."

"But Queen Annis is young. Queen Annis is healthy. Queen Annis may rule for thirty, forty or fifty years."

Wild Flower closed her eyes again, but – this time – they sprang open almost straight away.

"You're right. It does not make sense," she admitted.

"Well if *you* don't understand it, then…"

"Wait!" urged Wild Flower, holding up a hand, "It is completely and utterly strange!"

"Tell me."

"I see her wearing a crown and, then, only a short time later, I see her wearing a different crown."

"So, she has changed her crown. Surely she is allowed to do that?"

"It is a different crown and, yet, it is the same crown," Wild Flower muttered, half to herself.

"They are different styles?"

"Yes, but it is more than that. The second crown is far, far older than the first."

"Perhaps, the second crown has been dug up from somewhere? A crown of her ancestors, buried for a long time?"

"No, it is more than that..." Wild Flower began, before suddenly cringing and crying out in pain, "It hurts!" she cried, "It hurts for me to think about it!"

"Look there are geese, flying low above us!" shouted Logan, pointing into the sky.

Wild Flower turned to look, but could see no geese.

"Where? I don't see any," she replied.

"There are none, but you're no longer thinking about that crown and it's no longer giving you a headache."

Wild Flower gave a thin smile, "Thank you."

"Listen to me," said Logan, summoning her most authoritative and matronly voice, "And listen to me clearly: I want you to think nothing what-so-ever about Queen Annis or whoever might be her successor, and focus entirely on me killing bad men."

"Very well, come with me," her friend instructed, grabbing her hand and towing her back towards the house.

Logan did not protest, but meekly followed and said nothing. Wild Flower delivered her into her own chambers, where she sat her down in a chair before drawing one close up beside it, for herself.

"What are we doing?" she whispered, as if it might be a secret.

"You will see. Just relax and breathe slowly."

Logan did as she was told.

"Now," said Wild Flower, "Take my hand."

Logan took her hand.

"Now close your eyes."

Logan closed her eyes.

"Now, I want you to concentrate on your breathing. I want you to feel it coming in. I want you to feel it going out. Then, keeping your eyes closed, I want you to focus on a point directly in front of you, at knee height above the floor."

Logan obeyed.

"I want you to pay attention to your breathing and slow it down. Now, take note of your hand in mine. I want you to imagine a flow of energy, like the ripples on a pond, travelling from your hand up to your shoulder every time you breathe in."

Logan complied.

"Now, listen to my voice. As you hear it, draw it into you," Wild Flower instructed, "You are with me. We are together. Where I go, you go. We move as one. My footsteps are your footsteps. When I walk, you walk with me. Think... concentrate... breathe... listen."

Slowly, Logan saw a light waver and sway in front of her, in the space beyond her eyelids. It was like the light of a lantern that was swaying in a breeze."

"Where I go, you go," repeated Wild Flower, "We are together. We move as one."

Presently, despite her eyes being shut, she saw a girl ahead of her in the distance. There were two men with the girl. The girl looked frightened. The men were threatening her. The girl was crying. Tears were streaming down her cheeks. She was begging the men to leave her alone. She was beseeching them to let her go on her way. The men laughed and jeered at her. They began to tell her what they were going to do to her. They began to come very close to her. The girl was frantic. She was terrified of the two men.

"Leave her be!" shouted a voice.

Logan felt strange at hearing the voice. It sounded to her like her own voice, but how it might sound if she were older.

The men in her vision turned and looked at her. She felt no fear. She felt no discomfort. She sensed no danger. She felt completely safe.

"Did you not hear me?" Logan's older voice demanded, "I said leave her be!"

"Who are you to talk to us?" asked one of the men in a surly tone.

"Run away, right now, or you will regret it," said the other.

"Leave her. I have told you," said the woman's strong and confident voice.

"Shut your mouth," snarled one of the men.

"Or," the other glowered, "We will have to shut it for you."

"Very well, then you must pay the price," Logan's other self-announced.

She felt herself walk towards the men, down a shallow bank, and stand before them.

"Leave, now, or die," she told them.

"What?!" sneered the taller man.

"I'm going to break your face," growled the other.

Suddenly, Logan heard an unmistakable sound.

Shring!

Logan recognised it as a sword being drawn.

"The stupid wench has a sword!" cried the shorter man.

"Where did you get that?" asked the other, "Is it your brother's? Or is it your father's?"

"It is mine," Logan heard herself tell them, as she felt the grip of it in her hand.

The two men laughed, as if this were something hilarious.

"You should have run away when we told you," said one.

"Now," said the other, "We'll have to do to you, what we're going to do to her."

Logan felt herself turn to the side and step forward deftly, with the lightness of a dancer, and thrust in a graceful, powerful movement. The sword she had previously only felt was now visible to her. She saw it as its blade sank into the belly of the man nearest to her. Stepping backwards and leaning away, in a motion that felt practised and natural, Logan used her weight to pull the sword from the man, before suddenly jabbing it at him, blade turned flat to the ground, straight through his ribs and into his heart.

The other man gawped in shock at the spectacle and, struggling to gather his wits, attempted to grab his own sword, which he has stuck in the ground a step away.

Logan intercepted the man's movement, with an arcing cut that made a swishing sound as it sliced through the air. The man's hand was severed from his wrist. It fell to the ground with a thud. The man gazed in horror as blood gushed from his arm in a crimson torrent. He turned, in amazement, to Logan, then his eyes widened in terror. His distraction had cost him his life. He gave a yelp, but it was abruptly silenced as the point of her sword entered his throat, skewered up through his tongue and plunged up into his brain. He spasmed, gargled blood, then fell to the ground, dead.

The girl she had saved looked at her wide-eyed, scarcely able to believe what she had just seen.

"Go back to your village," Logan told her, "And spread the word."

The girl nodded, furiously and started to run.

"Tell them," Logan called, "That this country is no longer a safe place for men to treat women how they please."

The girl continued to run, calling back her gratitude as she went.

Logan wiped clean her sword and returned it to its sheath. Then, she began to walk back up the bank. Abruptly, she stopped and took at her sword again. She held it up, horizontally in front of her eyes, so that she could see her reflection in its polished surface.

To her surprise, the face that greeted her had a black mask across its eyes, with slots for her to see out. She also had a scarf tied across the lower half of her face to hide her features. Despite this, she was clearly a woman. There was no mistaking that fact. Logan angled her blade this way and that, endeavouring to see herself better, then drew it close and stared, intently, into her own eyes.

"Goodness!" she cried, taken aback by what she saw.

"Goodness?" asked Wild Flower from the chair beside her.

Logan jolted back to consciousness and leapt to her feet.

"What just happened?" she shrieked.

"What just happened was you," grinned Wild Flower, sounding matter of fact.

"Me? Yes! It was. It was me."

"You at sixteen years old," Wild Flower advised, "Making your first appearance as an avenger. That was you two years before you took on a certain name, the one you would become known by. That was you before becoming *The Flashing Blade*."

Logan smiled a huge smile. Wild Flower smiled back, sharing her joy.

"Tell me," asked Wild Flower, "Why did you say goodness?"

"You were there? You could see me? "

"Yes, I witnessed everything."

"It was definitely me?"

"Yes, of course it was you. There is no mistake about it."

"It was my eyes," said Logan.

"What about them?"

"My eyes are different when I am twenty years old ."

"They are?"

"Yes, they have changed."

"Changed?"

"Yes, I will have golden eyes!"

CHAPTER 10

"I am not convinced that this is a good idea," said Collym with a dour expression.

"Good idea or bad idea, it is what I intend to do," his employer replied.

"It is a very long fall."

"It is if I fall."

"If I looked down, from up there, I would piss my britches."

She looked down, giving her own britches close scrutiny, "It amazes me that a fashionable man would wear such a thing as these."

Collym screwed up his face, "Aye, but those with too much money often have too little sense."

She smiled and gave the slightest hint of a laugh.

"Is there anything I can do?" asked Collym.

"No, leave the rest to me. I won't need you any further."

"My Lady," replied Collym, tugging his forelock.

"Wish me luck?"

"Good luck, Mookey, and – if you fall – I hope the angels grant you a pair of wings in your next life."

She gave a little snort at his use of her childhood nickname, "If I end up with the angels, I hope to have the most glorious of wings!"

"I hope you will come back and fly around my head like the most graceful six foot butterfly that could ever be imagined."

She performed a little bow, "I shall. I promise."

"It is your height that helps you convince people that you are a man."

She scowled at him, playfully, "Surely it my convincing portrayal of a man that convinces them that I am a man," she retorted.

Collym chuckled, "Do the voice," he urged, "Please. Do the voice."

She gave him another scowl and made a small sound of annoyance, but — after taking a moment to compose herself — she did the voice.

"Which voice," she asked, speaking gruffly from her throat and the top of her chest, "This voice?"

Collym grinned and looked extremely pleased.

To further enhance her impression she slumped her shoulders, ambled forward in a mock shuffle, then reached down and roughly scratched one of her buttocks. She then hawked up some imaginary phlegm and made a spitting sound.

Still grinning, Collym led the horses away to the nearby line of trees.

Mookey stood a little while and let the minutes pass. She breathed in slowly, concentrating on the air that flowed in and out of her lungs. She was in no hurry. She didn't like to rush these things.

Eventually, she put on her belt and checked that her tools were each in their specific positions. Then, she approached the wall. She looked around and listened intently. There was nobody around. She listened again, for longer, until she was content.

With an elegant and well-practised move, she whirled her grappling hook around at the end of its rope. The swishing sound it made was barely louder than a sigh. With perfect timing, she released it. The metal device swept upwards, almost lazily, as if carried by a magical wind, and lodged itself in the wooden beam that laid across a pair of stone studs sticking out of the wall.

She quickly tied a loop into the rope at knee height and pushed her foot into it. Then, she jumped up and down to apply her full weight. Satisfied with its ability to carry a load, she leaned back and — with both feet against the wall — began to climb the rope.

Establishing a slow, steady rhythm, like the ticking of a clock, she stepped alternately with left and right foot as she hauled herself up the rope. Making the job look easy, she reached the top with impressive speed.

She didn't look down.

She never looked down.

Looping the rope a couple of times around one of the stone studs – which she knew to be called a corbels – she levered herself up until her knee was in the makeshift cradle she had created.

The wooden beam her grapple had found ran from left to right above a wide door that saw occasional use for bringing large pieces of furniture into the house. At either end of that beam was a large hole with a metal tube inserted into it. These holes were made to receive the heavy rods used to anchor an extendable pulley arm in place and prevent it from sway when raising heavy loads. By some uncanny luck, one of the sharply pointed claw legs of Mookey's grapple had found one of those holes. It had been an astonishingly effective throw.

The door was starting to suffer from the effects of the wind and rain, several parts of it becoming extremely weathered. There were signs of rot around both of the stout hinges, leaving the surrounding wood relatively soft. When she poked the wood with the sharpened tip of a metal bar, it began to splinter. After a little digging and levering at the edge of the door, it gave way around the lower hinge. She repeated the process with the other hinge and, before long, the door began to buckle in the middle.

Pressing her shoulder against the door, she could tell that the bar that was meant to hold it closed, on the inside, was missing. It had been removed. She smiled. Her spies within the building had done their work.

She pushed hard against the door, switching back and forth between pressure from her shoulder and pressure from her knee. After a while, she heard it start to splinter and, before long, it gave way. For one sickening moment, as she dislodged the door, she feared that she was going to topple backwards, but managed to stop herself. She waited until her heart stopped racing and clambered inside.

As promised, the next door, leading to the loft, had been deliberately left unlocked and she was able to exit into the narrow hall. She made her way along it and down the stairs, treading carefully so as to make no sound. At the bottom was another door. With exquisite slowness she turned the handle, praying that it would not squeak. The door opened.

She listened. She could hear voices. Two men were talking not far away. She tested the floor beyond the door to ensure that it would take her weight without making any noise. Satisfied, she crept along, keeping close to the wall, where the danger of shifting boards was the least. It was not long before she found the door she wanted. The voices could be clearly heard behind it. She crouched and put an eye to the keyhole.

There were two men in the room. They were stood by the fire. Each had a tall glass in their hand, filled with an amber liquid, which she took to be whiskey. As she watched, the men paused regularly in their talking to take gulps from their glasses.

The room was a large one. It was something like a library and had line after line of bookcases stretching into the distance. At the nearest end were several desks with comfortable, low-backed chairs. Closer still was an area for relaxation. This had four sumptuous red leather armchairs with ornate spiral legs. They were arranged in front of a roaring fire. The two men stood beyond these chairs, directly before the fire. One man had his back to her, the other was facing her.

She recognised the one who was facing her as being Rufus McKay. The other man, she knew, must be Ross O'Rourke.

O'Rourke suddenly stopped speaking and turned around to look at the door. She had an overwhelming urge to pull away from the keyhole, but she suppressed it. There was no chance, over such a distance, that he could ever be able see her eye peering through. None-the-less, he seemed to have some strange inkling of her presence.

She made a note to take extra care with him when it came time for him to die.

Rufus McKay seemed annoyed with O'Rourke's distraction and tugged his arm to regain his attention. O'Rourke turned back and resumed their conversation, but still seemed to be distracted. The conversation petered out, his mind appearing to be elsewhere.

"What's wrong?" McKay jibed, "Has somebody just walked over your grave?"

Ross O'Rourke gave a derisory grunt, "I dare them to try!" he snarled, "I'd reach up out of my box and grab their ankles," he declared, gesturing in the air, "And I would break their knees!"

The two men laughed.

"Let's make sure," McKay urged, "That this time tomorrow, we can all dance on the grave of The Queen of the West!"

"Aye!" the other agreed, "I will drink to that!"

With this he raised his glass and held it in the air for O'Rourke to meet it with his own. The two glasses clinked and their owners tossed the fiery contents of them into their mouths. Both made noises of appreciation as they swallowed.

McKay approached the mantle shelf over the fire and peered at the clock positioned above it.

"In an hour and a half, the first of the carriages will arrive with the guests for our banquet," he announced, "The banquet itself will arrive, half an hour later, in a carriage of its own. The food is being prepared, as we speak, by a group of the most accomplished and celebrated chefs. They are availing themselves of the fine kitchens of the local monastery, a little distance away."

"A feast fit for a queen!" remarked the other.

"Aye, as befits her last meal."

"And her last day on Earth," quipped O'Rourke, lifting his glass in a toast.

"It is a deplorable and shabby thing to kill a monarch, but we will be well rid of her."

"Well rid of her, indeed, for her tiresome obsession with the poor is a yoke around all our necks."

"We pay enough taxes to Scotland and to the Union," McKay complained, "Without her dipping her dainty hand into our pockets as well."

"Too true! May the Devil take her, I say."

There was a long silence as the two men brooded, independently, over their grievances with the Queen of the West. The silence was broken by a voice from half way down the long room, amongst the bookshelves.

"I've found it!" came the triumphant voice.

Mookey, now feeling cramp in her legs, adjusted her stance to one of kneeling on the carpet. During the transition, she skilfully maintained her eye to the keyhole. She made a very quiet noise of relief and allowed herself a little smile.

The two men had turned to the sound of the third man's voice. Presently, the bibliophile emerged into the open, carrying a book with such reverence, it might have been a holy relic.

"What were you seeking?" McKay enquired.

"A very special book," Sir Reginal Preece replied.

"Please tell me that it is titled *'How to Kill a Nuisance Queen'* or something very close to that."

The newcomer gave a little snigger, "Not quite, but I will still do the job every bit as well for you."

"I do not doubt it, or I would not have hired you for this task."

Preece bowed to them, formally, and waved an imaginary hat in the air as he did so, "I am hired. I am capable. I am her executioner."

"Not if I have anything to do with it," whispered Mookey under her breath.

Preece turned his head and looked towards the door.

"Not another one," she muttered, almost inaudibly, *"Two sensitive people in the room is twice the trouble I need."*

McKay looked at Sir Reginald curiously, for – he recalled – O'Rourke had done the exact same thing minutes earlier.

"Is there something wrong?" asked his hired killer.

"That's what I am wondering," replied McKay.

Within a moment, all three were looking towards the door. Like a runner who had, that instant, seen the starting flag swoop, Preece sprinted to the door. He reached it within moments and hauled it open. Swiftly he thrust his head into the corridor and looked both ways.

McKay and O'Rourke exchanged startled glances.

Preece waited a moment and then turned to shout over his shoulder.

"There is nobody there," he called, "It was just my imagination."

Immediately, he raised a finger to his lips, signalling the other men to be silent. Then, he made a pantomime of closing the door and walking away from it, before abruptly turning and tiptoeing back. Opening the door without a sound he stood and waited.

In the closet, only three paces away, Mookey stood holding her breath. With her mouth open as wide as it would go – looking like a gaping fish – she allowed herself a little air, but took in only the barest minimum she could. She maintained the pose, knowing it to be the quietest possible way to breathe, and let herself exhale.

She had heard the door open and she had heard the door close. She had heard the man walk away from it. All logic dictated that he had gone. Her senses, however, told her that it was still not safe and she did not question them. She waited.

Preece waited for a full minute, standing completely still. Eventually, he withdrew and closed the door for a second time, using infinite care to be soundless.

Mookey felt the danger pass and relaxed.

"What did you hear?" asked The Laird McKay when Sir Reginald joined them at the fire.

"I heard nothing," he replied, "But I sensed that we were being watched."

McKay laughed, "I have that feeling all the time. I think we all do. It's just our mind playing tricks on us."

"It wasn't that kind of a feeling," Preece objected.

"What was it then?"

"Something beyond that."

"But it has gone now?"

Preece looked back to the door, "No, it is back again."

Mookey pulled her eye away from the keyhole and placed a hand over her mouth.

CHAPTER 11

"Frankly, I don't give a mouse's tail what kind of plan you have," said The Laird Rufus McKay, irritably, "Just as long as you kill the queen."

"I am a master of my trade," retorted Preece, "And I do things *just so* or I do not do them at all."

"Well, do them. Do them just how you wish. Just kill the queen."

"She will die tonight."

"Good, that is all I need to know. My men will give you their full co-operation. They will do whatever you require."

"Then you will have her head in a sack before the night is out."

"Tell me, Sir Reginald," O'Rourke enquired, "Do you not fear her abilities with a blade?"

"No, I do not."

"What? Not even a little?"

"Not even a little."

"She is said to be formidable," McKay interjected, "And that is the word of men I trust."

"Have you seen her fight?" sneered Preece, "Have you witnessed her supposed ability with a sword?"

"No," McKay confessed.

"Then you can take it from me that everything people say about her is an exaggeration, an embellishment or completely fictitious!"

"Are you serious?"

"I am absolutely serious. A woman wielding a sword is as absurd as a donkey knitting a scarf."

Mookey, her eye still firmly at the keyhole, clenched her teeth in annoyance.

"Well, if you say so" McKay conceded, "It's just that..."

"My business is death," boasted Preece, "And if I underestimate anyone, then I endanger my life. Believe me, I am not underestimating this ridiculous fiction about the Queen of the West and her wholly invented swordcraft."

McKay and O'Rourke looked at each other for a moment and then both shrugged. They were more or less convinced by Sir Reginald's assurances. Neither could see any merit in having a disagreement with him.

Mookey shook her head, sadly and wearily, at their folly and arrogance.

Laird McKay went to a cabinet and took out a large ornate box and a rack of smoking pipes. Placing the box on the table, he opened it and removed several round jars with heavy lids.

"Gentleman," he said, "Come and select a pipe from my collection and join me in some of the finest tobacco."

The other two men approached, selected a jar each and sat themselves in one of the armchairs before the fire. There they proceeded to load their selected pipe with the dark, fragrant cargo from their chosen jar.

"What manner of pottery is this?" asked McKay holding up one of the jars.

"It is from China. It is called 'porcelain'."

McKay marvelled at the jar, turning it this way and that, and stroking it with relish.

"It is as if it were made from clay," McKay declared, "That is if the clay were half way to being glass."

"It is a most intriguing material," agreed O'Rourke, holding up his jar and turning it around.

"It is very hard to come by," The Laird assured them, "The method of its production is a closely guarded secret and the supply of it is scarce. Each piece commands a high price."

"Perhaps when I have slain this queen of yours," Preece suggested, "I can use some of your silver to acquire myself some..."

"Porcelain," McKay said obligingly.

"Yes, porcelain."

The trio sat in companionable silence for a little while, clouds of smoke wafting around the room from their pipes.

McKay offered around a decanter of whiskey. O'Rourke accepted a generous measure, but Preece declined, declaring that he was actually 'about his work' and that he was obliged to keep his wits sharp in his profession.

Mookey adjusted her stance at the other side of the door, moving her weight from her left knee onto her right and leaning against the door post as she flexed her foot to work out the effects of cramp. As she did so, her sword and two daggers, stowed in their scabbards at her back, began to dig into her.

Grimacing from the discomfort, she reached behind her and attempted some adjustments. Arching her back and twisting her shoulder, she had almost managed to put things to rights when her elbow slipped, causing her cufflink on her right cuff to strike the door.

Mookey stiffened, dread and horror sweeping across her face. There was no time for her to return her eye to the keyhole and the sound of Sir Reginald Preece rushing to the door told her everything she needed to know about the danger she was in.

She closed her eyes for a moment and attempted to draw upon whatever inner force she could summon, panicking as she faltered over how, exactly, to do it. She could feel as much as hear Preece. He was almost to the door. She reached over her shoulder and drew her sword. As she tried to scrabble to her feet, she abruptly slipped and fell onto her back, both shoulder blades against the floor.

She was appalled. How could she have been so clumsy? She stiffened. There was a darkness approaching. It was like the chill shadow cast across a sunny field as a black raincloud swept across the face of the sun.

It was not only her adversary that she could feel approaching, but the Angel of Death, too.

She looked up and saw the door knob jolt as it was grabbed from the other side. She gazed in wonder at the infinite slowness with which the huge brass orb began to rotate. Its progress was baffling. Then she heard her pulse in her ears. Instead of it pounding at the speed of a woodpecker's beak hammering on a tree, it was leisurely and unhurried.

Inwardly, she gasped, for in that second she knew the explanation. She was in the realm of perception where thought flew so fast that it seemed to bring time almost to a standstill.

She revelled in the lethargy of the long, drawn out seconds where each lasted for close to five or six, leaving time to elapse at a snail's pace. She watched as the door crept open, moving as if it were being dragged through treacle. It was intoxicating. It was mesmerising.

This phenomenon – so elusive and enthralling – could, she knew, terminate at any moment like a bubble bursting. When that happened, she would need to be ready.

CHAPTER 12

The door continued to open unhurriedly, progressing with an ostentatious lack of urgency. She waited and a face slowly appeared above her in the doorway. It was Sir Reginald Preece. He was looking ahead of him, as if expecting to find somebody who was standing upright. Finding no-one there, he cast his eyes down, seeking instead an attacker who might be kneeling. This did not bring his eyes downward enough. The fleeting moment that it took him to shift his gaze fully to the floor was sufficient to seal his fate.

Instinctively, Mookey had brought her sword up to catch the light from the lamps in the hall. Gently rocking the mirror-like finish of her sword, she skilfully caused a band of light to flicker up and down in his vision.

It was at that very instant that time shifted back to its usual tempo. Preece, who had screwed up his eyes against being unexpectedly dazzled, now opened them wide. His expression was like that of a rabbit trapped in the beam of a hunter's lamp.

The two seconds it took him to put a name to the "male form" before him amounted to one third of his remaining lifespan. She had performed the very action that had given rise to the name by which she was known. He murmured that name as her sword penetrated his chest beneath his rib cage, punctured his lung and entered his heart, stopping it mid-beat.

The last words he ever uttered were: "The Flashing Blade!"

CHAPTER 13

Neither Rufus McKay nor Patrick O'Rourke were able to credit what they had witnessed. A fearsome and formidable killer had just collapsed to the floor, dead, like a felled tree.

Sir Reginald Preece now lay in a lifeless heap before their eyes. Shortly, the shadows in the doorway and behind the furniture, seemed to liquify and ooze out like a black liquid that headed towards the corpse. These patches of blackness seemed to summon their fellows, for all around the room, shadows began to hurry across to form a pool around the dead man.

Presently, the black lake rose up from the floor, hung in the air for a moment, then fell onto Preece to cover him like an ominous blanket.

The Angel of Death emerged out of the air like smoke and had beckoned to the corpse of the man with a long, thin finger. Obediently, the whole of the blackness had risen up and followed Death as he disappeared, stepping through a hole that had conjured in the air.

The shadows, she knew, only came for those who were bound straight to Hell. No second chance, for them, to live a better life that might redeem them. The life that had just ended had been sufficiently vile to have guaranteed them a one way journey to the realm of sulphur and molten lava.

CHAPTER 14

Mookey turned to The Laird McKay and his joint conspirator, O'Rourke, then – with a speed that astounded even herself – she drew out a dagger and, holding it horizontally, flashed the reflection of the lamp above the fireplace into the eyes of The Laird.

The Laird staggered back a step and shielded his eyes, flinching in pain. Abruptly, he placed his other hand to the seat of his trousers and emitted an audible yelp as he had come too close to the blazing fire. The seared fabric conveyed still potent heat to his flesh beneath it.

"The heat of that fire is nothing compared to the one that Sir Reginald will very soon be enduring!" she laughed in her most manly voice.

"You!" gasped McKay, as she strode towards them.

O'Rourke looked bewildered.

"Who?" he beseeched.

"The Flashing Blade!" came The Laird's desolate reply.

At his introduction, Mookey paused to perform a rough little bow, using the bare minimum of grace.

"At your service," she grunted.

O'Rourke looked nervous, but his expression could not compete with the anxiety on his host's face. The anxiety, though, did not prevent him from snatching a pistol from a hiding place and levelling it at her.

The Blade gave a mocking snort at the weapon, quickly sinking back into the temporal dimension where time was tortoise slow.

She watched and waited as the slow speed seconds ticked by. Presently, she saw the flash of igniting powder and swiftly stood aside. The heavy lead ball streaked across the room, missing her by an arm's length and thudding into a window frame.

The Blade, still holding her dagger, threw it with casual precision and, as time returned to normal, felt satisfaction as it buried itself up to its hilt in her target's throat. Scarcely had his blood begun to flow before a second dagger was aloft and, with his arm now raised to his neck, flying to strike him in the heart.

The feel of her daggers always pleased her. They were heavy, but not so much that they were unwieldy, and – when they made contact – they carried a lot of force. The Laird McKay could testify to this as he crumpled to his knees and slumped forwards, face down, into an untidy heap.

O'Rourke took fright. Up to now, he had been able to compose himself, but quickly became frantic. Finding himself without a weapon, he lunged to take cover behind one of the large armchairs. At this point, The Blade was almost upon him. She took out her sword and described a circle in the air where he would be able to see it from his refuge.

"Your life was forfeit the moment you took sides against the queen," she told him, growling in a masculine tone.

There was no movement. She listened intently. She could detect no shuffling or crawling. Deciding upon caution rather than daring, she moved wide around the three armchairs. Doing so meant that she had to encounter the deceased Laird McKay. As she passed him she leaned over and slapped the side of his head.

"I don't hold with your opinions on women," she told him in a scathing, masculine tone.

She removed her daggers from his corpse, cleaned off the blood on his cravat and placed them back in her belt. On impulse, she stood and listened again. Somewhere close by, she heard the tell-tale sound of a sword being slipped from its sheath. O'Rourke, it turned out, had discovered another of McKay's hidden weapons beneath the armchair as he crawled under it.

The Flashing Blade cleared "his" throat, hoarsely, before speaking,

"I know you are unarmed, man," she announced, "Give yourself up and I will allow you an honourable death."

"I don't trust you," came the reply.

"You can trust me more that the queen could trust you."

"You will slash my belly, cut out my guts and leave me to die in agony."

Mookey stopped, again, and cocked her head. A noise had caught her attention. Her quarry had just tested the sharpness of his sword using his fingernail. It was a sharp *ping* sound and one that was unmistakable to her. It was one that she had made, herself, many times. The sound had just told her exactly where O'Rourke was hidden.

Resting her hand on the table, she crouched down, lowering her head towards the floor. She tried to look under the armchairs, but could not get low enough. For a moment, she considered dropping to her belly, but dismissed the idea. It would be best, she decided, if he thought himself to be hidden.

Deliberately walking her manly shoes in a way that would make them sound their loudest, she marched away from the group of armchairs, and paused. She counted to ten in her mind and then quickly raced back, treading as lightly as a dancer, before leaping through the air and landing with a foot on either arm of the chair that hid O'Rourke.

Looking down, she could see the edge of his face, including one eye. He was looking confused. He had heard her weight on the chair, but was unable to work out where she might be, for the seat was not depressed. He was holding the sword in two hands, level with the floor, ready to sweep at her legs to take her at her ankles if she came near enough. He was, she realised, intending to cut through her Achilles tendons, rendering her instantly lame.

She remained perfectly still, careful not to shift her stance and give herself away. The length of his sword, she noted, was something of a problem for him. It was too long to stop one end or the other from protruding. Keeping the blade out of sight meant that the handle was forced to jut out a little way between his chair and the next. Mookey looked down, gauged the length of the exposed handle and decided upon a plan.

"You have no weapon," she called, mockingly, aiming her voice to bounce off the fireplace, "And you cannot be far away from where I am stood."

She saw the corner of his mouth twitch in a smile.

"Listen, O'Rourke," she purred, oozing tolerant reason, "I only have to walk once around this room and I have you. Why don't you give yourself up and save me the effort?"

O'Rourke couldn't suppress another little smile.

"Very well," she told him, "Here I come."

She saw him grip the sword tighter, waiting for her to appear. She waited until her lack of footsteps caused him to become worried. Then, she took action. Stepping over the back of the armchair, and between it and the next, she landed with both feet on the handle of his sword, pinning it to the floor. He gave a cry of pain as his knuckles were crushed. Reaching and taking hold of her own sword with her right hand, she pushed the armchair over with her left. Like a beetle suddenly exposed to sunlight from under a stone, O'Rourke looked up in astonishment. Putting her full force into the movement, The Flashing Blade drove her sword through his right wrist, piercing it through.

Reaching down, she tugged at his scarf, pulling it out from under his chin, "What is this?" she asked in a scathing tone, "It looks like it's been knitted for you by a donkey!"

O'Rourke gasped in pain and uttered a strangled curse through clenched teeth.

"You are far too vile to die quickly, traitor," she cursed, "but I have always been burdened with a heart that is far too kind."

So saying, she pulled her sword from his wrist and drove a dagger through his heart.

CHAPTER 15

Logan Grant opened the front door to her home and stepped in. Closing it behind her, she rested against it with her back and gave a prolonged groan.

"So many enemies," she muttered, "So much killing."

She walked into the large front room. The lamps were lit on the walls and the table, but there was no sign of life.

"Am I right in thinking that you had full and absolute faith in me?" she asked in the empty room.

There was no reply.

Collym entered and set about helping her off with her boots, but – despite having clearly heard her question – it was obvious that he didn't believe it to be aimed at him.

"I take it you didn't fear for my life, then?" she chuckled.

Collym said nothing, but diligently undid the buckles and straps first of her left boot, and then of her right.

"Tell me that you were worried, at least for a moment, at some point!" she demanded.

Collym tapped her left ankle and she gripped the edge of her chair and braced herself. With a steady, even force he removed her boot.

"Were you not a little uneasy, maybe, when I fell flat onto my back?" Logan laughed.

Collym tapped her right ankle and, still holding onto the chair, she stiffened herself and held her foot, steady, allowing him to remove the remaining boot. Holding a boot in either hand, Collym stood and turned.

"Well," came girl's voice in cheerful reply, "perhaps I was, for just a second, but I felt sure that 'The Flashing Blade' could look after himself."

Collym took a step forward and then abruptly stopped, drawing back as his path was blocked.

"Don't do that!" he snapped, "Have I not told you before?"

"I'm sorry, I'm sure," grinned Wild Flower, curtseying and moving aside.

"One day," Collym protested, "You're going to stop my heart dead in my chest by suddenly appearing like that!"

Everyone laughed and Collym cuffed the little girl gently on the side of her head.

"I heard your voice and I rushed here without delay," said Wild Flower, giving Logan a hug, "But maybe a little carelessly," she added, winking at Collym.

As Collym hunched his shoulders and pretended to be in a huff, the two girls wrapped their arms around him and hugged him. Logan maintained the hugged a second or two longer than Wild Flower, causing her to tut and wag her finger.

"Oh, My Lady!" she said with a twinkle in her eyes, "You are so very familiar with your staff!"

"She's right," Collym agreed, crouching down on his haunches, "As your staff I should merit no more than a pat on my shoulder."

"Yes, I might do only that," Logan agreed, "And, perhaps, have you lick my boots clean to put you in your place."

This was greeted with howls of laughter.

"I was so proud of you, Mookey," said Wild Flower, placing a hand on The Flashing Blade's cheek, "Especially when you drove your sword clean through that nasty man on the floor."

"Traitors! All three of them!" the Blade cursed.

"Dead traitors! All three of them!" Collym mocked, imitating the voice used by Logan when she pretended to be a man.

There was more laughter.

As their merriment subsided, Collym stood stiffly and bowed.

"Would My Lady and her guest like some refreshments?" he enquired, "Some scones or cakes?"

"Can you eat?" asked Logan, looking quizzically at Wild Flower.

"I can when I am with you and my visit is not fleeting."

"The rules are baffling," Collym exclaimed.

"Listen to you!" Logan chided, "The first time she disappeared on you, you ran around the house, chasing from top to bottom searching for her, and refusing to accept that she could have just vanished."

"Well, I know a *few* more of the rules, now," Collym corrected, "But by no means all of them."

Logan pretended to shield her mouth and lean close to her valet, speaking in a hoarse stage whisper, "She doesn't understand all of the rules, herself!"

Wild Flower held up her hands in consternation.

"What can I say?" she asked, "I, too, am learning."

Collym held up a hand to muster their attention.

"So, is it scones and cakes or is it not?"

"It is!" chorused the two girls.

"Give me a minute or two and I will conjure them up," he told them.

Wild Flower put a hand to her mouth in a parody of shock, "Goodness! He does magic, too!"

"The only magic I do," Collym called back over his shoulder, "Is with dough, a rolling pin and a hot oven."

"It is magic enough!" declared Logan, licking her lips.

Wild Flower smiled, but then started to look a little melancholy.

"What is it?" Logan asked.

Wild Flower raised her hand and motioned for her friend to wait. She stood like that for around fifteen seconds before signalling that they were able to resume.

"What was wrong?" asked Logan.

Wild Flower smiled.

"Do you not remember your dream – when you were ten – about being The Flashing Blade? The first such one that you ever had?"

"I do!"

"You were here, just now. Your *earlier* self. In that dream you once had."

The Flashing Blade smiled, sadly, and seemed to descend into a daze as she recalled her childhood.

Wild Flower gave a little cough, "I went to see your grandfather's grave, a couple of days ago."

Instead of continuing in her sadness, Logan gave a huge smile, "The glorious Grant, you mean?" she asked, proudly.

"Yes, indeed, your glorious grandfather, the glorious Grant. It was he who restored your family name."

"Not just recovering it…"

"But elevating it."

"Yes, he was so proud."

"Yes, I recall."

"I am fairly sure, Wild Flower, that you had more than a little to do with that."

"Me? No. Fate dealt him the cards and he played them magnificently well."

"You say it truly?"

"I do."

"It was all fate?"

"Yes."

"That makes me even more proud of him, still."

"Rightly so."

Suddenly, Logan burst out laughing.

"What is amusing you so much, Mookey?"

"The thought that it is ten years ago that I first met you and that I hated you like poison!"

Wild Flower creased her brow, "It wasn't quite like that."

"I think it was."

"No, you made your very best effort to hate me, but you just couldn't quite manage it."

Logan pondered this for a little while, then her face erupted into a grin, "Yes, you remember it right!"

"You kept smiling and laughing."

"Yes, I did. I did a poor job at being nasty."

"You're just not a nasty person."

"Whoa! Stop! I *do* have it in me to be nasty!"

"It's true!" Collym confirmed, arriving back from the kitchen carrying a tray, "As her husband I can definitely confirm that she can be nasty when she wants to be!"

Logan feigned outrage, her mouth held wide in imaginary disbelief.

Collym looked mischievous, "I think she's about to do it right this moment!"

"I would run and hide if I were you," warned Wild Flower.

Collym pretended to have second thoughts. Spinning on his heels, he made as if to return to the safety of the kitchen. As he reached the door he stopped, came back, and placed the tray on a table.

"Can I eat before you flog me, please?" he asked.

"Only a mouthful," Logan cautioned, "And, then, I will get the whip."

Everyone laughed.

"If you were truly the bad person you once pretended to be, Mookey," said Wild Flower, pointing to the drawings and paintings hung around the walls, "Then you would, surely, not be able to do such beautiful art as you do. Your work is absolutely lovely."

"When you went off to serve the Queen of the West, my precious friend, I found that I had time on my hands and I took up art to absorb myself."

"You excelled."

"I like to excel. You gave me a taste for it," Logan confided, "As well as art, I took up archery. I was very good at that. I learned pottery and, I am told, I was very competent at it. I learned to weave and was very able, according to my tutor. Then, of course, I started killing people and that is where I really and truly became exemplary!"

This was the cause of even more laughter.

Collym rang a little bell and, with smiles on everyone's faces, they all sat down and tucked into the meal before them.

With an atmosphere of good humour, they ate, sipped wine and exchanged news and gossip as they did so. When they had finished, Logan would not let Collym clear the table, insisting that she and Wild Flower would do it. He was also forbidden from doing the washing up and banished from the kitchen while they put away the crockery and cutlery.

"You do like to drive your servant mercilessly hard, don't you?" Wild Flower joked, sarcastically.

Logan gave a little snort of amusement at this comment, "If it were not for him, I would not be anywhere near as active as I am in the role of The Flashing Blade."

"Then he is to be commended."

"The adventures of The Flashing Blade would be far more isolated if it were not for Collym's encouragement and support."

"Her other personality is kept quite busy," quipped Collym.

"At my count I have, so far, killed twenty two men who have plotted harm against my queen," said Logan, proudly.

"Twenty four," her husband corrected.

"Very well, twenty four. Each one a traitor to Scotland."

CHAPTER 16

Logan woke up with a jolt, sat up in bed and gave a cry of alarm. This instantly woke Wild Flower, who was "asleep" in the chair in the corner.

"I have just had the strangest dream!" exclaimed Logan.

"It wasn't a dream," Wild Flower assured her, "It was real. I was there, too."

"It was real? But I was twenty years old in my dream. I am only ten!"

"You were dreaming of the future. You were dreaming of things that are going to be."

"I was married! I had a husband!"

"You will be married, then, and you will have a husband."

Logan looked suddenly shy, "I loved him. I loved him very much. It felt wonderful."

"You can look forward to that, then!"

"I killed three people, one after the other!"

"Yes, you did. You were wonderful!"

"I was! My ability with a sword was amazing!"

"And then, when you went home..."

"You appeared to me! I remember. You were there. You appeared to me, in that time in the future when I am twenty!"

"Do you remember this? By the time you are twenty, you will have slayed twenty-four of the queen's enemies?"

"Yes! Twenty-four!" she said, proudly.

"Yet, just a few weeks ago, Logan, you would have scarcely credited yourself with the ability to slay a single one."

"That is exactly so, but that was before you told me of my fate and before you trained and cultivated me in my swordcraft."

"You also become quite the artist at the age of twenty. You are gifted with pencil, charcoal and a brush, if you recall?"

"Yes! Exactly so!" Logan chortled, "Which is quite some progress from the scribbles and scratchings that I am capable of at the moment!"

With this, Logan went to a drawer and took out a stack of papers which she proceeded to spread out on the table for Wild Flower to peruse.

"These aren't so bad," Wild Flower told her, looking through the pictures, "Especially this one, apart from the spelling, of course."

"What do you mean?" asked Logan, screwing up her face, "It's a drawing of a monkey. That's what the title says."

"No!" Wild Flower chortled, "Look! It doesn't say *monkey*, it says *mookey*!"

"Goodness me!" Logan giggled, "So it does!"

"Mookey!" laughed her friend, "Perhaps that is what I should call you from now on?"

They both froze and looked at each other, both with their hand over their mouth in surprise.

"*You do call me Mookey!*" shrieked Logan, "I remember it from my dream!"

"Yes! You're right! I used that name when I talked to you!"

They both marvelled at this astonishing development, fascinated at how life seemed to fit together like a puzzle with unlimited pieces.

"My skill as an artist, when I grow up," Logan declared, "Is wholly self-taught, but there was nothing self-taught about my skill with a sword. That was entirely down to you."

Wild Flower gave a little snort, as if she had been reminded her a private joke, "As you might imagine," she smirked, "I am not, in myself, an accomplished swordsperson."

"Yes, at six years of age that would certainly be unusual!"

Wild Flower gave a little chuckle, "You would never ever imagine from whom you *actually* learned your swordcraft."

"If it were not you, then who?"

Wild Flower grinned like a cat that had found a jug of cream.

"I had a lot of help," she winked.

"While it was you who was stood in front of me, Wild Flower, I quickly realised that it might not have been entirely you giving me my instruction."

"And who did I tell you was your real trainer, when you asked?"

"Did I ever hint as to my inspiration?"

"Yes, you did. You said that you owed your flair as a tutor to someone famous."

"Perhaps I should have been a little more honest with you."

"More honest?"

"Yes. You see that person was not merely famous."

"Really?"

"Yes, indeed, but I did not want to frighten you or ruin your concentration."

At this, Logan's eyes flicked around, here and there, but not seeing anything, as she dug into her memory for inspiration.

"Somebody not merely famous?" she queried.

"Yes. They were not merely famous. They were a legend."

Logan's eyes sprang wide in amazement, "Who?" she begged, "Please, please tell me!"

Wild Flower took a deep breath, then said: "It was Kiffan the Defiant!"

Logan's jaw sprang open and she gaped in amazement.

"You say this truly?"

"I say this truly. Every word. It was her life force that was inside me as you were trained."

CHAPTER 17

"I am completely shocked!" cried Logan, "To think that I was trained to use a sword by Kiffan the Defiant!"

"I cannot blame you!" chuckled Wild Flower, "It is a big thing to take in."

"Whenever we were about to start our sparring, you would close your eyes and stand still with a look of fierce concentration on your face. I knew that you were summoning something."

"I was invoking her presence. I wanted a very special mentor to assist you."

"You asked her and she agreed?"

"Agreed? No. She insisted."

"She *insisted!*"

"She was very fierce. She would not take 'no' for an answer."

"But why? What possible reason could she have?"

"She had *every* reason, Logan."

"So that I would slay her enemies?"

"Not *her* enemies."

"But is that not what I do? When I am twenty? I slay her enemies."

"You slay the enemies of the Queen of the West."

"*She* is the Queen of the West!"

Wild Flower looked exasperated, "There are things that you *should* not know, and there are things that you *must* not know."

Logan looked offended.

"Logan, I'm sorry. I should not have spoken so sharply."

"It is fine."

"In a few moments from now, you won't even remember that we had this conversation."

"I won't?"

"No, you won't. Because it is necessary."

Logan nodded, slowly, trying to process this absurd assertion in a mind. Then, she smiled, broadly and took up her previous conversation as if there had never been a pause.

"The instant you would open your eyes, before we sparred, I always knew that a part of you had become someone else."

"She could certainly be described as that!"

"That and more!"

"Yes, indeed," Wild Flower grinned.

"That and *much* more!"

"She was known as *The Greatest of the Great.*"

"Yes, I remember that title," Logan reminisced, "That is what my school books called her."

"When she fought, she was wonderful to behold."

"So they say."

"So I say."

Logan looked confused at this remark, "So *you* say? What do you mean?"

"I have met her."

Logan goggled at her in awe, "I am so very jealous!"

"It was *she* who trained *you* in swordcraft, so it is *me* who should be jealous!"

"You were somehow able to contact Kiffan, person to person, from eight centuries ago?"

At this, Wild Flower gave a quiet little smile to herself, as if it reminded her of a private joke, "Yes, but no."

"Which is it!" asked Logan, sternly.

Wild Flower held up her hands, "The truth is, I didn't, in fact, have any need to reach back eight hundred years to the time of Kiffan the Defiant to see her fight."

Logan blinked in surprise.

"You see," said Wild Flower, brightly, "I was actually alive in the year 793, when Kiffan took up arms against the Vikings."

"But, Wild Flower, you were always here, in 1622, in solid flesh and blood."

"Yes, I have grown into this time, but I was born in the far distant past. For me, I had to push through the curtain of time to the future, to be here in 1622."

"Yes," said Logan, with a sad smile, "Like when I visit myself when I am twenty."

Logan sat down with a thump, dropping herself into a chair like a sack that had been thrown onto it. She was on the verge of tears.

"I miss being the Flashing Blade," she confessed.

Wild Flower smiled and touched her cheek, gently, "You miss being someone that you have not yet become?"

"Yes. I miss everything about her. I miss the feel of a sword in my hand. At that age, I mean. It feels different… different to how it feels, now."

"When I am twenty, Logan, I have a sling. If I hold one, now, it just feels like sling, but when I am twenty," she closed her eyes and breathed in as if smelling roses, "When I am twenty, it is as if my sling is a part of me and I can hit any target just by looking at it. I just have to want to hit and I do."

Logan nodded, slowly and thoughtfully, as if she understood completely. Then she looked down at her hand, opened her palm and studied it.

"When I hold a sword, as The Blade," she murmured, "It is not as if I am merely holding it. It feels like an extension of my arm."

"Would you like to go back?" asked Wild Flower.

"Go back?"

"Yes."

"What do you mean?"

"Would you like to go back to when you are The Flashing Blade?"

"Yes!" she cried, without a moment's hesitation.

CHAPTER 18

"We spoke ten years ago," said Logan, proudly, "Yet I instantly remember the exact words we said."

"I would expect no less," Wild Flower grinned.

"Ten years ago and, yet, only ten seconds ago."

Collym looked up from the letter he was writing and across at the two women. He ignored that one of them had just materialised out of nowhere. He frowned and gave them a look of bafflement. For a moment, he appeared to try to make sense of their conversation, but quickly shrugged his shoulders, shook his head wearily, and returned his attention to his letter.

Logan grinned back at her friend, "I knew that there were strange and wonderful things about you from the moment you arrived in my life, but I never guessed that any of them would involve something like this!"

"What is any ten units of time between friends?"

They both laughed.

"The past, the present and the future," Wild Flower confided, "Are all places where I feel at home."

"That must be wonderful."

"If you wish," Wild Flower offered, "You can find out what it is like for yourself."

Logan looked dubious, as if someone were offering to barter a horse for a chicken.

"You witnessed yourself do something, Logan, four years in the past from this current date, but which has not yet happened."

"How can that be?"

"It sounds strange, doesn't it?"

"It *is* strange!"

"Well, as I said, you can see for yourself," Wild Flower retorted.

"I can see for myself?"

"Yes, or – more accurately – you *will* see for yourself."

"This has already been decided?"

"Yes, exactly so. If you recall, back when you were ten years old, I told you that, one day in the future, you would be The Flashing Blade."

"Yes. That's right. You did."

"I want you to look back from this age that you are now – which is twenty – and tell me when exactly you started making a habit of killing bad people? It was not so very long ago, was it?"

"No, it was not. I slew for the first time shortly after I became eighteen."

"That is a fine age to begin slaying wicked people."

"Is it? Truly?"

Wild Flower gave a little laugh, "Absolutely *any* age is a fine age to begin slaying them!"

"You're right!" Logan sniggered.

"Cast your mind back to when you were ten years old. Do you remember sitting with me, our chairs side by side, and me showing you your future self, killing two bandits? You killed them in the forest? They were about to do unspeakable things to a young girl. Do you recall?"

"Yes, I recall."

"How old were you in that particular vision of yourself?"

Logan concentrated, then looked surprised, "The me that I saw must have been sixteen, but that couldn't have been so, surely."

"Could you have been older?"

"No, not by much."

"Exactly so."

"But it makes no sense."

"No, it doesn't, but can you guess why you were that age?"

"No, I can't. Well, not properly so. The event you showed me doesn't measure up to the fact. I am twenty years old, now, and yet you showed me killing for the first time two years younger than was ever the case..."

A faint smile hovered on Wild Flower's lips as she waited for Logan to piece together the puzzle.

"The Logan I was destined to become, killed somebody at sixteen. The Logan that I am now – and the one that I have been for the past ten years – did not kill anybody until I was eighteen!"

"Yes, and it troubles you because you are as certain as you need to be that your memory is true."

"Completely true."

"You know, beyond doubt, that you didn't actually kill anybody at the age of sixteen?"

"Yes, of course, it is not something that I would be likely to forget!"

"And this is so despite the fact that, at the age of ten, you witnessed it happening in your future?"

"Yes, which makes it utterly baffling."

"That," Wild Flower announced, "Is because it hasn't happened, yet."

"What?!" cried Logan, making no attempt to hide her astonishment, "I am twenty years old, that killing occurred when I was sixteen. By any kind of logic and sanity, it must absolutely definitely have already happened."

At this, Wild Flower cupped her chin in her hand, and began to make thoughtful noises as she pondered and mused. Before long, she put up a finger, as if to pin a thought in place.

"I wonder if this is why we were drawn to have this conversation?"

Logan let out a sigh that inflated her cheeks and whistled through teeth as it came out. It was obvious that she was exasperated.

"I'm sorry!" said Wild Flower, looking contrite, "To you, all of this must seem like a cloud of total nonsense flying in circles around your head!"

Logan made a face and nodded her agreement, "Ever smaller circles and at risk of colliding with my head."

"I think, in this instance, it is just as I said: *You can see for yourself*. That is because I am now convinced that you are destined to go back to that time from now."

Logan pointed to herself – by prodding a finger in the middle of her own chest – and looked for confirmation.

"Yes, you. The two of us both saw you kill those wicked men when you were sixteen. If it is nothing that you remember, it is because it is only now – in this time and age – that you go back and do it."

"That's… That's…" Logan stuttered.

"Yes, I know!" smiled Wild Flower, "It is!"

Logan's brows furrowed as a dozen thoughts collided in her mind. Wild Flower reached out her hand and Logan gave it.

"Where," asked Wild Flower, "Do you feel most comfortable and relaxed? Where is there a special place that you like to visit to reflect and ponder?"

"The woods," Logan replied, "There is a place in the woods."

"Let's go there, then."

The two set off and made their way to a shady spot by a small pool. There, they sat down beneath a tree with fragrant low hanging branches.

"I can see why this inspires you," remarked Wild Flower, taking in the view, "It is a very tranquil spot."

"A tranquil spot for conjuring magic?"

"A tranquil spot for doing exactly what we need to do and – as far as I can understand – exactly what we were always going to do."

Logan gave her a questioning look.

"I think," said Wild Flower, grimacing as she grappled with the idea, "That if we were not here, in this very place, right now – here to do the very thing that we are about to do – then that girl in the woods, from ten years back, would have been raped and murdered by those two men."

Logan looked uncomfortable and anxious, "I'm twenty years old," she said, as if that were explanation enough.

"Yes, and you saved that girl when you were sixteen. We saw you do it."

"So...?"

"So, whatever is going to happen is going to happen," said Wild Flower, suddenly fully confident, "Now, take my hand and let us do this thing."

"You sounded just like Queen Annis!" Logan snorted.

Wild Flower laughed, too, "Yes, I did. Maybe it will bring us luck?"

The two women joined hands and leaned their heads back against the trunk of the tree. Both breathed slowly and deeply, relaxing their bodies and freeing their minds. Before long, they felt themselves begin to float in the air, a short distance above the ground. Despite the sensation, they could still feel that they were on the ground.

Suddenly they both stiffened. Something had happened. They could both sense it. They forced themselves to relax again and had just begun to achieve the state they wanted when they heard a far off humming sound. The sound began to grow in volume. It was soon too loud to ignore. Without warning it stopped.

They opened their eyes to find themselves in Logan's bedroom, back at the Grant stronghouse. They could both see Logan, at sixteen-year-old, asleep in bed.

CHAPTER 19

"I am sixteen years old," said Logan, with a tone of fascination.

"You're asleep," replied Wild Flower, "And you look to be very peaceful."

"Yes, I used to sleep extremely well."

Wild Flower knelt beside the bed, as if about to pray, and beckoned for Logan to do the same. Logan obliged.

"I want you to concentrate. I want you to focus on your sixteen-year-old self in front of you. I want you to push your thoughts into her mind."

Logan did so, finding it surprisingly easy.

"Now, I want you to go beyond your thoughts in her mind. I want you to enter her mind with the whole of your mind."

There was a prolonged moment of intense effort.

"Can you hear me?" Wild Flower asked the sleeping girl.

"Yes, I can," replied the twenty-year-old Logan, knelt beside her, "I can hear your thoughts from within the head of my sleeping, younger self."

"Now, think yourself beyond the walls around the garden of this stronghouse. Think of the shallow bank that drops down just beyond the trees. There is a path at the foot of it that leads to the Great Northern Road. You are standing at the top of the bank. While out walking, the sound of a girl crying in the woods has drawn your attention. You have walked towards the sound and you are now at the top of the bank."

Wild Flower thought herself to the very same place. Arriving there, she looked around, but could not see the younger version of Logan.

"Are you here?" she asked Logan's younger self.

"I am on my way. I will be there in a moment," came the reply, this time from the lips of the sixteen-year-old Logan in her sleep.

Wild Flower looked left and right and saw a far more youthful Logan step out from the shadows.

"It is nice to see you, Logan," said Wild Flower, smiling broadly.

"Is that you?" asked the sixteen-year-old, "Wild Flower, is that you?"

Wild Flower nodded, her smile widening still further.

"Oh, Wild Flower! Gracious me!" she cried, "I haven't seen you since you went to serve Queen Annis!"

"Even if I say so myself, I did serve her well."

Logan gave her an excruciatingly pained expression that seemed to be twisting her very heart, "I would never doubt it."

"She is far from the reach of any harm in this world, now."

Logan's expression turned to horror.

"No, no, no..." Wild Flower insisted, holding up her hands, "She is not dead! She is merely in hiding."

Logan looked relieved, "Far away?"

"Further than you would ever imagine," replied Wild Flower with an undecipherable smile.

Logan appeared reassured, so Wild Flower relaxed, her worry dispelled. The girl below them screamed, yanking them both back to their environment.

"I heard her cry out and begin sobbing," said Logan, "Which is what drew me here."

Wild Flower leaned very close to sixteen-year-old version of Logan and looked directly into her eyes, "Can you hear me?"

The young Logan recoiled from her, clearly worried by the strange behaviour, "Yes, of course I can hear you," she replied, indignantly.

"I'm sorry, whilst I was talking to you, I was actually talking to someone else."

"Someone else?" asked the young Logan, drawing back still further and looking even more uncomfortable.

"I'm sorry. Take no notice of me. I must seem strange. I am experiencing an awkward situation."

Suddenly, the Logan before her leaned forward and gave a very slow, very deliberate and very grown up wink. The kind of confiding wink, Wild Flower decided, that a twenty-year-old might give. It was now Wild Flower's turn to feel reassured.

The older Logan shot a hand to her face and prodded her eye accusingly with her fingers, "I just winked!" she cried in alarm, looking completely bewildered.

Wild Flower stepped forward and simultaneously hugged the two Logans, of differing ages but within the same body, "You have nothing to worry about," she urged.

There was another scream and they both looked down to where the girl in distress was trying to dodge the two men who were menacing her.

"What do I do?" asked the young Logan.

"I think you had better do exactly what you feel you should do. The less you think about this, the better."

Logan looked down and placed a hand on the handle of her sword that hung from around her waist, "I have my sword! I wonder why I have it?"

"Perhaps instinct told you to wear it?"

"Maybe so," murmured Logan, distractedly, as she watched the scene unfold, below.

Wild Flower patted her on her shoulder, encouragingly.

"I'm going down there," said Logan, abruptly filled with certainty.

Two men were threatening a girl who stood between them. The girl looked frightened. She was crying. She was begging the men to leave her alone and let her go on her way. The men laughed and jeered at her. They began to tell her what they were going to do to her. The girl was frantic. She was terrified of the two men.

"Leave her be!" shouted Logan in a strong and confident voice.

The men in her vision turned and looked at her. Neither of the Logans felt any fear. Neither felt any discomfort. They sensed no danger. They felt completely safe.

"Did you not hear me?" Logan challenged, "I said leave her be!"

"Who are you to talk to us?" asked one of the men in a surly tone.

"Run away, right now, or you will regret it," said the other.

"Leave her. I have told you," said Logan the threat in her voice unmistakable.

The two men were taken aback by one so young behaving so assertive and so sure of themself, and a 'mere' woman, at that.

"Shut your mouth," snarled one of the men.

"Or we will have to shut it for you," joined the other.

"Very well, then you must pay the price," Logan announced.

She walked towards the men, down the remainder of the shallow bank, and stood before them.

"Leave or die," she told them.

"What?!" sneered the taller man.

"I'm going to break your face," growled the other.

Suddenly, there came an unmistakable sound. The two men heard it, too. It was a sword being drawn.

Shring!

"The stupid wench has a sword!" cried the shorter man.

"Where did you get that?" asked the other, "Is it your brother's or your father's?"

"It is mine," Logan told them, relishing its grip in her hand.

The two men laughed, as if this were something hilarious.

"You should have run when we told you," said one.

"Now, we'll have to do to you, what we're going to do to her," said the other.

Logan twisted to stand sideways to the man and stepped closer. She moved with the lightness of a dancer. She thrust gracefully, but powerfully, at the man. She felt a thrill at holding her sword. She knew, beyond doubt, that this was her life's calling.

With great satisfaction, she plunged her blade into the belly of her adversary. Stepping back and leaning away, in a practised motion, Logan used her weight to withdraw her sword from the man. Like a snake striking, she jabbed it back into him, the blade turned flat and level, through his ribs and into his heart.

The other man looked astonished at what he had just seen and struggled to collect his wits. Suddenly, he reached to grab his sword, which he has stuck in the ground a step away.

Logan raised her sword and, with swooping cut that *whooshed* through the air, she severed his hand at the wrist. It thudded to the ground. The man gazed in horror as blood spurted from his arm like a red river. As he turned to Logan, his eyes sprang wide in horror. His loss of concentration sealed his fate. He gave a yelp, but it was cut short as her sword pierced his throat, cut through his tongue and penetrated his brain. His body jerked, he gargled blood, and he fell, dead, on the ground.

The girl Logan had just saved looked at her wide-eyed, scarcely able to believe what she had just seen.

"Go back to your village," Logan told her, "And spread the word."

The girl nodded, furiously and started to run.

"Tell them," Logan called, "That this country is no longer a safe place for men to treat women however they wish."

CHAPTER 20

Logan opened her eyes. She was back beneath the tree beside the pond, just as she had been. She immediately looked to Wild Flower and was glad to find her sitting next to her.

"That girl is still alive!" shrieked Logan, "I saved her life!"

"Yes, you did," Wild Flower agreed, "You were magnificent!"

"I vividly recall the time, back when I was ten years old, witnessing myself kill those men as a sixteen-year-old. Now, here I am, at the age of twenty and, just a few moments ago, I went back and did that very thing for real, fully in control of my sixteen-year-old self!"

"All that was meant to happen, has happened."

"So, when I killed those men at the age of sixteen, I was..." she said, halting as the right words defied her.

"You were spurred to do it by your older self."

"Yes! I was! I understand it now."

"Which was how you were able to behave the way you did."

"I was very confident and self-assured."

"Just so."

"In a way that would have been beyond the grasp of a sixteen-year-old."

"But not of a twenty-year-old who has slain many wicked men."

"It is a strange thing, Wild Flower, that while the act of killing becomes easier, the burden of having killed does not."

"Those men will have had no such trouble with their conscience."

"If they possessed one at all."

They both laughed.

"Do you recall, Wild Flower, that you told the ten-year-old me that I was inspired and that I had a gift?"

"Yes, I do. It was the truth and remains the truth."

"Exactly how inspired am I, and exactly how gifted?"

Wild Flower turned to her with exaggerated slowness, as if Logan were a snake that might strike at any sudden movement.

"Can I ask you something?" Logan enquired.

"Yes, you may."

"Where are you?"

Wild Flower turned away, then cast back a sideways glance from the corner of her eye. One she hoped her friend would not see. She saw it.

"I'm sat here, Logan, right next to you."

Logan waited a few moments, then asked the question, again, this time more insistently, "Where are you?"

"I'm sat beside you," replied Wild Flower, feigning innocence.

This time, the pause was shorter and Logan made no effort to suppress her annoyance, "Where are you?", she growled.

"Where else might I be but right here?" came the far more bashful reply.

Logan made the Scottish noise, the sound rumbling in her chest, then, placing a hand either side of Wild Flower's head, she turned her friend to face her.

"Very well," she said caustically, "*When* are you and *when* am I?!"

There was a ripple in the air as everything around them distorted for a moment, causing each other's faces to jump out of focus, then back again. Logan continued to look at her friend and saw the entire vista, to either side of her, undulate like waves on a pond. The next moment there was a humming sound, rising in pitch, as everything started to shimmer and sparkle. The next moment, it stopped and she found herself in her room at the Grant stronghouse. She was sat in her favourite chair by the window. Next to her sat Wild Flower, who was holding her hand in the exact same way she had when she had taken Logan to see her sixteen-year-old self slay the two men.

Wild Flower gave her a fake smile.

"I was twenty years old, not thirty seconds ago," said Logan, sounding dazed, "That's ten years away."

"You look nice at twenty."

"I do. I'm really pretty," she said before looking down and giving a cry of disappointment, "My hair has gone! My really long hair has disappeared! I don't have it anymore!"

"It was really impressive hair," congratulated Wild Flower.

"And shiny, too."

"Very shiny."

"But you only had your hair for a few hours…"

"Is that how long we were gone?"

"No… Yes… No but, yes, as well."

"Is that 'No' or is that 'Yes'?"

"As far as I can tell, an hour in some other time is just a minute, or maybe two minutes, in our time."

"I miss 1632," said Logan, wistfully.

"No you do not!" chided Wild Flower.

"I do. I miss my hair."

"They long hair will arrive…. Eventually." Wild Flower winked.

They both laughed.

Suddenly, Logan sprang to her feet.

"My grandfather!" she shouted, "My grandfather is going to die."

With this, she raced for the door and out into the corridor, heading for her grandfather's study.

"I need to hug him and tell him that I love him," she called over her shoulder.

"Right. Yes. That," said Wild Flower to the empty space where she had been, "I need to talk to you about that."

CHAPTER 21

"Why is it," exclaimed Logan, "That there is always a greedy duck that wants all the food it can get?"

So saying, she aimed her next handful of corn away from the creature in question and towards the rest of the flock. The greedy bird ran to push past the others and grab more than its fair share.

"It's like life," replied Wild Flower, "Ducks act like people."

"Dreadful people."

"Dreadful ducks."

The two girls sprang to their feet and, giggling and squealing, started flapping their elbows to mimic the ducks. The ducks jumped back into the river from the bank, deciding that feeding time had ended.

Once their frivolities had reached an end, Logan guided Wild Flower to sit under the trees in the shade.

"There is something I need to ask you," Logan announced in a serious voice.

"I don't like the sound of this."

"No, listen, there are things I need to know."

"No, listen there are things it is best that you don't know."

"When we went forward to when I will be twenty," Logan continued, undeterred, "It was for a very particular reason, was it not?"

"Yes, it was."

"And the reason?"

"We needed to put something right."

"What was that something?"

"You gained your courage from killing the two vile men who were going to beat and rape that girl."

"I sensed it happen. I felt suddenly empowered."

"Some things are inevitable, but that doesn't stop them from being a worry."

"A worry? You mean a worry that we are aware of them before our time?"

"Yes, that is exactly what I meant. Awareness of them is a worry and you are now aware of too much."

"I have a man in my life at that age," Logan sighed, dreamily.

"Yes, a good man. A very good man."

"One who loves and adores me."

"One who worships the ground you walk on."

"Oh! Glory! That is so romantic!"

"Yes, you will grow up, you will meet him and you will live happily ever after."

"Just like in a children's story?"

"Yes."

"What else will happen? What more is there to this children's story?" gushed Logan.

"This," replied Wild Flower, touching the tip of her index finger to her tongue, leaning forward and touching it to her friend's forehead, between her eyes.

Logan blinked, suddenly confused, and gave a puzzled look.

"What were we just talking about?" she asked, looking utterly baffled.

"I can't remember," said Wild Flower, shrugging her shoulders, "Blow me into the air like a feather if I can."

She waited a few moments, enjoying Logan's bewilderment before whispering to her confidentially.

"Do you think you will ever meet a boy and fall in love?"

"What?" exclaimed Logan, "Don't be so disgusting. I hate boys. They are nasty, grubby things."

Wild Flower gave a big smile.

"Why is my answer so amusing?"

"No reason. I'm just feeling silly at the moment."

Logan slumped back against a tree and looked up into the clear blue sky, something obviously on her mind.

"It's strange," she said, "I'm sure I was just about to ask you something."

CHAPTER 22

"Deep! Deep!" shouted Wild Flower, demonstrating the motion with her own sword, "Thrust deep!"

Logan looked perplexed.

"When you thrust, Logan, don't ever thrust your sword *into* someone, thrust it *through* them."

Logan nodded, fully understanding, but this didn't stop Wild Flower from continuing her tirade.

"When you thrust, you may only wish to pierce an organ or cause a wound, but there is a temptation to slow your motion as the tip of the blade enters them, losing the force behind it. To prevent this, you need to imagine that – when you aim for someone's torso – that you are *actually* aiming for their spine, behind it."

Logan gathered herself, padded lightly on her feet to the left and right of the suspended dummy, then drove her sword into it hard, causing it to sway back on its rope.

"Wonderful! Wonderful!" applauded Wild Flower.

"You are a wonderful teacher."

"Am I?"

"Yes, you are."

"Is it *me* who is teaching you?"

"No, now that you mention it, perhaps it isn't. You do that strange thing before we begin a lesson where you pause and seem to draw in some kind of force."

Wild Flower smiled a huge smile at this.

"It is very odd," said Logan, creasing her brows, "It feels like we have had this conversation before?"

"Does it?" asked Wild Flower, pretending to be intrigued.

"Yes. Have you never had that feeling?"

"Yes, I have, I know exactly what you mean."

Logan continued to hop and skip around, weaving to dodge the swinging dummy as Wild Flower pushed it at her, and delivering it savage jabs with her sword that fully impaled it.

"How does it feel to hold a sword, Logan?"

"It feels like I was born for this."

"Truly?"

"Yes, truly. No needlework, no tapestry and definitely no lacemaking for me. *This* is my chosen pastime."

"Your grandfather is very…" replied Wild Flower, searching for the word.

"Accepting?"

"Yes. Most definitely accepting."

"You told me my destiny. I know who I will become."

"You will be The Flashing Blade."

"Yes! I will be she!"

"Does that excite you?"

"Yes, it does because she will defend the true Queen of the West of Scotland *and* she will have golden eyes!"

"Which matters most to you?"

"Well…" Logan mused, rocking her head from side to side with indecision, "I suppose that killing traitors is a noble calling, but…. To be honest…. And I mean perfectly honest…"

The two of them descended into gales of laughter and laughed so much that they had to hold on to each other for support. All attempts to speak failed them, only causing further bouts of helpless mirth.

Eventually, having regained the gift of coherent speech, Logan adjourned their training to sit on a bench. Just then, a young servant girl arrived bearing their regular training refreshments, which arrived at intervals, and consisted of a large jug of fruit juice, sturdy tumblers and a copious supply of water melon cut into pieces.

The servant looked at her two mistresses a little dubiously. Both were wearing clothing very clearly made for men. They both had on thin cotton shirts with belled cuffs and a pair of thin cotton breeches. Their shirts were soaked in sweat, having dark patches beneath the arms, around the neck and in several places around the trunk. The servant's disdain was evident.

"Thank you, Bridie," smiled Logan as the girl set down a tray.

Bridie smiled uncomfortably. It was obvious that she found it awkward to be in the company of two 'ladies' who were dressed like men and who were drenched in perspiration. The look the girl reserved for their swords, however, was almost magical.

Seeing the way the servant was looking at it, Logan held up the sword and offered it to her.

"Would you like to hold it?"

The girl stepped back, as if she had been offered a red hot poker to grasp.

"Why will you not take it?" Logan asked.

"It is a sword. I am a woman," the girl replied.

"And women do not have swords?"

"No, of course women do not have swords."

"And yet, when you look at it, you do so enviously."

The girl thought for a moment, "I wish that women *did* have swords," she said, then quickly added: "But they don't."

"Very well. You may go. I will tell the housekeeper that you do your work very well and that you have perfect manners."

"Thank you, My Lady."

The servant curtsied and departed.

Once she was out of earshot, Logan turned to Wild Flower and, leaning towards her, confided: "No, of course women do not have swords."

"It is the way she has been raised."

"Because we live in a time of ignorance," Logan jibed.

"She has known nothing else."

"Nor has anybody, for the most part."

"But history *will* know women with swords," Wild Flower urged.

"History will know *me.*"

"Yes, it will."

"You told me that my destiny will be to slay the enemies of the next Queen of the West. You said that I will kill those who plot against her life."

"Exactly so."

"Then when will the *next* Queen of the West come to the throne?"

"In the not too distant future."

"That means nothing," Logan scorned, "You may as well have just barked like a dog."

"You will be an exemplary swordswoman by that time and well capable of the role."

"Woof! Woof! Woof!" said Logan.

"It will be when time and fate bids it to be so."

"Woof! Woof!" said Logan, snidely, "Would you like to hear me howl at the moon?"

Wild Flower gave a desolate sigh and shook her head, wearily, "If I told you, it would make no sense."

"Well, you're not making very much sense at the moment," Logan sneered, "So things cannot get any worse, can they?"

Wild Flower stared at her, wide-eyed.

"Or perhaps, Wild Flower, I should pick you up by your ankles and dangle you upside down, swinging you back and forth like the pendulum in a clock, bashing your head against yonder tree as I go, to get some sense out of you?"

Wild Flower stared with eyes that sprang wider, still.

"What is it?" Logan enquired, "Why are you looking at me that way?"

"You are ten years old. You have only a single decade of life behind you. You are only four years older than me. Yet, you are sarcastic, you are cocky, you are savage with your wit."

"I am?" replied Logan, startled.

"You are."

"Oh!" said Logan, blankly.

"It happens," retorted Wild Flower, choosing her words with care, "When someone is exposed to their older self, I believe."

Logan screwed up her face as if she had just put a spoonful of salt into her mouth, "Surely I don't have this kind of attitude when I am grown, do I?"

"No, only at first."

"Do I have long hair when I am grown?" Logan asked, gripping her hair and holding it out for inspection.

"You already have long hair."

"No, I mean very long hair."

"Why do you ask that?!" Wild Flower cried, louder and more sharply than she had intended.

"I don't know. It just leapt into my head," replied a crestfallen Logan.

"Tell me," Wild Flower smirked, "Why does your grandfather not allow you to mix with the *rude girls'* over at Glen Daglish?"

Logan gave her a furtive look as she answered, "Because if I mix with them too long, I will get like them."

"Aye," Wild Flower snorted, "Well, in that case, I think you've been mixing too long with yourself!"

Logan's face was a perfect picture of consternation. Wild Flower held up her hands, indicating her surrender.

"Very well, I will tell you all," she promised, "The next Queen of the West will take the throne before this year is out."

"Is Queen Annis going to die?!"

"No, that is not what is going to happen. It is far, far more complicated than that."

"It must be *extremely* complicated, because I am but ten years of age and I won't even be eleven until next year."

"That, Logan, is *exactly* how complicated things will be."

Logan's look of bafflement did not subside.

"The Logan you are today, at ten years old, and the Logan you will be when you are twice that age – at twenty years old – will not be complete strangers to one another."

"That sounds really strange."

"Your calling as The Flashing Blade is to protect The Queen of the West. Your calling will also involve protecting your ten-year-old self."

"I saw my sixteen-year-old self, Wild Flower, as completely real as if she were stood before me."

"That is true."

"Are you saying that it is possible for my twenty-year-old self to do the same and visit my ten-year-old self?"

"I know it is possible, for I have witnessed your twenty-year-old self visit and engage with your sixteen-year-old self."

"I can engage with my sixteen-year-old self?"

"Yes."

"And my sixteen-year-old self can engage with my older self?"

"Yes."

Logan held her head in her hands.

"I hark back, fondly, to the time when threading beads on string was the maximum challenge to my understanding that I encountered."

"You see! You're talking like her, again!"

"I'd like to meet her."

"You have."

"I have?"

"Yes."

"Would I not remember that?"

Wild Flower gave her a weak smile, "I don't think we can do this, can we?"

"Do what?"

"I have been shielding you from your twenty-year-old self and your twenty-year-old self from you, but it doesn't seem to work. It is as if the two of you need each other."

"Whoa! Stop! Wait!" Logan protested, "Please tell me that you didn't do the *'finger thing'* again!"

Logan touched her own finger to the tip of her own tongue and then held it up, accusingly, as if she were presenting an incriminating exhibit in a trial.

Wild Flower hunched her shoulders and crouched her neck between them. The seconds ticked by and then, with a look of resignation, Wild Flower touched the tip of her thumb to her extended tongue and then applied the thumb to the end of Logan's nose.

Instantly, Logan remembered.

"Oh! I see! Now I understand!" she laughed, "So *that* is why my hair was so difficult for me to forget!"

"There is no mistake that you grow into a woman."

"A woman with magnificent hair..." Logan cooed.

Her grin seemed to stretch from ear to ear, but it suddenly vanished as a worried look arrived on her face.

"It was me," she gasped, "Or, rather, her. Or, rather, me as her. Or rather her as the other me."

"Sorry? What?"

"It was me, now, who witnessed sixteen-year-old me killing those men, but it was twenty-year-old me who went back to my sixteen-year-old self to physically do it."

"Now *that*," trilled Wild Flower, pointing at her friend with both index fingers simultaneously, "Is the thing that I couldn't quite think how to explain."

"It is baffling and, yet – at the very same time – it is exquisitely elegant in its simplicity."

"That is *her* speaking, again, isn't it?"

"Yes, it feel like it. No! Wait! In fact it is *both* of us because we are one and the same."

"I see..." said Wild Flower, her tone making it abundantly clear that she didn't.

"I'm like you!" Logan shrieked, gripping the sides of her head.

"Like me?"

"Yes! You've never seen this done, have you? Yet you do it, yourself, all the time!"

"I do?"

"Yes. Because you," she said, patting Wild Flower on the top of her head, "Are six years old, but you are also – what? twenty-six years old? – at the same time."

"It is a way of life that I have started to take for granted, but now that you have pointed it out to me, I must confess that the older me does intrude on the younger me more regularly than I had appreciated."

"So me being ten years of age when I am slaying the queen's foes is just a physical, flesh and blood thing, because the real me – the one behind my actions – is the one who is double this age."

"If you recall the reaction of your maid to our possessing swords," said Wild Flower, thoughtfully, "She could see it was so, but found it a strange thing to accept."

"On the one hand, she seemed to like the idea of women having swords, but on the other hand, she was still uncomfortable with it."

"So, if *women* having swords is a strange thing, then *children* having swords must be stranger still."

"Therefore, if there were a killing, it would be *men* who would be the natural suspects."

"And a woman almost unthinkable as being the guilty party."

"But hugely less likely still, would be…"

"A child."

"And, even amongst children, the very least likely of all?"

"Would be a girl."

The two clapped their hands with glee.

"There is something just so deliciously perfect about this," said Logan.

"And please remember, I have met the twenty-year-old you, Logan, and she – as The Flashing Blade – is still undiscovered, her identity completely unknown."

"So if I remain undetected at twenty, it means that I was never detected before that."

"You say this truly."

"Indeed, I do, so let me say this even truer still: *Let us do this thing.*"

"Yes, Your Majesty," said Wild Flower, saluting her as if she were Queen Annis herself, "Your wish is my command."

CHAPTER 23

Gillum Dalry leaned in close to Padraic Howison, "It is the girl sitting next to The Laird Grant on his right side who is his granddaughter," he whispered.

Howison looked down the long banquet table and recognised her immediately, "She is just like her picture."

"Yes, it is a very good likeness."

"And the Laird is not suspicious?"

"No, not at all, he suspects nothing."

"Of course. Why would he? We are just two of his old friends who are passing through and who wish to remember the old days with him."

"Exactly so," Dalry agreed, "And he would scarcely be hosting a banquet for us if he knew anything."

"This is a good meal," Howison conceded, grudgingly.

"I think this surpasses a *'good meal'* by a very wide margin."

Howison smiled, his scheming mind hard at work.

"I believe," he proclaimed, with a raised voice, "That this is the best food I have tasted in half a lifetime."

All of the guests within earshot promptly voiced their own praise. They had learned that The Laird Grant's guests at the banquet were envoys of King James. It was for this reason that they had deigned to accept their invitations. They were all astute enough to recognise the dangers of snubbing representatives of the royal court.

As Howison looked around, many of the other diners were raising a glass to The Laird Grant in acknowledgement of the splendid feast. The Laird graciously accepted their praise.

"I cannot recall," one of them remarked, directing their words at the Laird, "When I have enjoyed a more consistently wonderful array of food. Course after course, each one outdoing the one before it."

Their host nodded politely to them and seemed to relish them showing respect rather than their more usual contempt.

Dalry, who had been keeping a careful watch on the other guests, very gently nudged his arm.

"The man with the pheasant's feather in his Tam O'Shanter is The Laird Grant's Sergeant-at-Arms," he whispered.

Howison turned casually to glance at the man and was greeted by his stony stare.

"Perhaps not the right moment to have turned," said Dalry, with a little smirk.

"You don't think that *he* suspects, do you?"

"No, I can't think that he does."

"He looks hostile."

"That might be because his master has shared our plan with him. Perhaps he does not relish the idea of yet more shame on Clan Grant if it fails and word of it escapes."

The Laird beckoned a servant and spoke a few words to them. The servant nodded, bowed and came to stand next to Padraic Howison. The servant shielded his mouth with a hand and discreetly relayed a message from The Laird Grant.

Padraic Howison stood up and made as to strike the handle of his dirk against a very ornate, half-empty silver bowl on the table. The man sat opposite gave him a thunderous look. Howison picked up a cotton napkin, draped it over the edge of the bowl, and – while the other guest glared at such a paltry precaution – proceeded to ring it like a bell.

All heads turned to him.

"Mnathan agus Uaislean," he began (this being the Gaelic for 'ladies and gentlemen'), "It is a great pleasure to be here with you all today to enjoy the company of His Lairdship the Grant of Garten."

There was a ripple of polite applause.

"The Laird Grant and I, along with my good friend sat next to me, spent some wonderful and memorable years together in the army."

This statement was met with general murmurs of approval.

"I may burden you, sooner or later in conversation, with some of our exploits. I guarantee only to mention the good things and nothing likely to cause dire embarrassment."

Several people laughed around the table, but this laughter immediately spread to everyone when the Laird pulled a comic version of a nervous face.

"I think I know which tale His Lairdship is thinking about," Howison added, to howls of genuine laughter from all.

After basking in the success of his humour for a little while, Howison sat down. The moment he did, The Laird Grant rose to his feet.

"I know you will all want to join me in welcoming these two bold and gallant gentlemen to the Highlands," he said, indicating Dalry and Howison.

There was restrained applause.

"And I must bind them to make no mention of those exploits that involved copious amounts of whiskey!"

This was greeted with unrestrained laughter.

"Or," added Howison, jovially, "Women of doubtful morals!"

The laughter died in a heartbeat and the most dreadful and appalling silence took its place. The ticking of the huge clock on the wall, previously inaudible, suddenly became almost deafening. The room was bathed in an excruciatingly brittle tension.

Grant suddenly gave a very purposeful chuckle and, in an instant, the whole room promptly erupted into hearty laughter.

Howison noted that even the two women at the table managed to abandon their reserved and aloof expressions and replace them with the hint of a smile.

Logan Grant, for her part, gave a little smile, too.

Wild Flower, sitting beside her, lowered her head and pretended that she had heard nothing.

His Lairdship pondered whether to continue with his response but – finding that the laughter was renewing itself, in fits and starts as people exchanged remarks – he discreetly lowered himself back into his seat.

Gradually, faces turned away from him and a low murmur began as people resumed their conversations.

Catching Wild Flower's eye, the laird beckoned to her. She slid off her chair and padded across to him in her stocking feet.

"Where are your slippers?" he asked.

Wild Flower shrugged, rocked her head and formed her mouth – sequentially – into the first syllable of three different explanations, one after the other. The Laird held up a hand to quell her attempts at a reply, opened his mouth to say something, then opted for smiling and shaking his head in amusement.

The two looked each other directly in the eye and Wild Flower heard his unspoken question. She cupped her mouth and he hunkered down in his chair to bring his ear level with her.

"The man Padraic Howison is up to no good," she whispered.

The Laird nodded, thoughtfully.

"The man with him," she added, "Is Gillum Dalry and he is cut from the same cloth."

"I thought as much. It means that my suspicions have good foundation."

"If anything, your low estimation of them falls short of the mark when it comes to their abundant capacity for treachery and deceit."

The Laird Grant guffawed. This caused Wild Flower to contort her face into an absurd approximation of offence, but it quickly turned into a smile.

"Your vocabulary is priceless!" he sniggered.

Logan, who had been overhearing, leaned close to the pair, "It's like conversing with a very erudite scholar!" she observed.

"You're getting as bad as each other!" he quipped.

"If you mix with them long enough," winked Logan, "You become like them."

"Well then," he cautioned, "Don't either of you mix with the two men who are our hosts."

"We won't," replied Wild Flower, very pointedly, "For Queen Annis will be the deliverance of your Clan."

The Laird Grant looked at her suspiciously, "What do you know of my dealings with these two men?"

"They wish you to join them in a plan they have formed."

"They do, indeed," he replied, then appeared to think for a moment before continuing, "We are – and we have been for centuries – in a feud with the Queens of the West."

"And that, of course, is hardly likely to be suddenly swept aside in the near future."

"No, exactly."

"And yet, this feud of such long standing is unable to summon your fullest vigour and enthusiasm."

"Is that a question or a statement?"

"It is less a question than it is a statement."

"Then let me give you more of an insight than a denial," he confided, "I have learned things that have sapped my hatred to the point where sustaining it feels like a chore. I feel like I am a storm that has blown itself out."

"Grandfather?" asked Logan, "Do we not hate the Queen of the West?"

"Yes," he replied, with scarcely a jot of conviction, "We loathe, hate and abhor her with a vengeance that devours our very soul."

So void of conviction were his words that Logan could not suppress a smile.

"Tell me, Wild Flower," he asked, "Why is it that you have not closed your eyes and concentrated so much as once during our conversation?"

"I am aware of events about to unfold and they are best left without my interference."

"Good events or bad events?"

"If you were given a wish by the gods, then this is the wish you would choose."

The Laird Grant scowled, "A huge wish, then?"

"It is a huge power that the gods wield."

"When and where will this be?"

"I cannot tell you when – though it will not be more than a week or so away – but I am able to tell you where," she replied, with a wry smile.

"Where?"

"On horseback, in the middle of a river."

The Laird's eyebrows shot so high that they risked ending up at the back of his neck.

CHAPTER 24

Once the impressive meal had finally drawn to a conclusion, The Laird Grant retired with his hosts to the opulent smoking room. There, they spent almost two hours talking, playing cards and drinking whiskey.

Eventually, The Laird Grant emerged and sent a servant to collect the girls from the games room. The valet returned with Logan and Wild Flower trotting behind him.

Logan and Wild Flower joined The Laird Grant in front of a roaring fire. Five minutes later, Padraic Howison and Gillum Dalry arrived at His Lairdship's door, wanting to speak with him privately.

When their knock came, Wild Flower stiffened and looked uneasy. Logan quickly moved to stand silently in front of her and gave her an enquiring look. Her grandfather paused, as he passed them on his way to the door, and looked at Wild Flower enquiringly. She shook her head and shrugged her shoulders, unable to muster any explanation for her anxiety.

Howison and Dalry had only exchanged a few words in lowered voices with His Lairdship before the two girls were sent off to wait in the library.

Closing the library door behind her, Logan took out two chairs from under a table and, arranging them to face each other, sat down in one and waved Wild Flower to sit in the other.

"There is something wrong, isn't there?" she demanded.

"Something very wrong," Wild Flower agreed.

"What is it?"

"I'm not sure. Things are foggy and unclear in my mind. Whatever those two men are saying, it is one lie followed by another."

"How so?"

"They are telling your grandfather one thing – and that is something that is bad enough in its own right – but the thing they are actually intending to do is far, far worse."

"What is it that they have in mind?"

"That's just it. I cannot tell. Whatever plan they are hatching, its consequences are so dreadful that it will change the course of history."

"I sense that there is great danger, too," said Logan.

"Yes, there is, indeed, for this could get your grandfather killed."

Logan's hand shot to her mouth, "What are we going to do about it?"

"Who? Us? You and I? A six-year-old girl and a ten-year-old girl? What are *we* going to do about it?"

Suddenly, they both laughed and clapped their hands in glee.

"A six-year-old girl…" began Wild Flower.

"With thirty years of magic and life knowledge behind her!" finished Logan.

"And a ten-year-old girl…" declared Wild Flower.

"With the ability and cunning of a much famed and much feared assassin at her disposal!" chirped Logan.

They both grinned.

"We need to refine our skills," said Wild Flower.

"Like sharpening the edge of a blade," agreed Logan.

"For we are not here to be idle."

"But to be harnessed."

"We are not here to be spectators."

"But to be participants."

They looked at each other in awe. Neither had needed any prompting to know either the exact words they had just spoken, nor the responses.

"I have a feeling," said Wild Flower.

"A feeling that we have been here before?" suggested Logan.

"Yes or, if not before, then…"

"Then we were always *going* to be here."

"Which is, of course, impossible."

"Completely impossible."

"And yet…"

"And yet…"

They shared a look of total wonder.

"And yet all who need to gather will gather…"

"And yet all that needs to be done will be done…"

They looked at each other and spoke the same words simultaneously: "The Quickening!"

"In a moment," said Logan, "There will be a knock at the door."

"And it will be the valet."

"Who will tell us that we are to retire to the bunk room to sleep."

"And then, a maid will appear carrying a pair of purple quilts."

"She will almost drop them and what will she say?"

"She will say: *Clumsy me!*."

A moment later, there was a knock at the door. The door opened and The Laird Grant's valet peered around it.

"Yes?" called Logan.

"Your grandfather will be occupied for a long time in his chamber," the valet replied.

"Oh, I see," said Logan.

"I am instructed to take you to the bunk room, which – I am told to say – you will find most comfortable as alternative sleeping quarters."

Logan and Wild Flower stood up from their chairs and made their way to the door. As they stepped into the corridor, behind the valet, a maid appeared. She carried a pair of purple quilts. As she attempted to adjust them, to take a firmer grip, she almost dropped them.

"Clumsy me!" she smiled, gathering them tightly as she followed behind them.

The two girls exchanged a glance.

The four marched off in a little procession towards the adjoining stables and up a short set of steps into the bunk room.

At the maid's direction, the valet pulled a set of ropes hanging from the wall and two beds descended, like a pair of castle drawbridges. The valet held the quilts while the maid took a pair of mattresses from a cupboard and fussed around placing sheets and pillows onto them. She then took back the quilts and placed them on top.

Logan leaned towards Wild Flower and, without speaking, mouthed the words: *'Milk? Hot chocolate?'*

Happy with her work, the maid turned to the girls, "Would you like any milk or hot chocolate before you retire?" she asked.

Logan looked to Wild Flower, who shook her head.

"Nothing, thank you," Logan confirmed, "But it is kind of you to ask."

The maid and the valet made their way back to the main part of the house.

"Is this a dream?" asked Logan, as the sound of footsteps receded into the distance.

"No, it's not a dream."

"So this is absolutely real?"

"No, I don't think it is quite that, either."

"Then what?"

"At this precise moment, I think it is reality, but *more* than reality."

"More than reality?" Logan queried, wrinkling her forehead.

She dwelt on the remark for a little while, then, raising her hand, she looked at her empty palm.

"I am imagining that I am holding a whip," she said, closing her hand around the handle of the invisible object.

After brief contemplation, she raised her hand. Then she jerked it up into the air, before snapping it down again. Half a second later – to the surprise of them both – the sharp crack of a whip could be heard.

Fascinated, Wild Flower held out her hand and made as if she were suspending a bell from it. She took hold of an imaginary metal rod and struck the air where – if it were real – the bell would have hung. Instantly, a loud chime note rang out.

CHAPTER 25

"I don't understand," protested the twenty-year-old Logan, stood in the bunk room next to the stables of her stronghouse.

"No, nor do I, to be honest," admitted sixteen-year-old Wild Flower, shrugging her shoulders apologetically.

"How can that be? How could *you* not understand?"

"Well, it's simply how it is."

"But how did you know that we had to do these things?"

"It just came to me. It jumped into my head."

"You had me crack this whip on impulse!" the twenty-year-old Logan guffawed.

"Yes and I rang this bell for no better reason!" the sixteen-year-old Wild Flower chuckled.

"And yet you don't understand why?"

"I have a very strong feeling that, if we wait, we will *remember* why we came here and did this."

"Well, one thing is for sure," laughed Logan, "Whenever you appear, my life is never the least bit boring!"

They both laughed.

Presently, Logan made a face and slapped a hand to the top of her head, as if something had just occurred to her.

"I *do* remember!" she cried.

"Yes!" blurted Wild Flower, "So do I!"

"It is a warning to our younger selves in our past. It is to spark a recollection. To show them that we know ourselves to be in danger."

CHAPTER 26

"In all my ten years of life," declared Logan, "I have never felt more certain that I have a destiny and a purpose to fulfil than I do now."

Wild Flower gave a twisted, impish smile in return.

"Would you like me to talk about the six years of this body's existence or the thirty years of my lifetime?"

"I think you have had a destiny since even before you were born."

"You believe in fate, Logan?"

"How many ten-year-olds have been known to debate the possibility of fate with a six-year-old and, furthermore, how many six-year-olds would even know what they were talking about?"

"I'm sorry," Wild Flower smirked, "You completely lost me after the first couple of words. Is that *grown up*, that you are speaking, perhaps?"

"You and I, Wild Flower, have not yet grown up, but at the same time, we have already grown up."

"Oh dear! That makes things complicated."

"In what way?"

"I know for sure that I live to the age of thirty and you know for sure that you live to the age of twenty."

The look of extreme worry on Logan's face prompted Wild Flower to hurriedly reassure her.

"I'm not saying that neither you nor I live any longer than those ages..."

"That's a relief!"

"But it does mean that we find ourselves in a very strange situation."

"Explain."

"Whatever we do to thwart the wicked plans of Howison and Dalry – and your grandfather's involvement in them – we know for sure that we will not die in the attempt."

"Because what *does* happen, is what *will* happen?"

"Yes."

"Unless, of course…"

"Unless, of course, what?"

"Unless, of course, we manage to change history because *that* is the thing that is required."

"We cannot change history."

"That is what you believe, Wild Flower."

"No. That is what I *know*."

"What if the change only involves you and I?"

"How is that possible?"

"What if you and I went to live in a cave in the mountains? Completely cut off from the world? If we had no contact with anybody, then if we were to die, it would have no impact on anybody else's life."

They both thought about this for a long time, walking back and forth, each behaving as if they were alone in the room.

Suddenly, Logan gave a cry of inspiration.

"Wait! If there were anything that we needed to know, then would we not get to know it?"

"Not necessarily," Wild Flower disagreed, "Only our future selves would know and, surely, would they not have tried to send us a warning."

Logan, growled and slapped her leg hard in frustration. The action made a loud crack, just like the noise of a whip.

"We did!" they both said together.

"Crack!" said Logan, making the motion of cracking a whip.

"Ding!" replied Wild Flower, making the motion of striking a bell.

CHAPTER 27

"So what warning were we sending to ourselves from the future?" asked ten-year-old Logan.

"I think – or I am inspired to think – that we were just warning ourselves to be careful."

"Warning ourselves to be careful?" asked Logan, looking sceptical.

"Either that or reassuring ourselves that we do, in fact, survive?"

"Why would we need to reassure ourselves that we survive?"

"Because our lives might be in danger?"

"How so?" scoffed Logan, before suddenly jerking in surprise and looking at Wild Flower fiercely, "No! Please! Don't say that!"

"Don't say what?"

"Don't say what you are about to say!"

"How can I promise that? I haven't even decided what to say yet."

They both gazed suspiciously around the bunk room, their eyes delving into every corner. Once they had both double checked that they were alone, they leaned close together.

"Are we watching ourselves?" asked Logan, warily.

"I don't know. Are we?"

"I mean from the future."

"Yes, that's what I meant, too."

"Is that possible?"

Wild Flower grimaced, "I no longer know for certain what is possible. I no longer know for certain what is impossible. Not anymore."

"Well, if *you* don't know!"

Wild Flower looked puzzled. Then, she held a finger up, suddenly inspired. She lowered the finger and positioned it to point at Logan.

"Wait!" she said, "What did you just say?"

"I said: *'Well, if you don't know!'* by which I meant..."

"That's it! I don't *need* to know! Neither of us needs to know."

"Because?"

"Because what needs to happen..."

"Will happen," Logan agreed.

"Yes."

"So we don't *need* to do *anything*, in that case."

"Whoa! Stop! Wait!" Wild Flower protested, "I don't think *that* is how this is meant to work."

It was too late. Logan had already sat down on the floor and crossed her arms in front of her.

"Please, Logan, we have to take some kind of action."

Logan abruptly leapt to her feet.

"Wait!" she urged, "Do you not remember? We already knew about this situation."

"We did?"

"Yes. We did. Think back."

Wild Flower thought. Then it came to her.

"Of course!" she trilled, "We are not here to be idle."

"But to be harnessed," Logan responded.

"We are not here to be spectators."

"But to be participants."

Delighted to have finally been able to work out some kind of perspective, they simultaneously reached their arms up and, lofting their hands, loudly smacked their palms together in a 'high five'.

They froze and looked at each other, panic stricken.

"What did you just do?" asked Logan, accusingly.

"What did *you* just do?" countered Wild Flower.

They paused distractedly, looking first at their hands and then up in the air, where they had just slapped one against the other.

"What did *we* just do?" asked Wild Flower, in a more conciliatory tone.

"I've no idea. It was strange. Very strange, in fact. Very strange, but oddly spontaneous."

"Yes, I know what you mean. Let's do it again."

They both reached up and re-enacted the gesture, this time with far less enthusiasm and making far less noise.

Logan looked at her friend with concern in her eyes. In response, Wild Flower motioned for her to wait and closed her eyes to concentrate. She began to draw upon her mysterious inspiration. It was something that she had promised herself she would not do, for fear of knowing more than she should, but she felt that there was no other way to proceed.

"I was born eight hundred years ago," she announced after a long pause, "And came to this time because I was drawn to it by a force that I could not resist."

Logan waited patiently for her to resume.

"There is something profound happening," Wild Flower disclosed, "And it is not just our lives in ten years' time that call to us. We are being hailed from a far greater distance."

Logan held her breath. Suddenly afraid to hear what might come next.

"It is the far future that hails us. Not ten years from now or even a hundred years from now, but four hundred years ahead of this time."

Logan's eyes sprang wide and her mouth dropped open. Wild Flower gleefully explained.

"In that time in the future, the motion we made will mean something to them. It is a celebration. An action signifying triumph. It is what they will do when Scotland is free."

"I don't understand," protested Logan, "Scotland *is* free. Why would we ever need to *become* free?"

"In 1707 England and Scotland will join together in a union that will make them as one nation. England, Ireland, Scotland and Wales will be joined as the 'United Kingdom' for over four centuries."

"We will be invaded? We will be taken over?"

"No, there will be much bloodshed, strife and many battles between now and then, some of them involving Scotland and some not, but it is as much the Scottish who take over the English as it is the other way around."

"We are happy to do this?"

"Neither Scotland nor England could endure alone. The wars that will sweep across Europe in the centuries that are to come will need them to be together, as one. The countries of the new United Kingdom will be victorious against overwhelming odds."

"So the Union is a good thing?"

"For a time."

"But not for always?"

"No, not for always."

"So we will break away?"

"Yes, we will break away, but we will stay together."

"Surely, we cannot do both?"

"No, I would not have thought so, but there it is."

"If something is impossible, then is it not impossible?"

"England and Scotland will remain together," said Wild Flower, with total conviction, "But both countries will be free of each other."

"But how can that be?"

"I do not know. It is a conundrum that I cannot solve."

"A conundrum?" asked Logan.

"A puzzle."

"Surely any puzzle has a solution."

"One would think so."

"It has to be so."

Wild Flower shrugged her shoulders and gave an enormous, long sigh.

"Think again!" Logan instructed, in a voice that brooked no argument, "Ask the future what happens to Scotland."

Wild Flower obediently closed her eyes. A full minute passed before she opened them. When she did, she laughed out loud.

"The solution isn't in the future!" she cried, "It is in the past!"

"It sounds to me like another impossibility!" Logan complained.

"There was once a man who liked to laugh. He liked to laugh loudly. He would laugh loudly with his English neighbours and he would laugh loudly with his Scottish neighbours. This man was Noory McGregor."

"And what of him?"

"He had the solution even before we ever had the problem."

"I want to ask you *'How is that possible?'* but I fear your reply…"

Wild Flower grinned.

"Well, Logan, this Noory McGregor was completely unknown to me, just a minute ago, but now I know all about him. He is a most fascinating person, especially with regards to his opinions about the relationship between Scotland and England."

"Tell me, please. I wish to hear."

"If you took a stubborn, pig-headed man from the Kingdom of Fife and married him to a stubborn, pig-headed woman from the Kingdom of Yorkshire, what do you think their child would be like?"

"They would be stubborn and pig-headed?"

"Exactly so!"

"But there is more to this?"

"Yes, far more! Just as those in Fife – despite their lofty and independent spirits – must somehow get along with the people around them in the rest of Scotland, those in Yorkshire – who, I must tell you, are every bit as lofty and independent in their spirits – must somehow get along with the people to living nearby in Lancashire."

"Tell me more."

"Eventually, assaulting each other, kidnapping each other and killing each other brought them so much misery that they could no longer endure it."

"And so?"

"And so, they had to eventually learn to accommodate each other."

"*Accommodate* each other?"

"Give in to each other without actually giving in."

"I see," said Logan, making it plain that she did not.

"To properly explain, I must tell you about Noory McGregor. The child of a Fife man and a Yorkshire woman."

"Please do."

"Noory was one of twelve children. Growing up, he had to learn – the easy way or the hard way – to get along with people. He learned to accommodate those whom he would like to punch, maim or kill."

"You mean the English?"

"No," replied Wild Flower, shrieking with laughter, "I actually meant his brothers and sisters!"

Logan laughed, too.

"Noory McGregor's parents lived for some time in Yorkshire, at the top of a range of hills called The Pennines. It was right on the border with Lancashire. Then, later, they lived at Glen Vale in Fife, near the waterfalls, right along the border with the rest of Scotland."

"It sounds like his family were attracted to border strife."

"Yes, it seems so, but Noory was able to smooth any argument and make peace between any parties. He had a rare talent for it, even from the youngest age."

"Where did he live when he grew up? When he had his own family?"

"He never married. He never had a family. Perhaps, after growing up in a crowd, he yearned for nothing more than to be alone?"

"So he didn't move to Glasgow or Edinburgh to live in a busy city?"

"No, after he had made his way in the world and put away enough money to own a home, he moved to Carter Bar in Roxburghshire, right on the border between Scotland and England."

"He really does seem to be drawn to borders!"

"Yes! Noory McGregor built himself not one but two houses. They stood side by side, sharing a common wall between them, and perfectly spanned the border between England and Scotland."

"So he lived in both countries?"

"Yes. In fact, he boasted that he would often eat breakfast in Scotland, in a morning, then walk next door to eat his lunch in England and, in the evening, return to Scotland to eat dinner and sleep. He claimed that would often move between countries completely at random."

"A real character!"

"He was a writer and philosopher, but he worked in Paris in France for some time, employed as a journalist on a newspaper there. In the year 1514 – which is one hundred and eight years ago – he wrote a very interesting poem. The poem explains to the French why the English and the Scottish were always battling each other, but why – without hesitation – they would rise to each other's defence in times of conflict."

"You wouldn't possibly know that poem, would you?" Logan winked.

"I know it word for word."

"Nothing about you surprises me anymore!"

Wild Flower cleared her throat, paused for dramatic effect, and then quoted, word perfect, Noory McGregor's poem.

> "We kill each other, from time to time,
>
> A Scot kills his and the English, mine.
>
> But God help he who kills a Scot,
>
> In the sight of the English! Fool, do not!

Nor kill the English in a Scot's own sight,
For dead as a stone will be your plight!
We reserve the right to kill each other,
Most jealously, as if a lover,
But with fury are these zealots prone,
To hold this right as just their own!"

When Wild Flower had finished, Logan applauded her. Wild Flower bowed flamboyantly and swirled an imaginary cape about her.

CHAPTER 28

"I have a question," said Logan, holding up her hand, as if she were a student in a classroom.

"Yes. The girl over there," said Wild Flower, in a thoroughly pompous tone, "You may address the class."

Logan's hand faltered in the air, raising and lowering, as if speaking to the entire class had prompted a bout of nerves.

"If you please," she said, timidly, "How does the poem written by Noory McGregor in 1514 relate to an independent Scotland so many centuries later?"

"I'm so glad that you asked that," replied Wild Flower, before abandoning her matronly tone to re-immerse herself in the story, "When he returned home from France, he wrote down his thoughts about the future independence of Scotland and of England in the form of several pamphlets."

"Pamphlets?"

"Small, folded documents of a convenient size for people to put in their pocket to read later."

"I see," said Logan, suddenly looking puzzled, "But there was no union between Scotland and England at that time."

"No, exactly so."

"So he knew that it was going to happen before it happened?"

"He saw it in a dream."

"Like *our* dreams? The ones *we* have?"

"Well, yes, considering he wrote about it in 1514 and it didn't happen until almost two hundred years later in 1707."

"Noory McGregor was a seer."

"I don't think he was a seer," Wild Flower replied, with a flicker of a smile, "But he certainly saw!"

"And what did he write?"

"He said that if a United Kingdom came about, and there were a single parliament making laws for both countries, then both countries – Scotland and England – should expect the exact same treatment from each other and that one should not seek independence *from* the other, but *for* each other."

"But Noory McGregor foretold that England and Scotland would become independent of each other, while each still remaining a member of the United Kingdom?"

"Yes."

"That is impossible."

"No."

"How can the impossible be possible?"

"Because we have Noory McGregor's word for it and he was a genius."

"He would surely have needed to be a miracle worker, too!"

"Even as a young child, Noory McGregor settled disputes. He was able to give people what they wanted without giving them what they couldn't really have."

"That sounds... baffling."

"I agree."

"So, what was his solution?"

"He said that when the moment came for Scotland and England to become independent, one from the other, they should give up everything that they should, but give up nothing that they shouldn't."

"The more you explain this, the more confused I become," laughed Logan, "What did he say should be given up?"

"All powers to make laws. Scotland should make all Scottish laws and the English should have no part in it. England should make all English laws and the Scottish should have no part in it."

"What are the things that should be kept?"

"He said that there should still be a common army, a common navy, a common authority to both look after the lighthouses and to guard the coastline and a common customs and excise force."

"A customs and excise force? What is that?"

"I have no idea," said Wild Flower, quickly closing her eyes to think about it, "They are like special soldiers who stop things coming into the country that are banned and who make people pay taxes on things that other countries are allowed to send here to be sold."

Logan sat deep in thought for a while and Wild Flower waited for her attention to return. When it eventually did, Logan had something important to address.

"This is my big question," she said, "What do you and I have to do with anything that you have spoken about? Why does it involve us? Also, why is the far future calling to us here in the year 1622?"

"Nothing of this made any sense to me, either, until something came to me: Noory McGregor was one of your ancestors. He is related to you through one of his sisters."

"Oh, I see."

"And where do you think all of his original writings might be?"

"I have no idea."

"Have a guess."

"In a museum in Edinburgh? Or, perhaps, in London?"

"They are all in a wooden chest in your grandfather's personal study."

"He inherited them?"

"They were passed down, generation to generation, and were ultimately received into the charge of your grandfather."

"That gives us a connection, but it doesn't exactly explain why you and I are involved."

"It is because Padraic Howison and Gillum Dalry propose to have your grandfather lend them Noory McGregor's papers. They intend to flaunt them to Queen Annis in order to deceive her that they are envoys of King James. It is a widely held belief – but a completely false one – that it is King James who has possession of those papers."

"I feel a cold chill, just thinking about it."

"And not without good reason."

"What is it that my grandfather believes they *actually* intend to do?"

"I cannot tell, just yet. When I try to see, my visions of the deed are misty and uncertain. Whatever it is, she is in danger."

Logan's eyes began to dart around the room. She turned her head to the door, then all four corners of the room.

"What is it?" asked Wild Flower.

"I am here," Logan replied, "I am here, watching myself."

Wild Flower looked around the room, "You are right. I can feel it too, now."

"But you do not see the older me, here?"

Wild Flower smiled and gripped her lower lip in her teeth, as if intrigued by something.

"I do not see your older self, because I cannot see my own other self. Both of our other selves are here, though, I assure you."

"We were here before, when we heard the sound of the whip?"

"Yes."

"We were here before, when we heard the sound of the bell?"

"Yes."

Logan went to sit at a little table and rested her hands flat on its surface.

"In that case," she announced, "I want myself to, somehow, show me that the future version of myself is here."

The two girls sat in silence. In the distance, somewhere within the house, they could hear the ticking of a clock. They had not heard it before. It was too far away. Now, the silence was so intense that the sound of it was clear.

Suddenly, Logan's index finger began to flex upward, off the table.

"Someone is touching me," said Logan.

The finger continued to rise, reaching its maximum possible extent – short of pain or discomfort – then, as if being deliberately released, it dropped back to the table making a loud noise that echoed around the room.

"Well," said Logan, "There is no doubt about that then, is there?"

CHAPTER 29

Padraic Howison leaned closer to The Laird Grant, "It is common rumour, Your Lairdship, that Noory McGregor's documents and papers are in the possession of King James. This being so, our presenting them to the Queen of the West will go a long way to convincing her of our authenticity."

"And," Gillum Dalry joined in, "We are very familiar with the royal palace in London. We have visited many times. We know how to behave, how to speak and how to dress in a manner appropriate to the roles we claim to hold."

"So the historical artifacts we will be bearing..." crooned Howison.

"...Artifacts kindly supplied by your good self..." Dalry interjected.

"...Will be the final piece in the puzzle that convinces Queen Annis that we are wholly genuine," Howison finished.

The Laird Grant rubbed his chin, thoughtfully, for a long time before replying.

"And all you require of her is to sign a treaty, already bearing what seems to be the signature of King James, that merely formalises what has already been agreed between her and the king?"

"Yes," the two men agreed, a little too eagerly.

"But the document – if I have understood you correctly – is carefully drafted..."

"Drafted with the most excruciating care and in the most painstaking manner!" advised Dalry.

"Yes, in that way, as you say," accepted The Laird, "But allowing for other words to be inserted after she has applied her signature."

"Yes," Howison beamed, "The text is precisely aligned and arranged to leave innocent looking spaces at the end of some lines. It does not look in the least bit suspicious."

"But," Dalry enthused, "Those spaces will furnish us with the precise room we need to insert an exact number of letters that will change the whole tone and content of the document."

"Turning it from an innocent agreement, to a complete and utter betrayal of the Highlands," confirmed Howison.

"And the king is happy to do this?"

"He is aware of only the broadest outline of our mission. We have kept the details of our plans secret from the king," said Howison in a sombre tone, "He will only find out about what we have done, when we have done it."

"The king is far too soft and far too weak to engage in such a plot as this," Dalry complained.

"We do, however, have access to a scribe who has practised the handwriting of King James to such a level of perfection, that his version of the king's penmanship looks more authentic than the real thing!" said Howison, proudly.

"I swear to you," Dalry chortled, "The king cannot come anywhere close to writing like himself, as this man!"

The Laird Grant grimaced, for the plan sounded just a little too easy to him, but – he told himself – these men would not have travelled all the way from London if there were any real chance of failure.

"Very well," The Laird announced, "You shall have these precious works of Noory McGregor. You may show them to show her. They will, indeed, add credence to your story."

"Scotland will thank you for this one day," Howison declared.

"And history will record you as having been a hero who did the right thing," added Dalry.

"A change in history's opinion of my clan would be welcome. I will not pretend otherwise."

"It is long overdue," oozed Dalry, fervently.

Dalry stiffened. The Laird Grant was fairly sure that Howison had just kicked his shin to quell his enthusiasm. Dalry looked glum.

"Discrediting and disgracing this girl who calls herself *'Queen of the West'* fills me with happiness," His Lairdship confided, "But, let us be clear, your plans go no further than that. You do not intend to do her any physical harm?"

The Laird Grant would later reflect that Howison's look of offence appeared just a little exaggerated and, perhaps, a little too theatrical to be entirely genuine.

"We wish to destroy her reputation, no more," Howison lied.

"You are men of honour," lied The Laird in return, "And I do not doubt you."

In response to this praise, Dalry almost squirmed like a cat. Howison, on the other hand, managed to mostly restrain his joy, manifesting itself only as a brief twitch of his eye.

The few moments that passed seemed prolonged and awkward. The Laird knew that what must come next left the two men were every bit as daunted as they were eager. He waited, thoroughly enjoying their discomfort.

Eventually, Howison decided to take the bull by the horns.

"When might we be able to accept your treasured archive into our care?"

The Laird allowed his face to progress through at least three unnerving varieties of concern – each of which caused them both to worry a little more than the last – before finally condescending to reply.

"I suppose I could muster my guards to convey them for you at my inconvenience."

Howison opened his mouth to reply, but The Laird cut him short.

"Instead, I feel it is more fitting that you take full responsibility for their care and security from the moment they leave my hands."

"Yes, of course. I fully understand," Howison responded, his relief palpable, "I would not dream of imposing on you to do otherwise. We will ensure that these priceless documents are shown the very greatest respect at all times."

"And," Dalry added, "We will keep them as secure as if they were the crown jewels."

The Laird narrowed his eyes, "Neither of you should be in any doubt that that I will hold you to that."

They promptly gave him their most obsequious assurances. After making a laborious show of reluctance and heartlessly prolonging it to dent their enthusiasm, he leaned forward as if to confide in them.

"Tell me, gentlemen, how can you be certain that I am not about to furnish you with mere copies of these famous papers? Brazen forgeries, if you will?" he demanded, relishing their panic, "For might I not have already had such counterfeits prepared?"

The two looked appalled and genuinely taken aback by his words. It was as if he had just thrown a bucket of cold water over them.

"Gentlemen, I jest!" he cried, after allowing them to suffer a while, "My sense of humour is perhaps, at times, a little too sinister."

The two looked mightily relieved. Whatever their plans, The Laird decided, they had evidently just run the risk of them coming unravelled.

As they gathered themselves and recovered their composure, The Laird Grant considered offering them some polite words of conversation to alleviate the tension. This idea quickly fizzled out. He had reached the conclusion that he didn't like them.

Back in his army days, these men had never showered themselves with glory. They had, he recalled, always had some kind of involvement with scandals, misbehaviour and the use of excessive force. No, he didn't like them, he concluded, and, if he had ever really liked them, he had been fooling himself.

He wondered if he would be willing to buy a horse from these men at a market. He decided that he would not.

CHAPTER 30

"You are very quiet, Wild Flower," remarked The Laird Grant.

Wild Flower looked up from her plate and realised that she had spent virtually the whole of breakfast in silence.

"I have that odd feeling that a person might get when a storm is gathering," she replied.

Logan laughed, deciding to make light of it, "I'm sure it is nothing more than the early hint of a cold or a runny nose on the way."

His Lairdship looked back and forth from one girl to the other, carefully scrutinising their expressions and demeanour.

"You, Logan, have hardly said two words to me, yourself."

Logan feigned innocence, "I'm sure I have chattered like a frog in spring, this morning."

"In which case," he replied, "You are an unusually quiet frog and it is an unusually cold spring."

With this, His Lairdship returned to his study of the two, convinced that there was something troubling them.

Logan gave Wild Flower a very pointed and meaningful look. Wild Flower crumpled her lips in reply and looked ill at ease.

"Grandfather," Logan announced, looking directly at her friend, "Wild Flower has something to tell you."

The Laird smiled, "Is it you, Logan, or is it she who has something to tell me?"

Logan gave the look of a chicken that had just spotted a fox, "It is both of us," she said quickly.

Wild Flower held up her hands as she spoke, as if she were surrendering, "The two men, Howison and Dalry. They fill us with dread."

"They are evil," added Logan.

"Well, girls, I'm glad that you don't feel the need to sprinkle sugar on your words."

"We don't know what it is that you have been discussing with them, grandfather, but they chill our souls."

"Do *you* not know what I have been discussing, Wild Flower?"

"No."

"That surprises me."

"It surprises me, too," Wild Flower confessed.

"You have no idea?"

"None."

"How can that be?"

"Because," she replied, "History is about to be made."

"Made for the better or for worse?"

"Whichever it may be, I am prevented from intruding."

"What? Even if you were to rush at them and poke your fingers in their eyes?"

"I'm sure I could do that, but I have no insight or inspiration about their intentions. If I were to rush at them, I would like it to be with a drawn sword."

"A six-year-old would not generally trusted to have such thing, Wild Flower," grinned The Laird.

"Nor are grown women!" Logan complained.

"If you wish for a sword," The Laird assured her, "Then you shall have one. I will see to that."

"Thank you, grandfather."

"You are welcome."

The Laird Grant looked down at his hand and clenched it. Then he held it upright, in front of him, as a fist.

"You have no idea," he murmured, "How good it feels to hold a sword."

Logan looked down at her own palm, curled in her fingers to grip something invisible, and smiled with what seemed to be great satisfaction.

Her grandfather frowned, "Unless, of course, you know already."

Logan raised her hand, as if dismissing it, and sprang its fingers wide apart before her, like an exploding star. The look on her face told him everything.

"You're ten years old," he gasped, "What need do you have of a sword?"

Logan looked suddenly shy.

The Laird added: "And wherever would you get one?"

"Your Sergeant-at-Arms is blameless, My Laird!" cried Wild Flower.

The Laird Grant scowled at her, trying to look angry, but then began to laugh.

"Of course he is!" he roared, pointing at Wild Flower, "He would have had no idea what-so-ever what he was doing! *You* would have made certain of that!"

"He is a *very* good Sergeant-at-Arms, Your Lairdship," Wild Flower declared, "And he keeps your weapons in the most perfect and exemplary condition!"

Logan raised an eyebrow and cocked a smile at her.

"It means outstanding or excellent," explained Wild Flower.

Logan nodded, "I knew that."

"Yes, of course," Wild Flower acknowledged, purposely looking at her blankly and without emotion.

"I sometimes forget," said The Laird, with a grin, "That for all your age is six, you are also as likely to be *twenty*-six."

"I am not the only one who can be precocious," replied Wild Flower, looking directly at Logan.

Logan, screwing up her face at the word 'precocious', responded in a flat tone, "Precocious? You mean acting older than my age?"

Wild Flower drilled her gaze into her friend, "You most definitely have your moments."

"Wait. Stop. Cease," cautioned The Laird, "This conversation is not about the subject in hand, is it? This is something more. What, exactly, is it that you are telling me?"

"Your granddaughter – by fate, by destiny or by divine will – is bound, in this life, to become of valiant and heroic service to Scotland."

"You say this truly?"

"I do. Every word."

"She will live a remarkable life?"

"She will."

"This is not merely likely or probable, this is…"

"This is inevitable. History will know her. Ballads and poems will be written about her."

"A Grant? A lowly Grant?" asked His Lairdship, "Or will it be that she marries and will be known by another name?"

"She will be married, Your Lairdship, but that man will shun his own name for the honour of taking hers."

"What do you say? The honour? Surely, you are mistaken! There is no honour in the name 'Grant'. There is only shame."

Wild Flower beamed at him, "That will not always be the case. Glory beckons soon in the future."

"And it is she, my granddaughter, who will bring this honour to our clan?"

"Her deeds will bring great honour, but not to the Clan Grant, for what she does she will do secretly, so as to avoid being discovered and having a price put on her head."

"Then who is it who will redeem my clan?"

"Why, Sir, it is you. None other than yourself."

"Me?"

"Yes, you. For there will come a wonderful day when the name Grant will not simply be made good, but made to shine like the sun."

"You say this truly?"

"I say it truly."

"I have had dreams of it. I have had the most incredible dreams. I know the outcome, but I don't know what is the route to it."

"You hear thunder in your dreams," asked Wild Flower.

"Yes, thunder. But is it thunder? Or does it just sound like thunder?"

Wild Flower paused and concentrated really hard. As she did so, her face began to contort and she looked confused.

"Yes," she said, at last, "There is thunder, but it is not thunder from the sky. It makes no real sense."

"Just so!" agreed The Laird, "It always seems to be coming from the sky, but I know that it is not."

"It is, indeed, strange," Wild Flower agreed.

"I cannot see what is going on. I can only see the rejoicing afterwards," he said, talking mostly to himself, "It is a most troubling thing to know only half a story."

He continued to mull over the matter, before abruptly jumping back to their previous conversation.

"What is it that my granddaughter does?" he enquired, "What deeds are they that mark her out so firmly in history?"

"In order to answer that question, I must tell you something of overwhelming importance."

"Do so, then. Tell me."

"Nothing that I say and no details that I provide can be anything that would impact on those things that must be and those things that must happen."

"I understand."

"Very well. Your granddaughter will become a woman both famous and feared for her great skill with any weapon that has a point or a blade."

"You mean a female version of The Flashing Blade, the heroic assassin that people talk about?"

"Exactly so, but perhaps in ten years or so."

"Does the Flashing Blade die?" asked The Laird, "He is extremely daring by all accounts."

Logan flinched at this remark and fixed Wild Flower with her eyes.

"No," replied Wild Flower, looking reassuringly at Logan, "The Flashing Blade lives to a ripe old age."

"And how does Logan, obtain her skills?"

"I have thought hard about this and the explanation that I have is that it is, for the most part, you who arranges her tuition."

"Me?"

"Yes. Do you not?" asked Wild Flower, sweetly, while looking deep into his eyes.

"Oh! Yes! Of course!" he exclaimed, a thought suddenly rushing into his head, "I do actually know somebody and, to be frank, they are absolutely ideal."

"That is wonderful. Who is it?"

"A young man with the most exceptional talent. I have encountered him a few times and I am very much impressed by him. I will, in fact, go and make arrangements for your training to begin as soon as possible," said The Laird Grant, rising and making for the door.

"Grandfather? What is his name?"

"His name?" replied her grandfather, stopping with his hand on the door handle, and turned, "His name is Collym McGrath."

Logan looked at her grandfather and blinked in astonishment at the name.

CHAPTER 31

"Tell me," quizzed Logan, "How old would a person be if they lived to *a ripe old age*, please?"

"Well, this body and I are currently six years old," Wild Flower replied with a smile, "So, to a child of that age, somebody of twenty years would most definitely have lived to a ripe old age!"

"So, the age at which I die will remain a mystery?"

"When *any* of us die *must* remain a mystery."

"Must it?"

"Yes, because – if not – it would prey on our minds and that knowledge would affect all of our actions. How could it not?"

Logan nodded, seeming to absorb her meaning.

"Tell me," asked Wild Flower, diverting her friend from those particular thoughts, "Did you have a dream last night?"

"I did."

"An amazing dream?"

"Yes, it was!"

"I want to let you know that it wasn't simply a dream."

"I got that idea, but I wasn't certain."

"Was the kind of dream you had the sort that might be called a '*come true dream*'?"

"Yes."

"You saw yourself kill Sir Reginald Preece?"

"Yes, I did. I was myself, but as The Flashing Blade."

"I want you to test what you might have absorbed."

"How?"

"In your "dream", I addressed you by your nickname. Do you remember that name?"

"Yes! I do! It was Mookey!"

Wild Flower made the motion of applauding her appreciatively. Logan grinned and made a little curtsey.

"Let *me* ask *you* a question in return," Logan challenged, "Does the name *Collym McGrath* means something to you?"

Wild Flower responded with a slightly shy look.

"I thought so," Logan smiled, "It means something to me, too."

"You remember him?"

"Are you asking me if I remember the love of my life?"

"You seem to recall a fair amount," Wild Flower winked.

"How is it possible?"

"The more time you spend in the *other you*, the more you absorb from them and – of course – it works the other way around."

"So, when you and I felt the presence of the *other us*, they were leaving us with an echo of ourselves?"

"An echo? Yes, that's a good way of putting it. They were, indeed, passing to us a tiny little bit of themselves and we, in the same way, were receiving a tiny little bit of them."

"So, in that case, you must…"

"Yes, very much so. I have absorbed so much of all those versions of my older self, that they and I are almost one."

"That must feel absolutely…"

"No! It doesn't! I promise you, Logan, it doesn't!"

"Not at all?"

"No, not at all. Nothing about it is fascinating."

"But what if…"

"It won't be a problem, because they will impart themselves to you by – in all ways that matter – by *becoming* you."

"That makes me a very dangerous ten-year-old!"

"Very dangerous, indeed."

"Am I right in saying that…"

"Yes, you are. We visited our future selves because it was necessary for it to happen."

"How do you cope with all of this, Wild Flower?"

"I often ask myself the same thing."

"Does it not torment your mind?"

"If I were to let it, then it would. There is no doubt about that."

"How do you prevent it?"

"I just tell myself that I am no more than a twig floating down a stream. Where I have been, I have been. Where I am going, I am going. I have precious little more influence on my situation than the twig. The twig, however, cannot think, so it doesn't think. That is an enviable advantage! So, I imitate the twig. If I don't think about things, then I don't dwell on them."

"And whatever must be, will be?"

"Yes."

"And wherever anybody must be, they will be?"

"Yes."

"How am I – or, rather, the far more dangerous version of me – going to be where I need to be? How will I, in this age and time, protect the Queen of the West?"

"Let us see, shall we? For, I believe, your grandfather is just about to return."

That very moment, the door opened and The Laird Grant strode in.

"I have sent a message to Collym McGrath," he announced, "And made him an offer that I sincerely believe he will find impossible to decline."

"There is no doubt about it," Wild Flower declared.

"You know this?"

"Yes, I do. In fact, I can guarantee it."

"This is excellent news."

"There is, however, the matter of Gillum Dalry and Padraic Howison."

"In what respect?"

"You have come to an arrangement with those two..." Wild Flower paused and grimaced, her tone changing to inject contempt to the last word, "Those two *gentlemen*."

"Are you able to read my life as if it were a book?" His Lairdship asked.

"No, but some things jump into my mind unbidden."

The Laird grunted, the sound containing a note of resignation, and replied to her mimicking Wild Flower's own emphasis on the same word.

"The two *gentlemen*," he said, "Are going to take charge of something of great value to me."

"But you do not trust them."

"No, I don't."

"They are worried about trusting you, too."

"They are?"

"Yes, they fear that you might betray them and inform Queen Annis of their intentions."

"I have given them my word."

"Men who are without honour have no real understanding of honour."

The Laird Grant shook his head dismally, "So what is to be done about it?"

"You will send your Sergeant-at-Arms with them, to guard your property."

"And they?"

"They will demand that you demonstrate to them your trustworthiness."

"How?"

"They will demand that you give them a hostage."

"A hostage?"

"Yes."

"Who?"

"They will — very unwisely — say that Logan must accompany them."

"No! Never! That is out of the question!"

"If you recall, I said that they would do so very unwisely."

"*Unwisely* in what way?"

"It will be their undoing?"

"Their undoing? How so?"

"The gods will be entirely with her and entirely against them."

"That is not enough. The gods are prone to whims and fancies"

"Then I will go with the both of them."

At this, his face softened and his jaw unclenched.

"You will?"

"Yes, I will. I will be visible at some times and invisible at others, but I will not leave her side. I guarantee it."

"No harm will come to her? No harm at all?"

"A bump or a scratch, here and there, perhaps, but no broken bones and no gushing blood."

He thought long and hard about it, but eventually relented.

"Very well. If it is necessary for this to happen, then I will not stand in the way."

"There is, of course, a very particular reason that I can be certain that her life is not in danger."

"And what is that?"

"It is as I said before, and it is the reason that you are making arrangements for her training with McGrath: She is known and celebrated in the future."

"So," cried Logan, "I could climb onto the roof of this building and jump off and no harm would come to me?"

Simultaneously, Wild Flower and The Laird Grant gave her a furious look of admonishment.

CHAPTER 32

"So, it is agreed," declared Padraic Howison, reaching to shake the hand of The Laird Grant, "We have a deal."

The Laird hesitated for a moment, looking at the other man's hand with fleeting distaste, before taking hold of it and shaking it.

"Yes, we are agreed. We have a deal," he confirmed.

"You need not fear for the safety of your granddaughter," assured Gillum Dalry, "For if you speak nothing of our mission and keep it secret, not one hair on her head will be harmed."

"I have heard word of armies on the move," said The Laird, "It would take one to shield you from me if she comes to harm."

"She will be completely safe."

"In the Highlands, Your Lairdship," said Dalry, "There are rumours of armies and there are rumours of rumours of armies. It is ever so."

"If we achieve what we seek to achieve," Howison assured, "Then the clans need no longer be at war with each other. They can be done with choosing sides – as they do now – to oppose or support that girl queen. For, if we can sully and discredit her reputation to the extent we intend, then her influence will be spent and the Highlands can have peace, again."

"That day cannot come soon enough," vowed Dalry.

"No matter how soon it may come," Howison cursed, "It will be long overdue."

The Laird Grant purposely remained silent, allowing them to suppose what they might from his lack of enthusiasm. After leaving them to worry for a little while he finally relented.

"Tell me, gentlemen," he asked, "Will you hire a gang of swords to accompany you or do you seek, instead, to draw the least possible attention?"

"There is much to be said for either approach."

"My Sergeant-at-Arms," The Laird advised, "Is little known in the lands that surround us, so none will associate him with me. I can assure you that he will give a good account of himself if you should encounter robbers. He is a man of considerable strength, having worked a good few years in a metal forge, and he is much accomplished with a blade."

The Laird took pleasure in their discomfort. He knew full well that his Sergeant-at-Arms would pose as much a threat as a reassurance to them. His concern would extend little further than be his master's granddaughter and his papers.

"We have a route that we intend to take that should ensure that we are reasonably safe," said Howison.

The Laird allowed himself a slightly puzzled look, knowing that it would make them ill at ease, then he rubbed his chin, thoughtfully.

"Are you going north and then west," he asked, "Or are you going south and then west?"

There was an awkward silence.

"Because," The Laird continued, mischievously, "If you start off northwards, into The Queen of the West's territory, you should be safe. She has no tolerance for bandits and robbers."

The two men shot each other an anxious glance.

"But, gentlemen, if you first ride south, you will soon find yourselves in the lands of the Clan Campbell. There, you run the risk of encountering any number of cutthroats."

Dalry looked to be contemplating a reply, but Howison – seeing the man's pained expression – raised a hand to quell him and spoke himself.

"We have given the matter some thought," Howison revealed, "But we have not yet committed ourselves to one route or the other."

The Laird pretended to ponder this impartially, before asking them the question he had intended to pose all along.

"Do the Campbells have knowledge of your endeavours?"

Padraic Howison responded as if he had been stuck with a pin.

"What? Who, you say? Who?" he blathered, "The Campbells?"

His Lairdship nodded, slowly, as if reasoning with a small child, "Yes. The Campbells," he confirmed.

"Oh, yes, them," mumbled Howison.

The Laird gave him a patient, encouraging look that seemed to unsettle him even more. It was clear that he had not prepared himself for such blunt questioning.

"Your Lairdship, we happened to encounter a Campbell scouting party on our way here," Howison lied, "And thought it wise to establish with them that we share the same enemy."

"But the Campbells were not a party to the formulation of your plans?"

"No."

"And King James knows nothing of what you intend to do?"

"No."

"Because he would prevent it if he did?"

Howison stiffened, "It is known that his attitude to this *girl queen* is far too tolerant."

"In your opinion."

"In the opinion of his advisors."

"You intend to discredit Queen Annis as much with King James as with her own followers?"

Howison looked like a rabbit caught in the beam of a poacher's lamp. His attempt at a reply was too slow. The Laird, weary of the tale they were weaving, fluttered a hand to indicate that he was not interested in a reply.

"Gentlemen, do what you will," he said, "And make haste about it."

So, saying he stood up to show that the meeting was at an end. The two sprang to their feet.

Escorting them to the door, The Laird Grant finally put them at their ease, "I will be off and away back to my stronghouse," he declared, "Within the hour my granddaughter will arrive here with my Sergeant-at-Arms. They will bring with them the chest that contains the papers that you seek."

"When we set off," replied Howison, "We will ride ahead of him with your granddaughter and he can ride behind us with the chest. If he approaches anywhere near us before we reach the queen's residence in Fort Augustus, we will regard it as a hostile act and respond appropriately."

"*Appropriately?*" The Laird mused, taunting him.

"Yes, appropriately," the other replied, daring to inject a note of defiance.

"I think you had best find yourself an army, because those are bold words for a man who doesn't have one!"

With this The Laird Grant spun on his heels and strode away.

CHAPTER 33

"So," said Logan, "From what you have told me, I am to be a prisoner, held by these two people – Howison and Dalry – to ensure my grandfather's good behaviour."

"A hostage," Wild Flower corrected.

"What?"

"You will be a hostage."

"What is a hostage?"

"It's a kind of prisoner."

"So I'll be a prisoner?"

"You'll be a hostage," Wild Flower persevered, "Which is a kind of prisoner."

"But a prisoner, all the same."

"You'll be a particular kind of prisoner."

"So still a prisoner?"

"Of sorts," said Wild Flower throwing her hands up in exasperation.

"I will be a prisoner, of sorts," Logan resumed, "And Michael Deedigan, our Sergeant-at-Arms, will ride nearby to protect me?"

"You will be a form of prisoner – often referred to as a hostage – and Deedigan will be somewhere close by to protect Noory McGregor's writings and journals."

"Not me?"

"Not you."

"That's outrageous," Logan objected.

"Some would think so."

"I would think so."

"The world is as the world is and not as we would wish it to be," replied Wild Flower.

"That's a quotation?"

"Yes, it's one of the things that Queen Annis likes to say."

"I like her," Logan announced, "She is a good person with a good mind."

"She would be delighted to hear that."

Logan looked offended, "There is a word for that kind of reply."

"There is?"

"Yes, it's the word I learned last week."

"And that would be?"

"Sarcasm."

"Yes, that would be it," Wild Flower smirked.

"Meanwhile," Logan continued, pausing to make comically wild eyes at her friend, "I am riding with nobody to protect me from two obnoxious men."

Wild Flower broke into wild applause.

"Wonderful!" she cried, "I was sure that you would forget that word before you got chance to use it."

Logan made an elaborate bow, "I thank you!" she chirped.

They laughed at length. Then, Logan frowned, having lost her train of thought.

"You were riding with two obnoxious men..." Wild Flower prompted.

"Yes, I was, riding with them and in danger."

"I think not."

"I think so."

"It will not be *you* in danger, Logan."

"It won't?"

"No, it won't," Wild Flower assured her, "These two men are chickens and they have invited a wolf into their henhouse as a prisoner."

"A hostage!" Logan corrected.

Wild Flower groaned, "A wolf."

"A chicken-eating wolf hostage!"

They both dissolved into fits of laughter. After several failed attempts to resume their conversation, Wild Flower managed to speak without laughing.

"There is little doubt," she said, "That if these chickens cause you to feel unsafe, they will find themselves being eaten."

"No matter how short or how long my life turns out to be," declared Logan, "I will most definitely be able to say that it was not a dull one."

"Some would favour a pointless and unfulfilling existence over a dangerous one," laughed Wild Flower.

"I'm glad that you have come into my life, my friend, and addicted me to danger. Then again, of course, it was always going to be this way, was it not?"

"That's the perfect attitude to have."

"Being ten years old, as I am, and knowing that I will live to be at least twenty years old could lead me into temptation, if I were the wrong kind of person."

"That is certainly so."

"A lesser ten-year-old, having the notion that she will live to be twenty, might find her head filled with all kinds of ideas, knowing that she could not die."

Wild Flower frowned at this observation, "I suggest that you don't drink poison, that you don't throw yourself from the battlements and that you don't leap into a pond with a millstone tied to your neck."

"If I were going to do that, then I wouldn't be alive when I am twenty."

"No."

"And I *am* alive when I am twenty."

"Yes."

"So I don't ever do that kind of thing."

"Yes, but..."

"Yes but what?" asked Logan, "We cannot change the future and the future cannot change the past."

Wild Flower shook her head, wearily, "You are right."

Logan grinned.

"But," Wild Flower insisted, "It is *my* job to make *your* brain hurt, not *your* job to hurt *my* brain!"

"I thought I would just flaunt my grasp of the Laws of Time."

"The what?"

"The Laws of Time," Logan repeated.

Wild Flower screwed up her face, "Yes, I suppose that *is* what it might be called, one day."

"Well, those 'laws' will affect the future of me as a...," she paused to laugh, "As a person held against their will."

Wild Flower closed her eyes for a moment.

"That's all very hazy to me," she said, "What is going to be, is going to be, but I can't really make out most of it."

"Let me help you," offered Logan, "Very soon, there will be a knock at my door and it will be time for me to leave."

"Are you sensing the future, Logan, or are you just supposing?"

"My grandfather is keen on things happening properly and without delay in this household. I am reckoning that this is about as long as it would take for all matters in hand to be completed."

A few seconds later, there was a knock at the door.

"Enter," called Logan.

A page boy entered and touched his brow in deference as he addressed her.

"Mrs McConnell says that she would be obliged if you would join her in the main chamber," he announced, "She would like you to make some choices of food and clothing."

"We will be there in a moment," Logan replied.

The boy touched his brow again and backed out of the room.

"I will select whatever seems to please her the most," said Logan, "For she has developed a talent for knowing my taste better than I know it myself."

In a cheerful disposition, Logan went to surrender herself to Mrs McConnell. Wild Flower accompanied her.

Once all choices had been made and Logan's bags had been packed, unpacked and repacked three times – until Mrs

McConnell was satisfied with them – they set off for Cullachie Lodge.

CHAPTER 34

Michael Deedigan looked long and hard at Padraic Howison and Gillum Dalry. The pair looked back at The Laird Grant's Sergeant-at-Arms, but — despite their best efforts — they failed to equal his disdain. Having been outmatched in this respect, they both resolved to look him up and down with the maximum possible contempt they could muster.

Michael was not a tall man. It would be charitable even to say that he was of average height. He looked disappointingly unimpressive for a man of his reputation but, despite this, he had a presence — some would say an aura — of profound ability. If it were possible to condense a fully grown bull into a body no larger than a donkey, then this was Michael Deedigan.

The Sergeant-at-Arms did not speak. The two heard not one syllable of his accent, still broad and unmistakable even after twenty years in Scotland. The eloquent look in his eye as he met the gaze of The Laird Grant, however, spoke entire chapters.

The Laird returned a disapproving look, for the benefit of Howison and Dalry, but — to all those who knew him — it was unmistakably a sham.

Michael Deedigan folded his arms and gave the two hostage-takers a steely look. They responded with their very best attempt at nonchalance.

Michael was used to being underestimated. It had always been that way. At first, it was something that he tolerated and endured. Eventually, it became something that he deliberately cultivated. He enjoyed it. It suited him just fine.

He took a step forward — narrowing the three strides between them — and reached out his hand as if offering to shake theirs. They faltered. He converted the forward motion of his hand into an upward one. As he did so, he modified his hand into a fist.

Howison and Dalry quaked and looked unnerved. Stood behind and between them, Logan gave a mischievous smile.

Logan knew Deedigan. She knew him well. He had trained her in lengthy and increasingly gruelling lessons, drawing out the very best from her and refining it to an astonishing level of skill and technique. The more her talent with a sword blossomed, the more Deedigan became impressed with her. The more he became impressed with *her*, the more she became impressed with *him*. The casualness of his exemplary abilities fascinated her. He was, she decided, almost lazy in the way he excelled.

She resolved to never confide in him that she was also being trained by Kiffan the Defiant.

CHAPTER 35

Logan had been puzzled by her grandfather's lack of worry or concern as she departed Cullachie Lodge. He had hugged her, kissed her head and bid her a fond and affectionate farewell, but had never seemed unduly troubled.

As if to answer her quandary, Wild Flower, who had smothered her in kisses and hugged her until she had been almost numb, had spoken words of peculiar reassurance.

"I will be with you, in spirit, every moment," she had said.

Logan had known that she had meant this quite literally and not as some misty-eyed sentiment. Her grandfather had grinned at these words. Their significance, of course, had totally eluded Howison and Dalry.

Michael Deedigan cleared his throat noisily to attract attention. When he had it, he addressed The Laird Grant while actually speaking to Howison and Dalry.

"I will take myself to the end of the meadow and will wait there, so that I can let these..." he paused, took a lungful of air and let it out as an audible sigh before continuing, "So that I can let these *gentlemen* get ahead of me."

Nobody failed to notice Deedigan's brittle and toxic pronunciation of the word 'gentlemen', least of all the pair in question. They promptly glowered at him. Deedigan gave them a wan smile as if he were oblivious.

Padraic Howison and Gillum Dalry climbed aboard the two horses they had borrowed from The Laird Grant, having claimed that their own were not yet fully rested.

Deedigan walked his horse forward. At a gesture from Howison, Logan obligingly fell in between them with her own mount. Dalry set off behind her.

At the bottom of the meadow, the two men studiously kept their eyes straight forward, as if Deedigan did not exist. Logan did the same, sitting stiffly upright on her horse, while looking haughty and aloof. Her mockery of the pair was exquisite.

Deedigan watched as they followed the track to the edge of the wood and disappeared into it. He had half expected Dalry

– at the rear – to turn around to measure how close he were riding to them, but he did not.

Deedigan turned to The Laird and, raising a hand, made a play of scratching his head questioningly. The Laird Grant shrugged his shoulders and waved a hand as if half-heartedly shooing away a fly. Deedigan gave a sly smile and urged his steed forward. His pack horse, with its twin panniers, obediently followed.

At the forest edge, he could vaguely discern the other riders ahead of him. As they passed through the odd patch of sunlight, filtering through the canopy, he caught sight of the head and shoulders of one or other of them. They seemed to sense his presence and picked up the pace. Deedigan was about to urge his horse on, when it sped up without the need. He patted its neck and tousled one of its ears and it made a snuffling sound in reply.

As they travelled, the River Spey would intermittently come into view through the undergrowth. Occasionally the sound of a waterfall could be heard or the sounds of splashing ducks and swans.

Presently, as the path straightened and the cover thinned out, he could see them clearly. He paused his horses and, listening carefully, he could hear Howison at the front having a conversation with Dalry at the back. Logan, riding her grey mare between the two men, appeared to be completely ignoring their exchange. Deedigan touched his horse gently with his heels and they moved away, again.

After an hour of riding, they reached the second set of shallows on the River Spey. This was a popular place for people to cross. Deedigan considered the situation. If it were him at the front, he decided, he would cross the river at least half way before stopping to wait for whoever was following. Instead, Howison and Dalry – with their captive – stopped at the shoreline. This was not a wise idea. Very soon, if he wished to, Deedigan would be able to pick off either of the men with a pistol shot and, very likely, reach the other with his claymore or – if he were so inclined – with his viciously long riding sword.

Deedigan stopped short of them, a good way further than they seemed to be expecting.

"You need to keep the lass closer to one or other of you," he shouted, "Or – at only another five paces – I would become a direct threat to you."

Dalry grunted with annoyance and propelled his horse to come alongside Logan.

"Wait there," called Howison, pretending that it might have been what he was intending to say all along.

Logan, wished that she had not been quite so offended by Deedigan referring her so impersonally as *'the lass'.* As quickly as it had arrived, the offence waned.

Then it suddenly occurred to her: *He was pretending to know nothing of me,* she decided. A ruse, she was certain, to shield any personal connection that existed between them. He was, after all, an employee of The Laird's household. She was The Laird's granddaughter. Under normal circumstances, they would be expected to have no more than a nodding acquaintance with each other. If even that!

The long hours of exertion and frequent bouts of exhaustion she and Deedigan had shared had generated a bond. He had coped admirably with her absurdly mature behaviour. This, she was sure, came from the strange connection she had with her twenty-year-old self. He had also been perfectly at ease with her grown up way of speaking. More importantly, he had been openly thrilled at the very rapid progress she had made in combat training. In return, she had made no effort to hide her utter awe at some of the more advanced moves he had demonstrated to her. This, she knew, had pleased him.

'There was more!' she told herself. They were fellow warriors. She had read, in several books, of the affinity that developed between fighters who shared hardship, like the punishingly long runs they had taken across the hills and down the glens and the prolonged bouts of hunger they had both endured when their hunting had delivered no quarry.

There were also their repeated practise – to the very brink of exhaustion – of a great number of coordinated advances against an imaginary enemy. They had stood side by side, pressing forward with a cuts, sweeps, thrust and lunges that were perfectly synchronised, until they had both been bathed in sweat.

Curiously, Logan reflected, Michael Deedigan had never treated her with contempt for being a "mere" girl and had never shown her disdain for still being a child.

As Howison and Dalry turned to look across the Spey, Logan caught Deedigan's eye and ventured a very slight, almost imperceptible nod. He returned the same.

"We will cross," ordered Howison, spurring his horse and striking out into the water.

Logan waited for his horse to take a few strides and, then, took to the water with her own. A few moments later, she heard Dalry's mount entering the Spey.

Once they reached the half way point, Deedigan ventured after them. He slowed as they reached the other bank and allowed them to make it out and onto the path before proceeding. He was both pleased and relieved that Logan persisted in ignoring him. He was certain that this tactic would pay off at some point.

They continued to ride at a reasonable pace, neither hurried nor casual. They seemed to be sticking mostly to the tracks that skirted the hills, forests and rocky outcrops, shunning the ones that crossed the open expanses of grass, out in the open. As far as Deedigan was concerned, however, the route was slightly bolder than he would have expected of people who were worried about discovery. They were, he felt, almost pretending to be cautious.

Deedigan began observing Howison and Dalry more closely. He noticed that they seemed unusually calm for their situation. Neither of them was as watchful as they ought to be.

Deedigan couldn't quite understand their behaviour. Suddenly, he spotted something. Initially dismissing it as his imagination, he caught another glint of sunlight reflecting off a cap badge. Someone was peering at them over a low ridge. He pretended not to notice. Soon after, he caught sight of a second observer, their head partly visible above a cluster of rocks. It was clear that they were under surveillance.

Despite their unconvincing pretence at alertness, Padraic Howison and Gillum Dalry excelled at ignoring their observers. Deedigan initially assumed that they knew they were being watched, but as he pondered it, he grew increasingly doubtful of it. The more he observed their behaviour, the more he suspected that they might be genuinely oblivious.

Logan, he was certain, was perfectly content to take no part in events. The two men had no apparent impact on her conduct. He had the distinct impression that she was engrossed in something. When he got a proper glimpse of her face, her expression was like that of someone absorbed in a conversation. He did not suspect that this was, in fact, *exactly* the case.

Later, just before dusk, Deedigan identified a third spotter hiding in a tree. The man was wearing black breeches and a black cloak wrapped around him, as if to hide his clothing. Despite this, Deedigan caught sight of a telltale length of exposed tartan and recognised it immediately.

Carefully controlling his horse by means of secret touches and nudges, Deedigan caused it to move from tree to tree, apparently haphazardly cropping grass beneath each of them.

Finally, they arrived at the tree that housed the observer. There, he acted out a very convincing pantomime of spotting an animal in the greenery. He very quietly dismounted, took out his pistol and pulled back the safety cover from the gunpowder pan. Looking back and forth between his weapon and the non-existent quarry, he pretended to have second thoughts.

With great care, Deedigan set his pistol aside, but still in reach, resting it horizontally between a pair of stubby branches. Still moving with great caution, he took his bow from his saddle and notched an arrow. Pulling it back, he aimed it at his imaginary target and paused to listen.

A little way above him, in the lower branches of the tree, he heard the very slightest noise as the man very gently flexed his leg to ease a painful cramp.

Lightning fast, Deedigan lofted his bow to point directly overhead and shot his arrow at the man. The arrow found his arm pit, buckling his arm and causing him to fall. In the brief moment it took for him to hit the ground, Deedigan had retrieved his pistol and had fired a ball into the man's head.

At a range of just an arm's length from him, the man's head exploded like a ripe fruit dropped onto paving stones from the top of a tall tower.

The noise was like a hammer blow on an anvil. It boomed off the nearby hillside and echoed, several times over, back and forth across the valley. This was deliberate. He wanted Howison and Dalry to hear it. He wanted the other lookouts to hear it. He wanted anybody else within earshot who wore the Campbell tartan to hear it, too.

CHAPTER 36

Michael Deedigan heard the pounding of hooves approaching and quickly reloaded his pistol. Not long after, Howison and Dalry came into view.

"What has happened?" cried Howison, obviously panicked.

"Why are you firing?" asked Dalry, equally worried.

"I've just shot a rat," Deedigan replied, "It was a big one."

"A rat?!" gasped Howison, "Are you out of your mind? Why would you shoot a pistol at a rat?"

"It was huge!"

"It must have been," Howison growled, "To warrant a damned pistol ball,".

"It was about as tall as you. Maybe a little taller," announced Deedigan, giving the corpse at his feet a hefty kick.

Both Howison and Dalry heard the noise of the kick and they also heard that it had made contact with something hidden in the long grass. They both looked baffled. Deedigan obligingly trod down some of the grass, flattening it out, and the dead body came into view.

The two men looked horrified.

"What is it that ails you?" asked Deedigan, "We were being spied on by a Campbell."

"A Campbell?" asked Howison, his panic now increasing.

"Yes, a Campbell," Deedigan confirmed, pushing open the corpse's clothing with the toe of his boot to display the tartan beneath it.

Howison and Dalry looked at each other in terror.

"Why?" Howison beseeched, "Why did you kill him?"

"He's a Campbell."

This elegantly simple explanation appeared to be lost on them.

"He was a Campbell and he was watching us," Deedigan ventured, "He can only have been up to no good."

"This is Campbell land," Dalry moaned, clutching his head.

"No it isn't," Deedigan replied, "It's not Campbell land until we reach the river that joins this one, further downstream."

"The Campbells *claim* this land," said Howison, in a state of agitation.

"Well it's not theirs and they *shouldn't* claim it!"

"They will have heard that shot!" wailed Dalry, looking to Howison for his reaction.

"This is a disaster!" bellowed Howison.

"What are we going to do?" begged Dalry.

"Let me think!" snapped Howison, "Let me think! We need to make this right…"

"I'll make this right for you," scoffed Deedigan, drawing his sword from the sheath attached to his saddle, "And it will cost every Campbell who hastens here, their life!"

"Calm yourself, man," shouted Howison, "This is no time for swinging steel around."

"This," insisted Deedigan, "Is the time for me putting steel into the front of a Campbell and out through the back."

"This is the time for…"

"Wait!" Deedigan interrupted, suddenly looking worried, "If the two of you are here, where is the girl?"

"She is safe."

"How is she safe if neither of you are with her?"

"She is only a little way away. You need not worry."

"I think I have *every* need to worry."

"There is nobody around. This place is deserted."

"Deserted?" scorned Deedigan, giving the corpse a vicious kick, "Does *this* says 'deserted' to you?"

"He is one man."

"One man? What about the two others who were keeping an eye on us from up on the hills? How many more are there lurking about?"

"I didn't see anybody," Howison protested.

"Nor did I," Dalry added.

"Then you weren't looking properly!" scolded Deedigan.

"Listen," Howison demanded, jabbing a finger towards the Sergeant-at-Arms, "After that pistol shot, everybody for half an hour's ride could be heading this way!"

"It darkens quickly at this time of year," Deedigan sneered, "And that will hinder them. I have a pair of hunting muskets. If they come with torches lit, I'll put a ball through the forehead of every man who carries one."

"We need a story to explain what has happened here," Dalry declared.

"A story?" snapped Deedigan, "The only story they need is the one that my bow, my sword and a horn full of gunpowder will tell them."

"Things are more complicated than you understand," barked Howison, his temper flaring.

"Complicated?" howled Deedigan, "How complicated is this: One of you get back to the girl and ensure her safety and the other come with me and we'll go and do some 'look and listen' for anybody approaching."

"If there are orders to be given," Howison brayed, "Then it will be *me* who gives them."

"Oh! So you fancy yourself in charge?" mocked Deedigan.

"I *am* in charge and *that* was clearly understood by your master before we set off!"

Deedigan flashed him a look of serene innocence, "He forgot to mention it to me."

CHAPTER 37

"What have they done to you?" asked Wild Flower.

Logan had been left tied up, with her back to a tree, to await their return.

"I am but a wench," Logan replied, sarcastically, "And big, strong men have left me thus while they strut around doing manly things."

With exquisite dexterity, Wild Flower undid the ropes around Logan's wrists. With a few more tugs she was able to remove the rest of her bindings and free her.

"Where are you?" asked Logan, "Are you here or are you not here?"

"I am not here," her friend replied, "I am sat in the far corner of the wood shed, at your grandfather's stronghouse, with a blanket over my head to hide me."

"There was a shot," said Logan.

"Yes, from Deedigan's pistol. A Campbell lookout, who he found hiding in a tree, now lays dead at the foot of it."

"The two oafs who are my travelling companions have rushed off to investigate."

"Oh, but is that wise?" asked Wild Flower, "If Deedigan is not permitted to approach anywhere near them, is it not folly for them to approach him?"

"I don't think they gave it much thought," chuckled Logan.

"I don't think they have gauged the character of your grandfather's Sergeant-at-Arms properly."

"It would seem that they have not gauged him at all," Logan grinned, nodding in the direction they had gone.

Wild Flower turned to see Howison and Dalry approaching, their hands raised above their head, and Deedigan marching them along at gunpoint.

Logan suddenly turned to Wild Flower, looking at her worriedly. Did she not need to hide to avoid being seen?

Wild Flower smiled and, making a quirky little smile, shook her head.

"So," Logan asked, "Which are they?"

"Which are they? What do you mean?"

"I mean are they hostages or are they prisoners?"

The two girls roared with laughter, causing Howison and Dalry to look at Logan as if she might be crazy.

"Mistress," said Deedigan, speaking formally, as he neared her, "How are you with ropes and knots?"

"Well, I escaped these knots without too much trouble," she lied, holding up the ropes that had held her, "So tying them myself should not be too much of a challenge."

So saying, she set about binding Howison's wrists behind his back and then to a loop of rope around his waist. Next, she turned her attention to Dalry and soon had him tightly restrained in similar fashion.

"That's good work," remarked Deedigan, accidentally walking straight through Wild Flower.

Wild Flower responded to Logan's alarm by giving her the sweetest, most angelic smile, but quickly contorting it into that of a clown. Logan laughed, causing – this time – all three of the men to look at her with worried expressions.

Deedigan herded the snarling and complaining captives across to a nearby ridge, beyond which a steep bank dropped away below them. There, he made them kneel at the very brink of it.

"Stay still," he warned them with a smirk, "And you may want to give your nasty mouths a rest."

The two men looked over their shoulders, straining their necks to look over the edge. They quickly pulled back, looking more than a little worried.

Deedigan fetched the horses across to stand close by.

"How do you propose to get us onto those horses, all trussed up like this?" demanded Howison.

Deedigan snorted, "Oh, I don't," he taunted, "The two of you will be walking."

The two men were outraged at this notion.

"When your master hears about this," Howison threatened, "You will be lucky if you are not flogged to death!"

"The Laird Grant's concern is for his papers and for his granddaughter. If both are safe, then he will care little or nothing for the likes of you."

"We have a bargain with him. It is one that he needs to honour!"

"Honour?" gasped Deedigan, "Does that word not sting your tongue when you say it?"

Howison gave him a thunderous glare, which seemed to have no other effect but to amuse Deedigan.

"I'm Irish," he announced, "So you'll forgive me if I don't take kindly to the English telling me about honour or find myself very much impressed by it."

Howison looked wild-eyed with rage, but held his tongue.

"Listen," Deedigan sneered, not happy that he'd quite provoked him enough, "All the honour in the both of you wouldn't fill a mouse's ear."

Howison clenched his jaw so hard that Logan feared his teeth might shatter. Then, she saw Wild Flower. Her heart missed a beat. Wild Flower had her arms held out, with a hand at each of the men's back. She was pretending to ready herself to push them over the edge.

Logan decided that the look on her face must have been frantic, because all three men – Deedigan, Howison and Dalry – turned and stared at her in alarm.

"There was a huge bee," she said, feebly, "I thought, for a moment, it was going to sting the nearest horse."

Howison made a sly dismissive noise, much to the Sergeant-at-Arms annoyance.

"The aiming pin at the end of this pistol" he snarled, "Is going to sting you in the middle of your forehead in a moment!"

Howison gave off the merest hint of unease.

"Gag them," ordered Deedigan.

Logan obliged, placing a couple of scarves across their mouths before tying them in place with absolutely no regard for their comfort.

Beside them, Wild Flower signalled furiously to Logan, indicating approaching troops. Logan jolted.

"We need to go!" she cried, "I sense soldiers are heading our way."

Howison and Dalry exchanged a furtive look. Its meaning did not elude Deedigan.

"You feel good about this, do you?" Deedigan asked, "It seems that the Campbells are no longer anything for you to worry about?"

Logan understood straight away.

"These men and the Campbells are in this together?" she asked.

"I would wager copper against gold that it is so," Deedigan replied.

Howison managed a throaty laugh from behind his gag at this.

"Mount up and take off, mistress!" shouted Deedigan, "We need to get away from here!"

As she climbed into her saddle to gallop away, Logan heard a couple of startled cries from Howison and Dalry.

"Why don't the two of you go on ahead of us?" Deedigan invited as he pushed the men over the edge, sending them tumbling down the slope, "Make haste! No delay!" he cried after them.

Leaping into his saddle, Deedigan shouted to the two riderless horses and the pack horse, which obediently followed.

After reaching the first bend in the track, Deedigan caught sight of Logan ahead of him, disappearing around the next bend. Speaking urgently to his mount, he urged it on. Around the bend, the track began to descend a hill, snaking back and forth to left and right in short stretches to absorb the gradient. Finding himself closing on Logan with every bend, he realised she was purposely allowing him to catch up.

Eventually, the track began to zig-zag less earnestly and slowly level off. By this time, Deedigan and Logan were riding side by side. Before long, they could hear the sound of a river not far away, the water cascading over a series of drops.

"We need to go upstream a little way from here," said Deedigan, setting off in that direction.

Logan followed and, after five minutes, Deedigan brought them to a halt beside a clearing. Standing up tall on his stirrups, he looked in every direction. Once he was satisfied that they were not being observed he dismounted and, instructing his horse to stay, walked with Logan into the lush vegetation. The sound of the river grew fainter behind them and the ground began to rise steeper and steeper.

Deedigan put a finger to his lips, urging her silence, then cupped his hands around his right ear, like a funnel, and slowly panned it from left to right in the direction from which they had come.

"I know where we are," he announced, "A little way along, to our left we will find those fine gentlemen Howison and Dalry."

Treading cautiously, they made their way back to the horses. The pack horse, having shunned the idea of fully keeping up with everyone, was just arriving. The other horses, on seeing it, walked to greet it. Deedigan made a quiet noise, which attracted the attention of the horses. Putting a hand firmly over his own mouth, he shook his head. The horses, clearly taking note of the gesture, refrained from whinnying.

Motioning for their mounts not to follow, Deedigan and Logan skirted the edge of the bushes, a little distance from the path, and made their way down river.

"They will be just beyond the next clump of trees," Deedigan assured her.

"You sound strangely certain."

"I am."

"How so?"

"Gravity!" he grinned.

Exactly where he had said, they found Howison and Dalry, sprawled on the ground, writhing in agony.

"If you two groan any louder," warned Deedigan, "It will be the very last sound that either of you will ever make."

The two men contorted their faces, closed their eyes and bit back the pain of their injuries.

"Do you see how quickly you got here?" asked Deedigan, "You did ever so well."

"You will pay for this with your life!" hissed Howison through gritted teeth.

"You will be hung by your ankles till your face turns black!" jibed Dalry.

"If the two of you don't be quiet," replied Deedigan, with exaggerated, patronising patience, "I will float you down the river."

The two men looked scared.

"I have two barrels, stashed nearby, for that very purpose," Deedigan assured them.

Unsure if he were serious or not, the two men held their tongues.

Deedigan called the horses with a whistle that sounded exactly like a bird, but none that anyone had ever heard before. Within a minute, in response, the horses appeared.

"Horses," explained Deedigan, addressing the question that hung in the air, "Are like dogs, with brains three times the size, but as intelligent as cats."

Logan, tilting her head from one side to the other as she weighed up the wisdom of this statement, eventually nodded her head in agreement. Wild Flower, replicating almost the same motions, nodded her head, too.

"On your feet, gentlemen," Deedigan ordered.

The captives struggled to rise and made it upright at their fourth attempt.

"There are some shallows, close at hand," he explained, "They are much loved by ladies of class and leisure. They like to feed the waterfowl, there."

Howison and Dalry looked at him as if he had taken leave of his senses. Deedigan slowly shook his head, like a disappointed parent.

"And there," he continued, "We will find some large stones, conveniently arranged to form steps, where you can mount your horses."

"What if we do not comply and throw ourselves off?" enquired Howison, defiantly.

"Well, on the one hand, the fall would be extremely painful for you," said Deedigan with a harsh, humourless laugh, "And on the other, I would very likely have to kill you."

CHAPTER 38

Gathered around the campfire that evening, Deedigan was not quite sure why the Campbells had failed to hunt them down. It was possible, he decided, that they had only made a half-hearted attempt at it. On the other hand, of course, it could have been because he had managed to evade them by being so resourceful and unpredictable. He preferred to believe the latter version.

As they took it in turns to cough and splutter from the smoke of the camp fire – depending on the direction of the wind – Deedigan congratulated himself on having lit it.

'*Surely,*' his enemy would think, '*Nobody would be foolish enough to light a fire if they feared being tracked and found!*'

It was, he told himself, either an act of utterly brazen audacity or nothing less than a master stroke of double bluff.

The two prisoners, who had been bound by their wrists and elbows, were now – instead – carefully bound at their thighs, knees and ankles before being relieved of their gags to allow them to eat. Between each mouthful of food, they proceeded to complain that their wrists had begun to prick and sting like a thousand pins from the earlier pressure of the ropes. Deedigan gave them no sympathy and, as soon as they had eaten and drunk, he reapplied their gags to shut them up.

Presently, as the fire died down, Deedigan stared dreamily into the flames. Methodically, he ran through the events of the past few hours in his mind, analysing each and every deed and word. He seemed to almost in a daze.

Logan kept her peace and made a point of not disturbing him. Just as she found herself about to doze off, she heard Wild Flower's voice in her head.

'*Just as he suspects, Howison and Dalry are indeed working hand in hand with the Campbells.*'

Happy that Deedigan was too lost in his thoughts to notice, Logan ventured a nod.

'*This,*' Wild Flower continued, '*Puts you both in danger.*'

"How so?" asked Logan from behind her hand, before realising that she only needed to think the words.

'At this very moment, the Campbells are closing in on you. They are not far away at all, now. When they find you and discover that Howison and Dalry are your captives, they may react badly to it.'

'How badly?' asked Logan, in her head.

'They will likely kill you both and send Howison and Dalry on their way to continue their mission.'

Logan's eyes sprang wide in alarm at this news.

'What are we to do?' she asked.

'There is only one thing to be done and that is to let them go.'

"What?!" exclaimed Logan, aloud.

Deedigan jolted and looked across to her.

"Is something wrong?" he asked.

"I was thinking," she explained, "And I shocked myself."

"What shocking thought did you think?"

"That these two men are working with the Campbells and that this is why they do not fear them finding us."

"And that is why you cried out?"

"No, it was something worse than that that made me cry out."

"How much worse?"

"Far worse."

"It can't be worse than the thought that came into my own head," Deedigan challenged.

"I fear it may be."

"Then let us count to three," he invited, "And we will say our thought to each other, both at the same time."

"One... Two... Three..." said Deedigan.

The two of them took a deep breath.

"We need to let them go!" they both said at once.

CHAPTER 39

Howison and Dalry were deeply suspicious at the prospect of being set free. It was clear that they feared being shot in the back. They required some serious persuasion to accept that it was not some kind of trap.

"Look," Deedigan explained to them, "You are two of the lowest forms of life that I have ever come across and nothing is beneath you or too disgraceful for you not to do."

The two men looked mildly insulted.

"But, as Sergeant-at-Arms to The Laird Grant, I am entrusted by him with the protection of both his most treasured historical documents and his most treasured granddaughter."

Warily, his audience nodded their appreciation of this fact.

"As his Sergeant-at-Arms, I have taken the decision that the safety of his granddaughter far outweighs the safety of mere ink and paper, so I am letting you go. By doing so, it allows The Laird Grant to keep his part of the agreement he has with you and show that he is a man of honour and it allows me to keep this lass alive."

Howison and Dalry nodded even more slowly, evidently giving his words grave consideration.

"This sounds all well and good, from your point of view," declared Howison, "But what if your master, The Laird Grant, decides to share details of our plot with the allies of Queen Annis? We wouldn't get so much as an hour's ride from her without having our throats cut."

"The Clan Grant has had a feud with the Queens of the West since the times of the Vikings," mused Deedigan, "Why would their Laird betray you and prevent his arch enemy from being slain?"

A fleeting look of confusion flashed across Howison's face before he regained his composure.

"Said like that," he admitted, "It sounds unlikely, but with our lives depending on it, we have no appetite to take such a risk."

"Soon enough," Dalry challenged, "We will be crossing into unfriendly territory and, there, we will have to watch our backs at every bend of the track."

"Oh!" remarked Logan, "So *these* lands, which belong to the Campbells, are *friendly* territory for you?"

Howison shot Dalry a vicious look. Dalry, realising his careless choice of words, looked embarrassed.

"My colleague," said Howison, with brittle annoyance, "Is…"

"Is," interrupted Deedigan, "Just like you, a bare-faced liar!"

Howison clenched his jaw and contorted his lips, "I am unwilling to take any chances."

"So you are refusing to be set free?" scoffed Deedigan.

"Well, no…" Howison faltered, "But…"

"But what? You would prefer to remain tied up as my prisoners?"

"No. Please release us."

"So that you can go running to your friends, the Campbells, and have The Laird's granddaughter and I killed?"

"I wouldn't do that," Howison protested.

"Said like that," Deedigan retorted in a mocking tone, "It sounds unlikely, but with our lives depending on it, we have no appetite to take such a risk."

Howison recognised his own words and scowled.

"If the Campbells slew you, then the Grants – once they found out – would definitely alert the Queen of the West to our intentions."

"Maybe you think you have time to reach the Queen of the West and kill her before our bodies are found?"

"An unwise gamble on our part."

"A ludicrous gamble on *my* part!" Deedigan snapped.

"Then neither of us, in this negotiation, has the upper hand."

"I am not the one who is tied up," laughed The Laird Grant's Sergeant-at-Arms, "So I don't think there is any question as to which one of us has the upper hand."

Howison fumed silently his face a picture of rage.

"It would seem to me," said Logan brightly and cheerfully, "That all four of us are of a common purpose and yet, despite being united in that goal, we are seizing on reasons to mistrust each other."

The three men blinked at her logic.

"At the end of the day," she continued, "If we are discovered, the executioner's axe – which most certainly hovers over us all – will care nothing for who was right or wrong in our squabbling and bickering when it parts our heads from our bodies."

The knotted eyebrows of her audience conveyed their astonishment. After many meaningful glances of silent consultation, all three of them saw the wisdom of her words.

"You're right," Deedigan conceded, "But I might just cut both their throats simply for my own amusement."

Dalry appeared alarmed at this, but Howison gave him a withering look of disdain.

"Cut away," he invited, "For then, Queen Annis is sure to live," before smirking and adding "I'm sure His Lairdship would struggle to find the right words to thank you."

Deedigan took out his dirk and handed it to Logan, "Here, you cut their bonds, it would sicken me to do it."

"No need," replied Logan, producing a broad-bladed dagger from inside her clothing, "I have my own."

At this, Howison and Dalry's eyes popped wide open, both having been completely unaware that she had been armed all along.

"You need to watch this one," chortled Deedigan, "She could have despatched the both of you from the moment we set out on this expedition, if she had wanted. A wee charmer she is! Imagine: Taking hostage what you believe to be an eel, holding it by its tail, only to discover that it is a venomous snake..."

Both Howison and Dalry looked at her cautiously, as if she were, indeed, a venomous snake and one they feared might strike.

"Mister Deedigan," she trilled, impishly, "If I accidentally cut them while hacking at their ropes, it won't harm them, will it?"

Dalry took a step backwards at this, but Howison – who had kept his eyes focused grimly on the ground – suddenly looked up, bristling with hostility.

"Are you really not going to restrain this crazy young lass?" he demanded.

"Crazy young lass?" Deedigan mused.

With a grim smirk on his face and a worrying twinkle in his eye, he walked across and sat down on the ground in front of them.

"Please go on," he invited, "This is wonderful entertainment. Far better than a carnival. Please do continue! The two of you are tied up and helpless, yet you are offending and insulting a girl who is about to bring a blade close to your hands. With the right provocation, she might even slit your wrists for you, right down to the bone!"

Howison seemed to deflate, crumpling up inside and somehow diminishing. His eyes returned to the ground.

Abruptly, there was a shrill laugh in Logan's ear and a smiling image of Wild Flower sprang into her head.

'Address the tall one,' she said into Logan's mind, referring to Howison, *'And tell him to stand in front of one of the trees and raise his hands above his head until they touch its trunk.'*

'Then what?' asked Logan, without speaking.

'Then throw your dagger, good and hard, at his hands. I will ensure that it doesn't strike them. At that moment, I will cause his bonds to fall free.'

Logan suppressed a grin as she issued those exact same instructions. Howison stood, in gruesome discomfort, as if he had the mother of all stomach aches and trembled gently from the fear that washed over him.

Logan drew back her blade, much to the amusement of Deedigan, and launched it at Howison with full force. The dagger flew straight and true to embed itself in the tree trunk. Instantly, Howison's ropes fell free and landed in the dirt, cleanly sliced in two.

Howison gaped at the bindings and nudged them with his toe, as if worried that they might be an illusion. He gulped and took in a deep lungful of air.

'And the next one, please,' whispered Wild Flower.

"Now you, if you will," she said, speaking to Dalry.

It was plain to see that Dalry was already a nervous wreck, having been unnerved by the spectacle he had just witnessed. Fearful of the consequences of any refusal, however, he duly moved into position.

As Deedigan threateningly unsheathed his sword at Howison, Logan recovered her weapon and returned to her previous position, some six or seven paces away.

She feigned preparation for the throw, then winced and rubbed the wrist of her throwing hand.

"Ouch!" she said, "I think I have a little cramp. I hope it doesn't put me off my aim."

Dalry almost wet himself in terror and visibly shook. Charitably, Logan hesitated only for a moment before hurling her dagger, again. Just as before, it sped across the distance between them, straight and true, to *'thwack'* into the tree. Dalry's bonds split and fell to the ground, where he gazed at them in awe.

"Gentlemen," said Logan, speaking to both of her former captives, "Let this be the last time, please, that you underestimate me."

CHAPTER 40

The four fellow travellers retired to their tents to spend the night in comfort, each taking with them a metal box of hot cinders from the fire to provide warmth. Before they split up, they each made meticulously certain that there were no gaps in the lids of their boxes that could allow poisonous fumes to escape, before each applied wet clay to eliminate any remaining possibility.

As they worked, Michael Deedigan regaled them with a story about his Great Uncle Fergus who, unbeknown to others in his party, was too drunk to properly seal his cinder box and was found, the next morning, dead beneath his blankets with a face glowing as pink as the flesh of a salmon. This prompted everybody to apply a second layer of clay to their boxes, just in case.

The fact that Howison and Dalry slept in separate tents amused Deedigan. During long hunting expeditions into the hills and mountains, Deedigan had experienced the traditional ritual of drawing lots to decide who shared canvas with whom. This would be done by the drawing of sticks of varying lengths. Only highly placed individuals would have their own, personal tent. For the rest, the groans and exclamations of distress that would accompany the matching of sticks would often be hilarious. For the bigger tents, that could sleep four, there would − for instance − be four sticks of the same size. Where there were multiple tents of the same sleeping capacity, the groups of sticks would have notches to identify them apart.

Nobody expected Logan to sleep other than by herself. This had been taken for granted. Deedigan had his own tent since it had originally been planned that he would be following up the rear.

The aversion that Howison held for Dalry's nocturnal company, however, only explained itself when Deedigan finally observed Dalry showing deference to Howison when they thought that nobody was watching. It was class! It was social status! Dalry was, Deedigan deduced, some kind of servant in Howison's employment and, therefore, to be looked down upon and held in contempt. Their deception, in studiously portraying themselves as *'colleagues'*, was a sham.

Deedigan smiled to himself as he snuggled under his blankets. His smile was due firstly to these two men pretending to be something they were not and secondly because he had given Logan a pair of pistols and – from his previous training of her – he knew that she would be very capable of using them.

As Deedigan drifted off to sleep, he gripped his own pistol underneath his blanket. His smile turned into a grin as he dreamily imagined Howison and Dalry attempting to kidnap Logan only to have their heads blown off.

CHAPTER 41

Logan was sure that she had woken early but, as she climbed out through the entrance to her tent, Deedigan had already lit a fire, fed the horses and was carrying water back for them from a nearby stream.

Howison and Dalry were eating porridge, sullenly, from metal bowls and not talking to each other. Dalry had, apparently been snoring loudly for most of the night, much to the irritation of Howison. According to Deedigan's version of events, Howison had almost been as much the offender as the offended, but would hear nothing of it from Dalry. Deedigan later told Logan that he had overheard Howison comparing Dalry to a farm animal.

Deedigan, after pulling down and packing away Logan's tent, made off through the bushes, returning a little while later with half a cup of honey.

Logan was fascinated as Deedigan recounted how he had burned a mixture of dry and mulched leaves in a metal pipe and propped it against the hive of a local colony of bees. After a few minutes, this had rendered its stinging inhabitants docile.

Deedigan liberally poured the honey over the porridge he was cooking on the fire. He resolutely did not share the syrupy bounty with Howison or Dalry.

Logan paid rapt attention to Howison and Dalry as, sitting in silence, they exchanged furtive looks at regular intervals. Stealing away to her saddlebag, she returned with the loaded pistols she had stashed. She promptly pointed them in Howison's and Dalry's general direction.

"Whoa!" shouted Deedigan.

The four horses all turned in unison to see why they were being called to halt when they had not even set off.

"What?" objected Logan with a sour face.

Both Howison and Dalry looked up from their porridge and froze in shock.

"Don't kill either of them. Not just yet. We need to talk to them."

"They are vermin and they need to be slain."

Deedigan huffed, then made the Scottish Noise in his throat, the rumbling sound being surprisingly loud in the now hushed forest.

Dalry started to raise his hands in surrender, but Howison batted one of them with his fist and Dalry put them both back down, again.

"Very well," snarled Deedigan, pretending to be in a bad temper, "We'll just drive them away. If you must, you may wound them, Mistress, but only in the legs, please."

At this, even Howison's composure wavered. Deedigan made the Scottish Noise twice as loud, then whirled around, a pistol in either hand.

"I suggest you both duck down," Logan advised Howison and Dalry.

The two men immediately fell forward onto the ground and stretched out flat on their bellies.

"You two in the trees!" shouted Deedigan, "We both have two pistols apiece and we are both very fine shots. I suggest you come out now if you wish to live."

There was a pause and, then, a pair of men emerged from the line of trees with their hands raised above their heads.

"If we do not return," one of them warned, "Then The Campbell will have you hunted down with dogs like you were gypsies."

"If you do not return," jeered Deedigan, "Then the Campbell would be well advised to run away as fast as his legs can carry him!"

The two men grumbled and cursed him.

"And as for your remark about *gypsies*, you'd best tread with great care and consult your maps a dozen times before you cross any river or a stream in this area!"

The two men looked mystified by his words.

"If you were to stray," Deedigan explained, "And set so much as a single toe into the territory of the Queen of the West it would be *she* who hunts *you* down and every one of your kind who spread hatred and loathing for gypsies, for Jews, for Arabs or for Protestants. She will have none of it – *none of it, I say!* – and nor will my master, The Laird Grant, for we are all born equal in the sight of God."

The swagger of the two Campbells vanished in an instant.

"I may have spoken rashly," said the senior of the pair, "With my tongue not properly connected to my brain."

Deedigan did not reply but made a shrug that communicated his grudging acceptance of the apology. The man straightened and looked sternly at Deedigan.

"You have killed one of my men," he reprimanded.

"I had no option, for he was doing his job far too well!"

This prompted a laugh from the man's companion, for which he was scolded by a searing look.

"The Laird Campbell will take it as a grave offence against him."

"The man had first spied me at such a distance that I thought him blessed with the eyes of an eagle. I felt certain that I would have been a mere speck on the landscape. Even so, he held me in sight for the whole way. How could I let a man like that stay alive to send word of my direction once I had passed?"

The man scowled, "A killing is a killing."

"And it should not have been needed to be done. You could have let us pass across '*your*' lands without the threat of your eyes in every clump of grass, every bush and every tree."

"I have my orders."

"So do I, and if I obey them, exactly how they were given to me, the two of you will be stone cold dead in a moment."

The other gave a hollow laugh, "Do you seriously think that we have come alone?"

"Do you seriously think that I care?"

He laughed, again, "I may have twenty men behind me. I may have fifty. I may have a hundred."

"And do you think that *we* are alone?", Deedigan enquired, gesturing towards Logan, Howison and Dalry.

"I *know* you are alone," the man replied.

"Are you sure?"

"I am absolutely certain."

"Good," smirked the Sergeant-at-Arms, "That is exactly what I intended you to think."

"You're bluffing."

"Am I?"

"Yes. You are."

"Are you willing to stake your lives on it?"

"Without hesitation."

Deedigan smirked again, then moved across to Logan, walking sideways like a crab, both pistols remaining trained on the newcomers.

"Where is she?"

"Who?"

He asked her, again, more insistently: "Where is she?"

"I don't know who you mean," Logan lied.

Deedigan raised his eyebrows and crinkled his nose.

"She's close," he announced.

"She is?"

"Yes, I can feel it."

"How recently have you seen her?"

"She was stood by the oak, over yonder, only a quarter hour ago," he said, nodding in that direction.

Logan looked at him, unable to keep her curiosity from her face, *'What does this man know?'* she wondered, *'Is there something he has discovered?'*

"Oh, yes," Deedigan added, "An oak. That would be magical."

"What do you know of her?" Logan enquired.

Deedigan smiled from behind his scarf, but it twinkled in his eyes.

"My master... The Laird... your grandfather, due to my role and my status of trust, keeps very little from me. I even suspect that he keeps nothing at all from me."

"He has great faith in you."

"A Sergeant-at-Arms is of little use if he didn't."

Logan nodded slowly, appearing a little distant, as she tried to work out just how much he might know. She pondered whether she should *fear* that he knew everything or *hope* that he knew everything.

"What did my grandfather say about her?"

"He said that I should regard her as a pixie, as an elf or as a goblin, but of human size and in human form."

Logan sniggered, "Do you believe in all that folk nonsense and superstition?"

Deedigan spoke earnestly, "Every bit as much as you do."

Logan processed this declaration for a few moments.

"Wait!" she cried, "You walked right through her!"

Deedigan laughed, "I didn't see her in time. It was too late to turn aside. It felt like I'd passed through a warm breeze."

"She's back," said Logan, nodding towards the oak.

"That's a pretty dress she is wearing ."

"It is."

"Now that she's here, we need fear nothing."

"How do you know?"

"It is what your grandfather said."

This time, it was Logan's turn to raise her eyebrows, "And you believe that?" she asked.

"Why would I not?"

"Yes, indeed, you are right. My grandfather's word is as strong as iron nails."

"Tell me, can you speak to her?"

"Yes."

"And she can speak to you?"

"Yes."

"That is good."

"It is better than you think, for conversations are not usually even needed. If you think it in your head, she just knows."

"Belief in someone – total and absolute belief – enhances the power of the person in whom you believe."

"I am impressed by your philosophy, Mister Deedigan."

"I trained for a little while. I am from a good family. A good family that fell on hard times."

Logan looked down at her arms. They were both covered in goosebumps and the hairs on them had just stood up on end.

"What does this mean?" she asked nodding towards her arms.

"It means that the power is close. It is like when a hot cake comes out of the oven and you can feel the heat."

The Campbell who had been the spokesperson for the pair spoke up, jovially imitating annoyance.

"Are we to stand here all day, at gunpoint, while the two of you chatter aimlessly about the weather and what socks you have on, today?"

Deedigan grinned at the man's charm and his aura of good nature.

"Speak a little more harshly to me, Campbell," Deedigan grinned, "For it is easier to hate you if I am not tempted to like you."

"It is a pity that we should find our clans so..." the man paused as he mustered the right word, "So indisposed with each other."

"In another life and in another world, perhaps things could be different."

"In this very same life and in this very same world," the man of the Clan Campbell insisted.

"Now, there you go, being all charming again. I'm going to feel really bad about shooting you, now."

The man laughed and it was entirely genuine. His companion joined in and, he too, seemed properly amused.

Deedigan turned to look at Wild Flower and fixed her with his gaze. Looking straight at her, but speaking to the man who wore the Campbell tartan,, he posed a question.

"What if I were to prove to you that I have one hundred troops, ready and eager to deploy to our aid, and – thus – show you the wisdom of you withdrawing and leaving us to our business?"

"You are weaving a fanciful tale, Sir, if I may say?" replied the other, "But I will indulge you, if you wish. Please, be my guest, and go ahead."

Wild Flower grinned with a grin as wide as a bear trap.

CHAPTER 42

To the last day of their lives, none of those one hundred musket men would be able to explain why they had been there, that day, and why they had done what they had done. It would remain a complete mystery to them. None-the-less, they each felt a little pride that they *had* been there and that they *had* done what they had done. That would just make the strangeness of it all the more appealing.

The flag bearers had not been called. There was no reason to believe that a conflict was in the offing. Living on the border of Campbell land, though, the militias in those parts were always vigilant.

Each had come from their town, their village, their hamlet or even single croft, drawn by some irresistible force. They had found each other on the paths and tracks and begun to march in order. Their lieutenant, having been taken by the fancy to parade himself in his uniform, had also found himself marching to the very same field.

They gathered, that morning, by the bank of a wide stream and, at the command of their lieutenant, they had prepared their weapons and made them ready to fire. None of their number were surprised to see others there. It was their unanimous belief that they were meant to be there.

Lieutenant Higham McIntosh arranged them in ranks. Once he was happy that they were ready to fire the practice volley that they all felt so very sure they were meant to fire, he lifted his sabre in the air and held it ready.

CHAPTER 43

Michael Deedigan made great play of setting his two pistols back into their holsters. Following his lead, Logan did the same.

The Sergeant-at-Arms extracted a whistle from his inside pocket, put it to his lips – having no idea what he might blow on it – and took a deep breath.

Wild Flower, leaning nonchalantly against the oak tree, raised a hand and fluttered her fingers in the air as if shooing invisible mice. Deedigan instantly understood that he need not worry about doing the right thing. Holding his breath for just another couple of seconds, he blew three short notes and a long one.

The very moment the last note ended, there was a loud boom, like rolling thunder, as – just the other side of the stream and down through the trees – one hundred muskets fired in unison.

The two Campbells leapt into the air from shock.

Deedigan found himself counting the seconds aloud and had reached fifteen when – at a moderate distance from all parties – a loud rattling, clattering and cracking of branches and twigs erupted as one hundred weighty metal spheres gave in to the power of gravity.

The two Campbells were aghast, looking for all the world like a pair of chickens that had gone to sleep in a hen house and woken up in a cage full of wolves. It was clear from their expressions that they did not have any of the soldiers behind them that they had boasted.

The pair slunk away, their hands held aloft until they were out of sight.

CHAPTER 44

The atmosphere was almost surreal. Howison and Dalry looked as if they were unsure whether they were awake or asleep. Deedigan swaggered around as if he had just felled a giant. Logan appeared to be calm and collected. Wild Flower, suppressing a simmering angelic smile, appeared to be more concerned with examining her fingernails than with what had just happened.

It was a long minute before anybody spoke.

"I thought you were bluffing," Howison remarked, "I was convinced of it."

"We should play cards together some time in that case," Deedigan laughed, "I could take all your money."

Howison gave him a weak smile.

"Shall we be off, then?" asked Dalry, suddenly perky, pointing to the horses.

"Yes," Deedigan confirmed, motioning in the air as if he were shoving them away, "Get yourself up the track."

"We take the papers?" asked Howison, uncertainly.

"Of course."

"And you follow well behind?"

"Of course."

"And the lassie? Once our backs are turned, she will not just head away home? She will continue the journey."

"I guarantee it," Deedigan confirmed.

"So do I," added Logan, testily.

Mounting up, Howison steered his horse in a circle to pass the pack horse and took up its reins as he drew alongside. With a sharp word to the animal, he led it away, handing it over to Dalry as he reached him.

Watching them go, Deedigan and Logan exchanged a congratulatory smile.

"You lose a cargo of priceless, historical relics in exchange for just a wee bairn," Logan observed.

Deedigan flashed her a wry smile, "I think I have myself something of a bargain. You are destined for great things."

"You think so?"

Deedigan threw back his head and filled his lungs with the air of the forest, before letting it out, dreamily.

"Do you not feel it?" he asked, "The almost unspeakable magic of the place?"

"You're turning out to have something of a deep soul, Mister Deedigan."

"Being in a forest, for me, is the same thing as being in a cathedral."

"That is a fine sentiment."

"Here, I can feel my soul. It tells me that you have a destiny."

"Has my grandfather said something to you?"

"About such a topic? No."

"Has Wild Flower said something to you?"

"She and I are not in a habit of speaking. I am, no matter how grand my title, no more than a servant, and she is an honoured guest of my master."

Logan looked at him curiously. She studied his face. He seemed to be utterly serious. Deedigan held his expression. He fought to keep it perfectly set. He steeled himself to endure and not to waver. Abruptly, he lost all restraint and burst into bellowing laughter. Logan laughed, too. They laughed so much, they thought they would never stop. They laughed so much, they laughed until they cried. They cried for joy.

Just as they were recovering, Logan blinked and became totally rational again.

"You do know, do you not?" she demanded, "That nobody else but the people around us, this side of the stream, heard those musket shots?"

He contorted his face into a whimsical expression, "Yes, in a strange way, I do."

"I don't know how much I can trust you, Mister Deedigan."

"I'm offended!"

"I'm not sure if you being offended should matter."

"I'm even *more* offended!"

"There is so much at stake. There is so much to lose."

"For you, M'Lady, a lot. For me, *everything*."

"How so?"

"You will be away from here, soon enough."

"I will?"

"Aye, I have dreamt it."

"That is interesting!"

Deedigan gave a little grunt and – while she suspected it – she couldn't be certain if it were derisory. She waited for him to follow up his noise with actual words, but he didn't. She drew in a deep breath and let it out as a sigh. Then, dramatically, as a ten-year-old might well do, she slumped to the ground in a heap.

"The future of Scotland..." she began.

"Hangs in the balance," he completed.

"How could you know that, Mister Deedigan?" she asked, looking up at him sharply.

"How could anyone who loves Scotland *not* know that?"

"You have gifts?"

"My grandmother had gifts. My mother, not so much. But they say that it sometimes skips a generation, don't they?"

"Yes, they do."

"It is said, that when the time comes..."

"Stop! Please!" she shouted, louder than she had wanted, "Say no more."

He frowned at her, confusion written across his brow in bold letters.

"For... for all..." she hesitated, "For all I know you could be a spy."

"What!" he exclaimed, genuinely shocked.

Logan sprang to her feet, throwing her arms open, "Well? Hello?" she shouted, seemingly to nobody, "Are you just going to leave me here?"

Deedigan stood stiffly, his awkwardness evident.

"Well?" she demanded, again, "Are you going to let me flounder? Or will there be some participation?"

There was a merry chuckle, from somewhere in the air.

"Participation?" giggled Wild Flower, "Now *there* is a word for a ten-year-old!"

Wild Flower materialised right in front of them, within touching distance and – much to Logan's annoyance – Deedigan didn't seem the least bit perturbed.

"Well done," he congratulated, while silently applauding, "Those musket shots were most impressive."

"I can't actually take credit for those," Wild Flower admitted, "For the force behind this world had already delivered the troops who fired the shots, to the field. I simply willed that, the moment having already been created, that they would do what we needed them to do."

"To assemble all of them would have been a monumental task."

"Monumental for our world, perhaps, but not for a power that came from outside this realm."

He nodded, mulling over those facts at length, before changing his tone and changing the subject.

"Howison and Dalry are far enough ahead of us, now," he announced, "And we don't want them to think that we are not following."

Logan looked at him blankly, tempting him to own up to his abrupt swerve, but he chose to ignore her.

"Very well," she said climbing into her saddle, "But just hold that thought that you were having."

Wild Flower slowly dissolved before their eyes, casting them a wave at the last moment. Logan turned to Michael Deedigan and gave him a measured, steady look as their horses navigated back onto the path.

"What?" he asked, trying to look completely innocent, "I've seen her appear and vanish quite a few times."

"And you didn't think to make any kind of mention of it to me?"

"No matter how lofty my title..." Deedigan began.

"Yes, yes, I know," she interjected, "But you are my grandfather's closest confidante."

Deedigan blew a noisy puff of air, dismissively, at this.

"I think you'll find that he has an advisor, already, in his cousin Gordon."

"He listens to you in preference to him."

"You flatter me, Mistress."

"I'm telling you something that you already know."

"Gordon has a wise head on his shoulders and is very well educated. He was schooled in Winchester, in Salisbury, in Dublin and in Paris. He even speaks Greek and Latin."

"Something tells me that none of this actually impresses you, Mister Deedigan. You are simply recounting items on a mental list."

"How old are you, My Lady?"

Logan turned to him, her eyes flat and without emotion.

"No, My Lady, you are not."

"I didn't say anything."

"You didn't need to say anything."

"I would have told you that I am ten years old if you had given me enough time to speak."

"Yes, which is exactly what I meant. That is the age of your body. That is how long it has been since your flesh, blood and bone entered this world."

"I thought I knew you, to at least some extent, Mister Deedigan, but it appears that I never knew you at all."

"You don't talk like a ten-year-old."

"You flatter me, Sir."

"I'm telling you something that you already know."

She beamed at him, realising that they had just respoken part of their previous conversation, but from opposite sides of it.

"How does *she* speak?", Logan asked.

"Mistress Wild Flower?"

"Yes."

At this, Deedigan burst out laughing.

"Well," he grinned, "Isn't that just it all? Isn't that just everything? The two of you, I mean, not just her."

Logan looked at him with the glimmer of a smile.

"I am thirty-eight years old," he resumed, "My body is thirty-eight years old. So is my mind. You and she, however, have a long, long way to go if your bodies ever have a hope of catching up with your minds!"

He laughed and Logan could not help laughing. too.

"I have experienced some very, very strange things since the day that Wild Flower arrived," Logan confessed, "She, herself, by all accounts, has experienced things that are even stranger still!"

"Do you feel a sense of purpose?"

"Yes."

"Do you feel like you were *meant* to be here?"

"Yes."

"I feel the same. I feel like everything I am doing matters."

Without a further word, they set off after Howison and Dalry.

CHAPTER 45

To Logan and Deedigan it seemed to take an age for them to catch up with Howison and Dalry. When the two men finally came into sight, they could be seen casting nervous glances about them. On sighting Logan and Deedigan, they could be seen to relax. There was no mistaking that they were hugely relieved.

After an hour or so of further riding, Howison and Dalry moved off the track onto a wide verge and came to a halt. Dismounting, they began to rummage in their luggage, producing bundles and wrapped packages that turned out to be food.

"It looks like they are hungry," remarked Deedigan.

"If you listen carefully, you might hear my stomach rumbling."

"Shall we join them?"

"Join them?"

"Yes."

"We can't *join* them, surely."

"There is no reason why not."

"There are plenty of reasons why not," Logan frowned, "Do we not have an agreement with them?"

"Oh, I wouldn't worry so much about the agreement. I would wager that its importance to them has severely diminished. They have been riding ahead of us for long enough, by now, to be more worried about falling prey to bandits than any threat that we might pose."

With great reluctance, Logan joined him in walking their horses slowly towards the two men. As they approached, both looked up, but neither made any complaint. Logan remained in her saddle. Deedigan dismounted and addressed them.

"Any band of robbers would look to take you both from the front," he said, "And from behind. Seeing the two of us, with four pistols at the ready, they will have had second thoughts and let you be."

"Do I look like a man who is worried?" Howison challenged, haughtily, adopting his bravest face.

Deedigan raised a hand and put a finger to his lips for hush, looking around – left to right – as if he had just heard a noise in the greenery. In response, Howison and Dalry both froze and looked uneasy.

Observing their reaction, Deedigan smiled, "Yes, you do," he replied.

Howison gave him a vexed scowl and went back to eating his bread and cheese. Dalry glanced about, a little longer, before returning to his own meal.

Logan, dropped from her horse into a crouch, a pistol held out before her, concentrating her attention on a nearby bush. Stepping towards it with exaggerated stealth, she repositioned her pistol in line with her eye, as if aiming it.

"I am going to count to five," she announced, "And if you don't come out, I am going to shoot."

Howison and Dalry stopped, mid bite, and turned in her direction.

"One... Two... Three..." Logan counted.

Howison and Dalry were frozen as if they were made of stone, gazing fixedly into the undergrowth.

Deedigan gave a chortle and shook his head.

"Don't be so mean," he told Logan, "Let them eat in peace."

Logan laughed and slipped her weapon back into her tunic. Howison and Dalry silently seethed with fury at having been humiliated by a young girl.

For the next twenty minutes, Howison and Dalry spoke sparingly to each other while, a couple of paces away, Logan chatted amiably with Deedigan. The short distance between the two pairs might as well have been an hour's ride.

Once everyone had finished eating and drinking, they all cleared up, packed away and got back onto their horses.

Unwilling to entertain any further silent hostility, Deedigan loudly addressed Howison, acting very convincingly as if the recent spate of ill will had never happened.

"A half hour, now, to the river crossing and then we are in the lands of The Queen of the West. No fear of bandits there. Her Lairds use them to decorate the trees."

Howison looked momentarily confused, but quickly recovered himself. Dalry was less ashamed of his ignorance.

"What manner of decoration might they be?" he asked.

Howison turned, slightly, to make sure that he did not miss the reply.

"This side of the river," Deedigan quipped, "Robbers and cutthroats pay with coin to be allowed to conduct their business… while over yonder, at the far side of the river, people who conduct such business pay with their lives," – Deedigan left a few moments for his words to sink in before continuing – "They swing in the breeze, dangling by their feet from a bough."

"I thought that Queen Annis was timid about such things," said Dalry.

"Not a bit of it," Deedigan corrected, "She understands what she can change and she understands what she cannot change. She accommodates herself to the blood and gore as a necessary display of resolve. Make no mistake, though, when it comes to despatching someone condemned to death, she isn't afraid to swing the blade herself."

"She has more to her than I had imagined," Howison grudgingly admitted.

"She has more to her than *most* people imagine," replied Deedigan.

"You seem to know a lot about her?"

"I know little or nothing compared to some."

"Yet enough that you seem to admire her."

"You will admire yourself, soon enough."

"I am here to kill her, Mister Deedigan."

"I wish you success."

"That's good to hear, because I was starting to worry that your resolve was failing you."

"My resolve is firm."

"The firmer the better, Mister Deedigan, for I haven't journeyed here all the way from London for…"

Howison's voice trailed off, his attention focused on Logan.

"What is it, girl?" he demanded.

"It is nothing," Logan assured him, "My mind was wandering, that's all."

"You were looking at something. You were looking intently. It didn't seem like nothing to me."

"I thought I saw something, but I think my mind may have been playing tricks on me."

"Something in the sky? You were looking up," Howison quizzed, his patience – what little he had – wearing thin.

"What is it you thought you saw?" asked Deedigan, his voice kind and reassuring.

"I thought I saw an arrow, in the sky, but with a tail."

"A tail? You mean streamers?"

"Yes."

"What colour?"

"A line of black and white that alternates from one colour to the other."

'Alternates!' laughed Wild Flower, both in Logan's head and in Deedigan's, *'Now, there is a fine word for a ten-year-old to use!'*

Taken by surprise, Logan and Deedigan immediately looked at each other with startled expressions.

Howison opened his mouth to speak, but Deedigan lifted his hand, palm towards him, urging his silence, while he pretended to listen intently.

'Sometimes,' Wild Flower's voice continued, *'Knowing things before they happen can cause things that must happen, to not happen. So I apologise for being unable to warn you of what is about to occur.'*

"What is it?" Howison demanded, "What's wrong?"

"It is a signal," Deedigan explained, "An arrow with a black and white streamer is an advance scouting party calling for the forces to their rear to hasten forward to provide assistance."

"Who are they?" Howison demanded.

"That's not the right question," Deedigan reprimanded, "What we need to know is what is it that they have seen."

"I think your question is answered," said Logan, pointing along the track.

Approaching them were six men on horseback, claymores drawn and shields on their arms.

"Campbells," said Dalry.

At this news, Howison looked relieved. Deedigan gave him a scornful look.

"You might not look so pleased in a moment or so," he told him.

Howison ignored him. As the riders neared, he waved an arm in greeting, "A good day to you. We are friends."

The big man on the lead horse – the one plainly in charge – growled his animosity and spat on the ground before responding.

"You are no friends of mine."

"You are of the Clan Campbell are you not?" Howison asked, suddenly less assured.

"I am," the big man replied, but without any great enthusiasm.

"Our group is passing through these parts with the blessing of The Laird Campbell, himself," Howison announced.

"If it is him you have paid, then he hasn't passed on any of your coin to me."

"We have paid him nothing, for our mission is one that enjoys the full support of The Campbell."

"You have a warrant bearing his seal to say that this is so?"

"I have no warrant. The Campbell has said what he has said and he believes that his word is good enough."

"The Campbell's word may be good enough, but that doesn't mean that *your* word is good enough."

"We travel with his assurance of safe passage," Howison protested.

"His assurance carries weight in his vicinity, but his assurance is of less and less value the further away you get."

"Are you prepared to cross him?" asked Deedigan, speaking for the first time.

"Are *you* prepared to cross *me*?" the big man challenged.

Deedigan ignored his words, declining to succumb to a confrontation, "You learned of our approach?"

"I did. Word travels fast, hereabouts."

"Did you learn that we are not alone?"

"Any escort you may have would have been pushed to the far side of the water as it widened and deepened. They won't have transgressed onto Campbell land."

"You seem very confident about that."

"I *am* very confident about that."

Deedigan's mind spun like a sycamore seed whirling and spiralling to the ground but, despite this, he managed to snatch a thought as it flew past.

He knew that, if the arrow with the black and white tail had come from friendly forces, that he must get closer to them. The trees along his flank hid the river from view, but he could hear the sound of the water gurgling over and around rocks and the distinctive sound of water cascading over falls. He needed to move these six Campbells along the track to the shore and the crossing that lay ahead.

"There are six of you and four of us," Deedigan observed with a perfectly calculated amount of contempt, "Do you not think that you should have come with more men?"

The big man growled and gnashed his teeth.

"Do you count the wee lass in your number?", he asked, before spitting copiously on the ground.

This reaction was exactly the one Deedigan had wanted.

"The wee lass?" he asked, before throwing his head back and laughing, "Is that how you see her?"

A moment of confusion flickered across the big man's face, and he looked Logan over more closely. A second or two later, his previous look of disdain was restored.

Deedigan looked to Logan, then slowly to the big man, then back to Logan.

"No! No! No!" Deedigan chastised, wagging a finger at her, "Don't even think of it. Not even for a second. Get that thought out of your head."

Picking up on and joining in his playacting, Logan adopted a suitably disappointed face.

"Please Uncle," she pleaded, addressing him as a relative on a whim, "Can I not kill just *half* of them? The other three can run away."

The big man glowered at her with a cold fury, unsure if she were worthy enough of his time to bother with a reply. The five men behind him seethed and fumed, too, their eyes wide and their jaws clenched.

Deedigan, acting casually, made the Scottish Noise and shook his head as if in sorrow. Logan folded her arms, lifted her chin and – with an exaggerated motion – shook her long hair like a whip, causing it to slew over her shoulder.

"Very well," she snapped, impetuously, "But at least let me kill *one* of them."

At this, the big man could no longer contain himself.

"Shut the lass up or I will slit her throat from one ear to the other!" he shouted.

Logan sniggered as if this were the best joke she had heard in ages.

"Yes!" Deedigan grinned, "Why don't you come and do that? First, though, make sure that one of your party has a spade. We don't have one."

The big man looked quizzical. Deedigan took malicious pleasure in offering him an explanation.

"I presume that you'd like to be buried and not simply left for the birds?"

The man contorted his face with such grotesque contempt that it was as if he were trying to force his own brains out through his nose.

"I might just crush your Irish skull between my hands," he said, gesturing to show how it might be done, "Just before I rip the young lassie in half," he snarled, adding a second gesture for good measure.

"Calm yourself," Deedigan urged, "These are the last words that you may ever speak. Choose them wisely. Very soon, you will be laid out – flat on your back – with your empty, dead eyes staring up at the clouds."

The big man bared his teeth and began to make a rumbling noise, but Deedigan waved him to stop.

"This mud," said Deedigan, gesturing to the ground, "It is almost black. It will ruin your tunic when you're laid out in it. Once you're dead, I intend to use it for rags to clean my horse's hooves. Let's move up along this track to the shore, by the river. We'll find nice clean sand, there."

"We will stay right here."

"Uncle!" cried Logan, her shrill impatience impressively authentic, "It matters nothing to me where he dies! I will take him down in the mud, if he wishes. Just let me kill him."

"Hold your tongue!" Deedigan replied, "If you tripped over his corpse, while you were mutilating him, and you were to fall into that mud, your mother – my sister – would have me flogged!"

"Enough of this!" the big man boomed, "I have no more patience left!"

"Very well, have it your own way," cried Deedigan, "I will kill you, myself, right now. Then, we can move up to the sand by the river and she can kill which ever one of your remaining men she chooses."

With this, he gently stroked his steed's belly with the toe of his shoe in a very particular way. In response, his horse began to take a series of sideways steps towards the big man.

The leader of the Campbell fighters laughed, despairingly, and his men joined in.

"But," Deedigan insisted, "Let us make this clear: Your last order to your men, before you die, is that – whatever happens – they are to nothing more here, but are to ride along the track until they reach the sand by the river?"

"If it is so damned important to you," the big man snarled, "Then, before *you* die, my order is exactly that."

"That's fine then," said Deedigan, as casually as if he had just agreed an order for ale at a tavern counter, "All that remains, now, is for you to die."

Deedigan reached backwards, up over his shoulder, and grasped the handle of the weapon that was tethered there. The big Campbell watched him, eyeing the opposite end of the scabbard, gauging the length of the weapon within it, and feeling a pang of pity for his opponent's stupidity.

'What idiot,' he mused, *'Who would draw a long, riding sword at such close quarters and think that they would have any hope of wielding it?'*

Deedigan paused and braced himself, as one might when preparing to apply a lot of force, then he tugged at the handle of his weapon and pretended that he couldn't budge it. He stiffened, allowing momentary panic to show in his eyes, before looking down with dismay at his other sword, which was now awkwardly positioned to access it.

Seeing an opportunity, the big Campbell did not hesitate, he spurred his horse forward, and – levelling his sword at his opponent – lunged hard to skewer him in the heart.

No sooner did the Campbell move, than Deedigan yanked the handle of his weapon for real, lofting it into the air above his head, while simultaneously delivering an instruction to his horse with his toe. The horse promptly took a single step backwards and, lowering its head, dropped to its knees.

Deedigan ripped the twin bladed battle axe from the imitation scabbard where he had stowed it. Swinging it in a long arc, he lunged out of his saddle and fell forward. This well practised motioned transferred the combined force of his own bodyweight and that of the descending horse to the edge of the axe blade.

The axe caught the man just above his ear, slicing it from his head, before cleaving through his jaw, severing part of his tongue, hacking through the side of his neck and severing his windpipe. The force taken to deliver the blow was momentous, the accuracy of it precise and the result utterly devastating.

The five men to his rear sat motionless, each temporarily entranced by what they had just witnessed. They were all seasoned mounted troops, well familiar with dozens of different forms of assault from the saddle – rider to rider – but Deedigan's transition, before their very eyes, from hapless victim to elegant and exquisitely capable executioner had left them enthralled. Their natural instinct to surge forward and attack was completely extinguished by their common sense of horror. They were no more mobile than statues.

CHAPTER 46

Assembling on the fine sand beside the fording point, the five Campbells were a little subdued. Deedigan had insisted that they bury their leader and not leave him for the birds and the animals of the forest. This they had been eager to do. It had been an act of chivalry they had received with appreciation. Still more impressed were they with the fact that Deedigan, himself, had joined them in the task, taking turns to dig, industriously, with the spade that he had denied possessing.

The five lined up on their horses, looking sombre. Deedigan felt a wave of sympathy for them. They were unmistakably men in the early stages of mourning. The man who had died had clearly left a huge hole in their hearts. Their duty was, now, to kill the girl, the Grant Sergeant-at-Arms and their two companions but they seemed to have no great appetite for it.

"Turn and go," Deedigan instructed them, his tone soft and almost friendly, "There is no need for any more death, here."

One of the men flinched at the suggestion.

"I thought your little girl was going to snub one of us out like a candle?" he scorned.

Deedigan gazed at him, then spoke kindly and without malice.

"Go home to your families. I give you your lives."

"Are you insane?" asked another, suddenly provoked, "We are more than a match for you and those three."

Deedigan turned and looked around. Five strides ahead of him were the five Campbells. To his right was Logan. To his left were Howison and Dalry. Behind him was the river with five strides of pale, yellowish sand between him and the water.

Deedigan dismounted.

"I have two axes," he told them, "Which is enough to take down two of you. She has two heavy throwing knives. That accounts for another two."

The men sneered at him and shook their heads as if listening to the ramblings of a lunatic.

"Our two companions," he continued, waving towards Howison and Dalry, "Should be more than able to take care of the last of you… and that's if she or I don't decide to slay them ourselves."

The five Campbells exchanged glances, then one of them declared their shared conclusion.

"You are bluffing."

Howison and Dalry looked at Deedigan pityingly. Deedigan dismounted and confidently walked towards the Campbells with no weapon drawn.

"It is no bluff," he insisted, "I'm letting you go."

Howison and Dalry both looked suddenly unsure and shifted in their saddles uneasily. The five Campbells seemed to lose their bravado.

Deedigan approached the first Campbell rider, reached up and offered his hand. The rider shook it. He walked to the second rider and made the same gesture. The rider looked at his hand suspiciously for a moment, but then shook it. The third rider made as if to shake Deedigan's hand, but then caught him by the arm, twisted him around and held a dagger to his throat.

"Kill him!" shouted Howison, "I have no need of him. He is yours."

"Kill him slowly," urged Dalry.

Logan shot them a look of incandescent rage.

Behind the Campbells, the pack horse, which had been grazing in a leisurely fashion amongst the long, sweet grass, suddenly looked up and fixed its gaze next to Logan. Following the direction of the beast's eyes, Logan saw Wild Flower stood on the ground beside her horse.

Wild Flower gestured to the horse, indicating where she stood, then motioned to what lay between her and it, before pointing out the path she wished it to take to reach her. The horse studied her directions for a few seconds, then nodded its head enthusiastically. Wild Flower went into a half crouch, as if making ready to break into a run. The horse nodded, again.

Deedigan – all the while with a knife at his throat – looked at her curiously, wondering quite what it was that she was doing.

Raising her hands in front of her, Wild Flower smacked her palms together, loudly, making a noise like a pistol shot.

The pack horse leaned forward, stamped its hooves into the ground and broke into a sudden trot. Following the precise line indicated to it – and veering not one bit to left or right – the horse sped past the man who was holding Deedigan. The wooden crate strapped to its left side struck the man's elbow with its sharp front edge. The man's arm broke immediately, his knife jumping away from his prisoner's throat. Deedigan lost no time in diving to the ground and rolling to safety.

Logan threw a knife, hitting Deedigan's attacker in the throat, directly under his chin. He tumbled off his horse, gripping his throat with the hand of his good arm, as a torrent of blood erupted from it. As the man next to him drew his sword, Logan launched a second knife. The knife struck him at the base of his neck. As he struggled to remove it, an axe – thrown by Deedigan – took him squarely in the chest. He keeled off his horse and was dead before he hit the ground. Another axe whirled through the air, taking another of the Campbells in the ribs, beneath his arm. The man slumped forward and slid sideways to the ground.

As the remaining two Campbells spurred their steeds forward, brandishing their swords, Deedigan and Logan chose a man each as their target. Both hoped, fervently, that they had not chosen the target of the other.

Logan drew her sword, took a deep breath, and said a little prayer. As the Campbell closed on her, she braced herself and lifted her blade to rest flat against her left shoulder. The charging Campbell – lifting his sword to deliver a sweeping cut – wavered for a second before committing himself to his move. As the blade swept towards her, Logan threw herself backwards, arching her back to accelerate herself. The back of her head hit her horse's hind quarters with a slap.

With all her might, Logan forced her free hand against the hilt of the sword she held in her other. Grunting with the effort, she levered her blade out and around, flat to the ground, into the path of the oncoming rider.

Too late to stop himself or to change course, the Campbell was impaled. The tip of her sword entered him just above his navel and came out of his back a thumb length from his spine. As his own blade passed over her, it came so close to her head that it cut off a lock of her hair.

Deedigan stood stock still as the Campbell rider approached him. The rider raised his sword, ready to strike. Deedigan, calmly and without fluster, slipped a hand inside his tunic as he sidestepped his adversary's blade, then turned to face his back as he passed. Deedigan pulled out a pistol, swept back the lid from over the ignition pan, and squeezed the trigger. The firearm kicked and belched flames from its barrel. A moment later, a bloody hole appeared between the rider's back shoulder blades, and he crashed to the ground.

"You had a pistol?" Howison shouted, angrily, "All this time, you had a pistol?"

"No," replied Deedigan, "This is yours."

Howison frantically forced a hand into his left saddlebag, then his right, and looked furious that his pistol was missing.

A few paces away, one of the dying Campbells attempted to get to his feet, but fell back to his knees in the attempt. Deedigan reached into the other side of his tunic and, producing another pistol, readied it and fired it at the man, killing him instantly.

"And this is yours!" Deedigan cried to Dalry.

Dalry performed his own hectic search in his saddlebags, then looked every bit as annoyed as Howison had at having been robbed.

"They need reloading," Deedigan called, throwing them in the general direction of their indignant owners.

The two took a couple of strides towards their property and then stopped, staring at their weapons suspiciously. Their striking the ground appeared to have made it shake. As they gazed in wonder, the ground rumbled and shook still more.

Just beyond the thin strip of trees, clearly visible through their sparse branches, came the source of the tremors. A dozen or more riders were pounding towards them at a gallop. From the tartan they wore, they were unmistakably Campbells.

Suddenly, a powerful voice boomed out, its source to their rear, across the river. So loud was it, that it echoed like thunder, setting a hundred birds to flight from the surrounding trees.

"Cleave!" shouted the voice, the word urgent and deliberately prolonged.

Obeying without thinking, Deedigan ducked close to the ground, ran to the left and threw himself onto his face. Logan sped her horse to the right, hunching down in the saddle as she went, before sliding off and into the tall grass. Howison and Dalry looked stunned. They paused, appearing distrustful, but moved none-the-less and deposited themselves in a patch of ferns.

Just then, the Campbells burst through the brush, swords held aloft.

"Loose!" came the same voice from beyond the river.

A moment later, a blizzard of fifty arrows came thrumming through the air. They flew like a swarm of angry insects. The Campbell riders seemed to dance in their saddles as arrow after arrow found its mark, lurching them this way and that before sending them reeling backwards, to land on the ground in contorted, lifeless heaps.

After a few seconds, another wave of arrows was launched. They found their targets with the same merciless accuracy. Those of the enemy who were not already dead, died.

Howison got cautiously to his feet, disregarding Dalry's shouts for him to remain under cover. Hearing the sound of footfalls swishing through the grass towards him, Howison whirled around. His reaction was too slow. Deedigan struck him squarely in the jaw, felling him, unconscious, straight onto his back.

"No use for me, is it?" cursed Deedigan.

Dalry jumped into the air like a frightened cat and turned to flee. Before he could escape, Deedigan landed a blow on the side of his head that sent him reeling. He blacked out, his limbs going limp as he sprawled on the grass.

"Kill him slowly, indeed!" Deedigan snarled.

CHAPTER 47

It did not take long to identify the army that had felled the attacking Campbells from across the river. The MacDonald Tartan they wore left no doubt.

Their rescuers waited patiently for Deedigan and Logan to cross the river at the fording point and made a point of staying at their own side of the water. This far upstream, apparently, it really *did* divide them from Campbell territory.

The sight of Howison and Dalry bound and gagged and securely tethered face down across the saddles of their horses caused them great amusement.

"I see you have fallen out with your travelling companions," joked Finlay MacDonald, "Did they lose at dice and refuse to pay their debts?"

"They played a game more serious than that. They sided with our enemies in a fight," replied Deedigan.

"And," added Logan, "With your very kind assistance, they most definitely lost."

Howison and Dalry writhed and wriggled, while doing their best to curse, but the gags around their mouths reduced their words to grumbling noises.

"They seem like sore losers!" laughed Heather MacDonald.

Logan hurriedly dismounted and dropped to her knees.

"Your Ladyship," she blurted, "I apologise that, until you spoke, I mistook you for a man by your clothing."

Heather MacDonald laughed, again.

"And, until *you* spoke, I mistook you for a child, young lady," she responded.

"I am ten!" Logan responded, indignantly.

"Ten, maybe, in years of life, but fifteen by the way you talk and, surely, not a day less than twenty by the way you fight."

"Thank you, Your Ladyship."

"What about you, lassie?" Heather enquired, looking to Logan's right, "Are you wee or girt?"

Both Logan and Deedigan whirled their heads to see whom she was addressing. To their great surprise, she was looking at Wild Flower who had appeared without them noticing.

"Sad so say," Wild Flower replied, curtseying, "I am likely afflicted with the same mature tongue as my stepsister."

"You have a twang to your Gaelic," replied Heather MacDonald, "That I cannot identify."

"I am from here, I am from there and I am from everywhere."

"You raised your hand and made a gesture in the air, when the arrows flew."

Logan and Deedigan looked at each other, for they had not even seen her at that point.

"Did I, Your Ladyship?" Wild Flower asked, innocently.

"Yes, you did."

"It must have been a tick or a twitch."

"It was no such thing," Heather protested, "It was very deliberate."

"Oh! Then I must have…"

"You must have what?" Heather enquired, "For one hundred arrows were fired, and not an arrow less, yet not so much as a single one of them struck a horse."

Wild Flower threw a hand to her mouth and looked embarrassed.

"Oh!" she exclaimed, "That is… errrr… very fortunate."

"Tell me this," Finlay challenged, "You have no horse and you did not share a saddle with any one of these, and yet you have come across the water, from one side to the other, without getting your feet wet."

"Bite my thumb!" Heather demanded, holding out her hand.

Wild Flower stepped forward and, happy to oblige, she bit it, gently.

"Bite mine, too!" Finlay commanded, offering the said digit.

Wild Flower turned to him and bit it, a little harder than she had Heather's. Finlay flinched and shook his thumb, as if to dislodge the pain.

"I feared you had no form," Heather announced.

"She has form," chuckled Finlay, "And I can very much assure you, so do her teeth."

"Who are you?" asked Heather, looking at her closely.

"You know me," replied Wild Flower, flatly.

Heather came closer still and studied her.

"You are the girl from my dreams," she gasped.

"And from mine," said Finlay.

"And they?" asked Wild Flower, pointing to the squirming forms of Howison and Dalry, "Are they in your dreams?"

"I cannot be certain," replied Finlay, approaching them as if they were animals he feared might have fleas, "It is hard to tell."

"I'm not sure," Heather agreed, "I would not put a wager on it."

Wild Flower allowed them to ponder and puzzle for a little while before interrupting them, "We have work to do," she said.

"Yes, we do," they both agreed.

Wild Flower smiled. All thoughts of her inexplicably dry feet were forgotten.

Everyone mounted up, Wild Flower on a borrowed horse. Just at that moment, the pack horse, which had been delayed cropping the most succulent grass at the other side of the river, came plodding out of the water onto land.

"Is he in your dreams?" asked Wild Flower.

Heather turned to look and so did Finlay.

"He is certainly in *my* dreams," Heather declared.

"And most *definitely* in mine," Finlay assured.

Deedigan looked at the pack horse, and then at Heather and Finlay, in turn. He wondered why neither had asked what the pack horse was carrying in its bags and crates.

CHAPTER 48

"We were lucky that you were nearby," Deedigan told Finlay MacDonald.

"I don't think luck had anything to do with it," the man replied, looking to Heather MacDonald to gauge her opinion on the matter.

"We headed this way on impulse," she told him, "We were drawn here."

"And, then, there were the dreams," Finlay offered.

Heather made a face at this. It was apparent that she did not feel the moment had arrived for such frankness.

"We felt that this was where we needed to be," Heather declared.

An awkward silence brewed. Deedigan respected it, for a while, before piercing it.

"We saw your arrow," he said.

"Our arrow?" Finlay asked evasively.

"Your signal arrow."

"Oh, yes," replied Finlay, looking puzzled, "But that could have only been visible above the trees, for…" he described an arc in the air with his finger while mechanically counting the seconds up from one to five, "For five seconds," he announced.

"We happened to look up," Logan told them.

"Just at the precise time it could be seen," mused Heather, dubiously.

"When the time comes," Wild Flower quoted, "All that needs to happen, will happen."

Finlay MacDonald, Heather MacDonald and their two senior officers simultaneously drew their steeds to an abrupt halt. Deedigan, Logan and Wild Flower did the same. Behind them, the column of troops, on foot, came to a stop, too.

"Those are famous words," said Heather, accusingly.

Wild Flower gave her the best and sweetest smile she could muster, "Yes, indeed," she confirmed.

Finlay and Heather gave her a stern look of reproach. In response, Logan gave a loud, impatient sigh.

"Shall we, perhaps, agree not to play these word games?" she asked, "For we all know the significance of those words."

This time, it was Finlay and Heather's turn to sigh.

"Wait!" Deedigan interrupted, "You never asked us who we are."

"Do you want to tell us?" Heather snapped.

"No," replied Deedigan, sullenly, "I don't."

"Well, there we have it then," said Wild Flower, merrily, "There it is."

Nobody moved. Each rider held still. Their horses remained rooted to the spot. Finlay and Heather looked thoughtful. They seemed to be either trying to work out a problem or recall something to mind. Eventually, the two exchanged a tentative glance.

"Falbh!" said Wild Flower, quite loudly, this being Gaelic for 'go'.

Obediently, the horses all started forward. Heather shot her a look of annoyance. The look Finlay gave her was unmistakable one of disgust. *'How dare you?'* he seemed to be thinking.

Their horses to continue on, picking their way carefully through a patch of rutted mud and small boulders as they went, displaying all the concentration of acrobats walking a tightrope. Several of the riders patted the neck of their mount in encouragement or acknowledgement. The horses snuffled happily at the gesture.

Once the track had become less rugged, Finlay instructed one of his officers to wait for the foot troops, while he roused everyone to a more rapid pace. After half an hour of this, he drew the riders off the road onto a patch well-trodden earth. Here, the horses were watered in a stream a few paces away, before being set to graze along its bank.

"You could be any kind of traveller at all. Am I right?" Finlay asked Deedigan.

"Yes, just so."

"But you are not. You are most definitely not."

"How can you be sure?"

"We… That is my cousin and I…" Finlay declared, nodding towards Heather, "Have ridden down to that crossing and brought with us a small army not once, or twice, but three times over the last month. On each occasion we have not known why, but we have known that, eventually, we would have to use our soldiers in anger."

"I see."

"Today, however, we knew for certain that today was that day."

"It was the right day for us, too," Deedigan professed.

"It was the right time for everyone."

"I'm not sure that the Campbells would agree with you, there!" laughed Deedigan.

Finlay joined in the laughter and his cousin strode over to see what was the cause of mirth.

"You, Your Ladyship, felt compelled to go to the crossing today?" asked Wild Flower.

"Oh, he told you, did he?" she replied, casting a disapproving look at Finlay.

Finlay frowned at her, "Does anyone know of such a thing as recalling the future before it can have happened?"

"Yes," replied Deedigan.

"Yes," replied Wild Flower.

"Only too well," replied Logan.

"How so?" Heather asked.

Logan couldn't suppress a smirk as she replied, "I seem to have that feeling at least twice a week, recently."

"The sense that you have experienced a situation, already, that could not yet have happened is a strange one," muttered Finlay, to nobody in particular.

Logan became aware that she was being stared at by Finlay. Moments later, Heather noticed it, too.

"What is it?" she asked him, while looking intently at Logan.

"I have a strong feeling that I am recalling the future right now," Finlay announced.

"In what way?" demanded Heather.

"Her eyes," he replied, looking even more intently at Logan, "They are worryingly familiar."

Heather moved to stare into Logan's eyes, "You are right, I can feel it, too."

"Wintryth," called Finlay, hailing one of the soldiers close by, "Come here, will you?"

Wintryth stopped what he was doing and walked across to stand by Finlay.

"What can I do for you?"

"This girl," said Finlay, pointing to Logan, "Look at her eyes and tell me if you have seen her before. Look deep into them. Think really hard about it before you answer."

Wintryth did as he was asked and spent fifteen or twenty seconds looking intently into Logan's eyes. Then, suddenly, he laughed.

"Aye, I've seen them, so I have," he confirmed, "But, if you will forgive my words," Wintryth explained, pointing in the general direction of her crotch, "The owner of such eyes will have had a cock down there instead of a girl's parts."

"Wintryth!" cried Heather, astonished by his coarseness, "I think that will be all we need of you!"

Wintryth shrugged his shoulders, grunted and wandered off back to where he had been.

"I'm sorry!" Heather apologised to a blushing Logan, "That was a little crude!"

Logan looked down at her feet in embarrassment.

"But he is right," Finlay agreed, "For if you imagine those eyes, if they were transferred into the face of a man of roughly twice her age, they would be the very person I am recalling. Yet, it is someone that I could have never possibly met."

Fascinated, Heather placed a hand on Logan's cheek and gently moved her head to face her.

"You have it exactly right," she gasped.

"Let me see," said Wild Flower, staring into Logan eyes and giving her a discrete wink, "For these eyes have, beyond a doubt, the very same look as those of The Flashing Blade."

CHAPTER 49

The MacDonald troops waited on the track as their leaders and their guests moved off the road and onto a broad, flat apron that ran beside it to the top of the rise ahead of them. A group of servants began to unpack some things from the back of a cart. Their party, Deedigan concluded, were going to stop for a while.

"If your companions wish to be presented to the Queen of the West," Finlay advised, looking more than a little displeased, "I regret to say that there will be no alternative but to untie them."

Deedigan put his hands to his mouth, mimicking shock.

"Seriously? You think so?" he asked, giving a wry smile, "That's horrifying and very disappointing."

Howison and Dalry wriggled and grumbled, venting their anger with an incomprehensible stream of noises that sounded very much like swearing. Deedigan looked pleased.

"Your mission..." said Heather MacDonald, "The one in which you are engaged..."

Deedigan cocked his head, enquiringly, to prompt her to continue.

"It is, you have said, a closely guarded secret?"

"Yes."

"One that has the blessing of King James?"

"Yes."

"And your *companions*," she asked, loading the word with contempt, "They have a warrant from the king? A warrant with his seal?"

"Yes," Deedigan confirmed.

Howison and Dalry started making muffled noises, again, but their attempts to communicate were in vain.

"There are many Lairds," Finlay pointed out, "Who are displeased at Queen Annis' continued loyalty to King James and who would wish to thwart it."

"That is the truth," Deedigan agreed.

"Amongst them, there are those…" Finlay began, pausing when Heather raised a hand.

Deedigan looked to Heather MacDonald with renewed interest. A question crossed his mind. It was obvious, he noted, that Finlay MacDonald was in charge. It was equally obvious, however, that he gave very clear deference to this woman. Most women would never dare to hold up a hand to silence a man who was speaking, not without risking their wrath and, very possibly, the back of their hand.

"There are those," said Heather, taking over speaking, "Who would very much like to stop talking and direct themselves, instead, towards eating."

Finlay motioned to a group of men – dressed in cooks' hats, aprons and oversleeves – who had gathered a few paces away. They had brought lidded churns that were gently giving off steam and a most delicious aroma.

"No," said Deedigan, holding up his hands, "I must decline. You have no need what-so-ever to feed me."

"I insist," Heather purred.

"You are our guest," agreed Finlay.

"I really cannot impose on you," Deedigan protested.

"It is no imposition," replied Heather, "It is our pleasure."

Deedigan looked almost ill as he surveyed the stew being ladled out into bowls and the hunks of bread and cheese being set onto plates.

Finlay glanced briefly at Wild Flower, moving his gaze to Logan, but drew it back again. Wild Flower has an unusual look in her eyes. Finlay looked more intently at her. It was as if the little girl were relishing the sharing of a mutual secret. Finlay looked back to Deedigan, whose discomfort was unmistakable.

Heather was unable to ignore Finlay's sudden distraction and looked at Wild Flower, too. It took Heather but a moment to interpret what she saw, causing her alarm. Finlay's eyes shot to Heather and, in a moment, he had drawn his sword.

"No," said Heather, "Let him give an account of himself."

Finlay, very reluctantly, re-sheathed his blade.

Deedigan looked pained, his face suddenly pale.

"I am not hungry," he said, unconvincingly.

"Is that so?" asked Heather, in a mocking tone.

Finlay's sword hand twitched, eager to grip his weapon again. Deedigan turned to look at Howison and Dalry, his face tightening slightly and the contour of his lips becoming grimmer.

Heather noted his demeanour and looked back to Wild Flower, who met her gaze with an unspoken question: *'Do you see what is before you or not?'*

It was like a pile of painted wooden bricks toppling over to form a picture.

"Maybe," suggested Heather, "Your appetite would return if we took your two companions back across the river and abandoned them on the track. The thieves and bandits who frequent it would welcome victims who are bound and gagged."

"I have given them my word."

"You can take back your word."

Deedigan looked insulted, "No, I cannot!"

Finlay grunted contemptuously, "If they were in your place, they would not hesitate."

"It is I who am in my place."

"Then none of you will meet Queen Annis," said Heather, "For if you cannot share a meal with us – which worries me with regard to your intentions – then you must be slain or banished."

"Is that how your dream ends?" demanded Wild Flower.

Heather and Finlay both turned to her as if she had pricked them with a pin. Slowly, they looked around them, as if assessing everything that met their eye. Heather took Finlay to stand a little distance away and motioned for Wild Flower to join them. She did.

"Am I asleep?" asked Heather, earnestly.

Finlay looked down at his hand and pinched it firmly. His resulting flinch confirmed that he was awake.

"What is happening?" he asked, warily.

"You know what is happening."

"I do?"

"Yes, you do."

Finlay looked to Heather, as if she might know the answer.

Heather looked at Wild Flower with a hint of suspicion.

"You know who I am, don't you?" Heather asked, making the question sound more like an accusation.

"Yes."

"Have we met before?"

"No."

"You know me from a picture you have seen?"

"No."

"Then how?"

"I just know."

"How is that possible?"

Wild Flower looked at The Laird MacDonald's daughter steadily and patiently.

"Your dreams," asked Wild Flower, "What are they about?"

Heather raised her shoulders, then let them slump. Wild Flower decided upon a different approach.

"A little earlier, just before your very timely arrival, My Lady, we heard the sound of hooves coming towards us, rapidly. We did not have to look to know that horses were approaching."

Heather looked intrigued.

"Perhaps, My Lady, you have a sense of what is approaching without needing it to present itself to you?"

Heather's look instantly became one of concern. She turned and locked eyes with Finlay. He appeared to be worried about something.

"These men" he said, nodding towards Howison and Dalry, "They are on a mission of their own?"

"They are," replied Wild Flower.

"And he," Finlay continued, nodding in the direction of Deedigan, "Is he on the same mission?"

"He is accompanying them on their mission but he is not part of their mission."

"He is guarding them?"

"No, he is guarding her," Wild Flower explained, indicating Logan.

Suddenly, all fifty of the soldiers dropped to one knee. Seeing them do so, Finlay and Heather did the same. Logan, as she watched Wild Flower drop into a curtsey, took in the expression on her face. Logan glanced around, from person to person, and noticed that all eyes were fixed on a point above her right shoulder. She realised that somebody had come and taken up a position behind her. She turned and quickly adopted a curtsey, herself.

"I am surprised that you need guarding," said the young woman who faced her, "For you fight with a strength and agility that is astonishing."

The person for whom the soldiers were kneeling was on horseback, wearing gleaming armour and had long blonde hair that fell in a cascade down to her waist.

"Your Majesty," said Heather MacDonald.

"Your Majesty," said Finlay MacDonald.

"Your Majesty," said Michael Deedigan.

"Your Majesty," said Logan Grant.

"Your Majesty," said Wild Flower, with an impish twinkle in her eye and the merest hint of a smile.

The Queen of the West barely managed to disguise that she shared Wild Flower's amusement, before she inclined her head to accept everyone's respect and gestured for the troops to stand. She gave Heather the tiniest of smirks, that seemed almost conspiratorial.

"Your Highness," said Finlay, "We have travellers who are on their way to present themselves to you."

The queen glanced at Logan, Finlay and Heather before moving her attention to Howison and Dalry.

"Those two appear to be in no situation to present themselves to anyone or anything," she remarked, "Unless it is to their horses' hooves."

"They are temporarily restrained, My Queen," Finlay advised.

"Their rope bindings speak for themselves."

"Yes, Your Majesty, of course. These men had a falling out with their companions."

"Well, I'm glad they don't travel like that for no reason," she replied.

Finlay hesitated, not sure if she were joking. The queen smiled and gave him a little laugh to set him at ease. Finlay smiled in relief.

Swinging her leg from her saddle, the queen dismounted. She moved with a fluid grace, landing lightly on her feet, despite the weight of her armour.

"She fights like you," said the queen, addressing herself to Heather.

"And I, Your Majesty, to some feeble extent, attempt to fight like you."

"Your attempts are more than a little successful."

"If you say so, My Queen."

"I do say so, I do indeed, and you," she said, prodding Heather between her eyes with a finger, "Need to put a little more effort into your modesty if you are to make it appear truly convincing."

Heather, taking offence, narrowed her eyes at the queen. The reprimand she conveyed was dramatically at odds with her earlier deference and formal curtsey.

"Unbind and ungag those two men," the queen instructed, "And, when they are in a fit state, bring them before me."

Finlay promptly set about issuing instructions accordingly.

"If you will follow me up to the top of the rise?" invited the queen, setting off at a casual stroll.

Logan, Deedigan and Wild Flower obediently set off after her in a line. They had hardly taken three strides before half a dozen burly soldiers had sprinted out of the greenery either side of the track to take up protective positions around the queen.

After several minutes of walking they arrived at the brink of the incline. Before them, in the distance, lay the royal stronghouse of Faiche Samhraidh – *or Summer Meadow in English* – its pale yellow walls illuminated with a golden glow from the rays of the sun.

"It is a wonderful sight, is it not?" the queen enquired.

"It is Your Majesty," agreed Logan.

"It is beautiful," swooned Wild Flower.

"Fit for a queen," said Heather with a tiny hint of sarcasm in her voice.

The queen shot her a stern look and Heather lowered her head.

CHAPTER 50

At Faiche Samhraidh The Queen of the West, who retired briefly to her chambers, reappeared in a sumptuous gown of silk and lace.

The welcome that everybody received was beyond friendly and beyond generous. All parties were overwhelmed by the kindness of the staff and the kindness of their hosts.

Deedigan, Logan and Wild Flower were given refreshments in the lower hall and given facilities to freshen themselves after their journey.

Meanwhile, Howison and Dalry, who had eaten lunch with the queen in the upper hall, accompanied her to her study. On entering, they gazed in amazement at the thirty towering bookcases, each eight shelves high, that lined the walls.

"I think it is fair to presume that you enjoy reading?" quipped Howison.

"Yes, I do. Very much."

"I am guessing that you have not actually read all of these?" he joked, gesturing at the enormous bookcases.

"I have read every one of them," she replied

"What? *All* of them?" gasped Dalry.

"Yes, all of them. I often read a book in a day. Sometimes two."

Howison and Dalry exchanged looks of surprise and gawped in awe at her personal library.

The queen pretended to clear her throat to regain their attention, "I have looked through the very impressive collection of Noory McGregor's works that you have brought with you," she announced, "And I have had them scrutinised by a scholar who has great expertise in this subject."

Howison and Dalry stood with expectant faces, neither having any real clue as to the absolute authenticity of the papers.

"And," the queen continued, "I am assured that there is no cause what-so-ever to doubt that they are genuine."

"They are from the private collection of King James himself," boasted Howison, knowing it to be untrue.

"It is inspiring to see the words of Noory McGregor written on the page by his own hand, revealing his deepest thoughts to the reader."

"We have gazed at his words in awe, countless times, Your Majesty," Dalry invented.

"He had a fine hand," she replied, gazing at the page she held, "Intricate and yet, at the same time, somehow quite simple."

They waited as the queen browsed through the contents of the crimson leather wallet they had presented to her.

"There are, Your Majesty, another fifteen volumes of Noory McGregor's works," he intruded.

She nodded, absentmindedly, seemingly absorbed by a particular volume.

"It is fascinating," she declared, "To see the pages written alternately in Gaelic and English, one language on the even pages and the other on the odd."

"A man of many quirks and foibles," suggested Howison.

"He was, but he had a fine mind," she insisted.

"Yes, a fine mind, indeed," agreed Howison.

Dalry opened his mouth to add his own opinion, but Howison waved a hand to discourage him. Dalry remained silent.

"As I have already mentioned, Your Majesty, we have brought with us a very particular document from the royal court for you to examine."

"From King James, you said?"

"Yes, from the king and bearing his signature, with ribbon and seal."

"You saw him put his signature to the document?"

"I did, indeed," lied Howison, "And, having done so, he handed it to me, himself."

"You are close to King James?"

"No, I would not claim be, Your Majesty, but I have a cousin who serves at the Royal Court and it was he who recommended me when the king was seeking a trusted courier for a particularly important job."

"How did you come to be travelling with the big Irishman and the two young girls?"

"A haphazard arrangement, Your Majesty. It came about due to a lapse in our better judgement," Howison pretended, "When the possibility of our travelling together presented itself, it seemed to be a great deal more practical than it turned out to be."

The queen looked at him with an unyielding, penetrating gaze. It was accompanied by the vaguest trace of a smile. Howison became uneasy under her scrutiny. His explanation, he decided, had sounded far more believable when he had been making it up in his head than it did when it came out of his mouth.

"Your little band appears to have had a falling out."

"Yes, it did. We caught the Irishman cheating at cards. We challenged him and he took it badly. Later, he took us by surprise and attacked us."

"That is not the version of events that my scouts brought me," the queen replied, dubiously.

Howison had to fight to control his expression. He had not thought that he would have been caught out so easily.

"The truth is that we were a little more to blame than I have made out" Howison declared, "The dispute over the card game wasn't today, but yesterday evening. We taunted him about it a little too spitefully and a little too long."

The queen frowned at him.

"We told ourselves that it was simple playful teasing," he continued, "But, to be completely frank, it was no such thing. In the end, our words proved to be too cruel and his temper too frail, and he flung himself at us in a fit of rage."

The Queen of the West gave him a long, steady look that felt to Howison as if it lasted for an hour.

"Very well," she said, clapping her hands, "Let me sign the king's treaty."

Just out of sight, a servant – who had been hovering attentively – sped off to fetch the queen's advisor. A minute or so later, the advisor arrived bearing the parchment and spread it out flat on the table before the queen, weighting it down at each corner with a cube of iron.

With elaborate formality, the advisor placed a heavy square of crimson cloth on the table and arranged on top of it a spirit burner, a tiny ladle, a block of blood red wax, a flask of yellow fluid and an ornate knife with a deer antler handle. Removing the lid from the flask, he used it to measure out a portion of fuel for the burner and poured it into the device with a funnel that looked as if it belonged in a dolls house. Using a spill of wood, he carried a flame from the fire in the hearth to the burner and lit it. Next, he carved off a little chunk of wax from the block and placed it carefully into the ladle. He, then, added a cube of resin to it. Happy with the proportions of the mix, he placed the ladle into a holder atop the burner.

The advisor, with great ceremony, took out a sturdy black box covered with intricate carvings and removed from it a writing quill, a bottle of blue-black ink, a bottle of red ink, a short length of red ribbon and a pen knife. With great care, he first sharpened the quill and then cut a triangular notch into the bottom of the ribbon. Dipping the quill into the blue-black ink, he shook off the surplus drops and handed it, reverently, to the queen. She took it and, with a sure, steady hand, applied the words *Annis, Rex, AD1622* at the foot of the paper.

The advisor waited, seeming to count away the seconds, before producing from the box a polished piece of wood that was shaped like a quarter section from a wheel of cheese. Along its rounded surface was a pad of felt. He place this object on the parchment, directly over the signature, and rocked it back and forth to absorb any surplus ink.

The advisor reached back into the box and took out a heavy rod of metal, unscrewing a cap from its end. The queen took the object from him and examined it. Happy with what she saw, she held it in the open palm of her hand.

The advisor took from the box a pair of brass hoops that looked like they might fit over a pair of very fat fingers. He positioned one of the hoops flat on the parchment, beside the royal signature, and poured the, now, liquid wax from the ladle into it. After waiting a precise amount of time, he deftly removed the hoop and placed the upper half of the crimson ribbon into the still soft wax. Placing the second hoop over it, he poured another quantity of wax into it.

With great precision, which she had practised over and over, the queen gripped the metal rod like an enormous pen and pressed it down on top of the wax. She held it in position for precisely fifteen seconds before lifting it away.

As everyone gathered there knew, the signature of a monarch was one thing, but the seal of a monarch was another. The seal was far more the monarch's identity than any mere mark of ink on parchment.

She waited for the wax of the seal to set then, taking up a fresh quill, dipped it in the red ink. To the complete and utter horror of Howison and Dalry, she drew a bold red line around the words of the agreement, forming a scarlet perimeter, and looped it into her signature.

Howison and Dalry looked as if they had been punched in the belly, slapped in the face and poked in both eyes.

CHAPTER 51

Michael Deedigan wiped his mouth with a very plain and ordinary napkin then, leaning back in his very plain and ordinary chair back from the very plain ordinary oak table, embraced his belly with both hands and let out a satisfied groan.

"Food fit for the gods!" he declared.

"Wonderful food, wonderfully cooked," answered Logan.

"It was completely delicious," Wild Flower agreed.

"If I ate another morsel, I would burst," Deedigan warned, seeming to relish the idea.

Suddenly he froze, whirled to stare at Wild Flower and reached out with the flat of his hand to gingerly press it against her face. His hand made contact with flesh and blood.

"You are here!" he cried.

"I am" she confirmed.

"Yet we left you behind, with my grandfather," said Logan.

"Things have changed."

"In what way?"

"Heather and Finlay MacDonald are too sensitive to things beyond this realm. I had to deliver myself here in body for risk of them discovering me to be an apparition."

"You can do that?" asked Deedigan.

"I am discovering my limits," Wild Flower grinned, "And they are not as limited as I believed them to be."

Spontaneously resuming their conversation about food, they chattered for several minutes, exchanging their favourable impressions on those things they had particularly enjoyed and their common approval of everything they had eaten.

"Magnificent food," Deedigan observed, "But served in very humble surroundings."

"There is much splendour here," Logan replied, "But, outside of it, there is a theme of unassuming modesty."

"The queen has indulged in opulence and grandeur only where it serves to impress her guests and project her status to them in the way they expect to see it," Wild Flower responded, "But everywhere else, we see nothing but restraint."

"The furniture and fittings beyond the public areas are well made and in good taste," said Logan, "But none of it is expensive. I find it to be very refreshing."

"Your grandfather spent far more money on the decorating of his stronghouse than has been spent here," Deedigan marvelled.

"As I have said," Logan replied, "I find it refreshing."

"Her Majesty regards every coin spent on this palace as one less coin spent on the welfare of the poor," Wild Flower told them, with a slight edge to her voice.

Deedigan took her admonishment in good humour.

"It is not a criticism," he insisted, "But an observation. I was wondering how this place compares to the dwellings of her lairds? I feel sure that most of them will have spared little expense on their own homes. I wonder how her rejection of luxury chimes with their apparent love of it?"

"I am sure there are those who will not be happy about it," Logan suggested.

"There are those who go beyond that," Wild Flower replied, "And who are hostile to it."

"And, yet, she does not bend to them," said Deedigan, admiration in his tone.

"She does what she believes to be right," Wild Flower assured him, "As her mother always did."

"I can think of two people who are only too happy to do wrong, all the way from morning until night," suggested Logan.

Her reference to Howison and Dalry was not lost on her companions.

"They may be dining with the queen," Deedigan assured them, "But they won't be eating any better than us."

Logan looked at her plate, "You're right. This was absolutely delicious food. In fact, this meal was superb."

In reply, Wild Flower closed her eyes for a moment.

"We have eaten exactly the same food as they have eaten," she revealed, "Merely from plainer plates and with simpler cutlery."

Deedigan's face fell and he looked offended.

"I am done with this!" he growled, thumping his fist on the table.

Logan and Wild Flower, jumped at the sudden noise, turned to him in surprise.

"I will not sit idly by while those two weave their mischief," he continued, "For I would never have a night of peaceful sleep, again, for the rest of my life if I did."

CHAPTER 52

Howison and Dalry had spent the afternoon and early evening in their appointed chambers, mostly in the two mutually accessible areas that linked them. They drank whiskey, smoked cigars and played an endless succession of card games. They had finally migrated to the day room, where they sat themselves on the opulent couches, both wearing the splendid dressing gowns provided by the queen's staff.

Howison leaned close to Dalry, placing his mouth beside the other's ear.

"That is it, then," he hissed, "We have no option. She has to die."

Dalry nodded his agreement, "When she drew a red line around the wording of the document..."

"Yes," fumed Howison, not bothering to let him finish his sentence, "I almost leapt out of my seat and hit her!"

Dalry's face fell and he raised a hand in caution, "There are more guards here than a dog has fleas," he warned.

"That may be so, but some things are almost worth the doing, no matter what the cost!"

The two stewed in their thoughts for a little while before Dalry seemed to remember something.

"You have the ring?" he enquired.

"Aye, I do, indeed."

Howison raised a hand and wagged the finger on which he wore it.

"There is enough poison in this to slay a bull," he declared.

"Then we will be rid of her."

"We will, indeed," he replied holding up his palm, then flopping it forward to indicate a person falling to the ground.

Dalry silently applauded.

Howison stretched back to rest his head against the wall behind him and slapped his belly. The motion spurred a comment from Dalry.

"If the midday meal we ate is any kind of a measure," he said, "Then the evening meal that we are just about to have is going to be completely wonderful. We are going to dine like kings!"

"They do muster a fair spread," Howison replied, grudgingly.

"If you have eaten any better than this, at any time in your life and anywhere that you have been, then I would be most surprised indeed."

Howison's face tightened. He was very much averse to criticism. Just then, a gong sounded, somewhere far off. Both men rose to their feet, took off the robes the queen's staff had provided and threw them dismissively and discourteously to the floor.

At the door, the queen's butler greeted them, studiously pretending not to notice the two garments so contemptuously cast aside, and escorted them to their dinner with the queen in her private dining room.

CHAPTER 53

The evening meal was magnificent. Even Howison seemed to be impressed, though he made great effort to hide it. Dalry, however, was charming in his compliments on the fare. This drew a look of acrid rebuke from his companion.

The queen was gracious and regal and ate delicately with impeccable refinement. This reminded Dalry of the more modest aristocratic ladies of King James' royal court. The ones who did not worship themselves in the mirror at every opportunity and who did not constantly preen themselves at every break in a meal.

Dalry regretted that they were about to kill her. Howison appeared to have no such qualms. From the look in his eye – a look with which Dalry was familiar – he was relishing the secret that she was unwittingly dining with her executioner.

If the guards posted around the chamber had discerned anything that was inappropriate about Howison's demeanour, they did not betray it. They were vigilant – their eyes everywhere at once – but they were not on edge. They were all young, Dalry noted. Not one of them could have been over thirty.

Padraic Howison had also appraised the queen's guards. He had also noted their ages. He had also noted their constant vigilance. He had noted their stance and evident readiness for anything that might happen. Unlike Dalry, however, he had not been fooled by them. Padraic Howison had known, within moments, that these men were frauds. These men were not the queen's personal guards. More importantly, nobody in the room was her close bodyguard.

CHAPTER 54

The meal progressed with only occasional conversation that was always eminently suitable, restrained and thoroughly polite. They talked about absolutely nothing in particular and said not one word of any actual importance. The charade that played out was a familiar one to all involved. They all feigned interest but took no interest. They all laughed or chuckled at the right moments, but found no humour in anything that was said. It was as if they were actors in a play, all well versed in their lines and familiar with their cues.

Howison looked around nonchalantly. He knew for a fact that the three men who served them food, were not actual servants. They would be specially chosen guards with prowess in combat at close quarters. Howison could see the carefully concealed daggers they carried and had been able to make out the subtle outline of the stilettos hidden in their sleeves. Their hands, he observed, were not soft enough nor their grip weak enough, to be simple table staff. Howison knew all three of them to be a threat to his plans.

Around and about them, skilfully pervading an air of bored detachment, stood the other guards. They were, Howison knew, not at all bored and not the least bit detached. They were alert. While none of them were tense, every one of them was in a state of readiness. Mostly relying on reflections in mirrors, glass doors and ornaments, Howison studied them, with very infrequent covert glances. He was certain that none of the men had the kind of muscles that came from long hours of hard practice wielding a full sized claymores and battle shield at arm's length.

'Where are your real bodyguards?' Howison asked himself, unable to subdue his curiosity.

As the meal drew, eventually, to a close, Howison found his mind working furiously to determine his best options.

The big Irishman, whom he hated, and the two girls would, he knew, be dreaming peacefully. They would all be sprawled out on the woven furniture positioned on the stone-paved frontage of the stronghouse. This was Dalry's doing. Dalry had carefully cultivated a superficial friendship with the queen's butler and – as Howison had been reading studiously in the vast library – he had managed to apply a very special sleeping draft to the ale of Michael Deedigan and to the lemon water of Logan and Wild Flower. This potion was slow to work, but was very precise and very predictable. He knew that it would have only taken effect within the last twenty minutes. He was sure that, because all of their party were honoured guests, the royal staff would have made no effort to wake them. Out of politeness, they would have done no more than light the brazier and cover the three of them with blankets or rugs.

Waiting for the queen to rise from the table first, Howison and Dalry then got to their feet and bowed deeply to her. She acknowledged the gesture with the merest hint of a nod.

Moving around the table, Howison – with the precision and accuracy of a surgeon – caught a jug of wine with his cuff and sent it toppling to knock over the queen's own chalice. He quickly shouted for a nearby junior maid to attend them and barked for more wine. Deftly setting the queen's cup back upright, he poured more wine for her from the fresh jug brought by the panicked servant.

The party moved away from the table – leaving the spillage to be mopped up by a gaggle of house staff – and headed in a sedate procession to the queen's evening room. Wordlessly taking the queen's wine from her, a guard – posing as a servant – looked at it suspiciously and furtively poured it away. Replenishing it from the jug from the dining table – that was now following them, carried close behind by a page boy – the soldier covertly handed it back to the queen. Howison missed nothing.

When they sat down, Howison gave Dalry the tiniest of winks, then tapped the ring that had contained the poison against his cheek, confirming that the deed had been done.

As they sat before the crackling blaze of a log fire in the hearth, the queen described the hunting available in the nearby forests. Presently, she began to recount stories of her feats of archery, telling how she had taken quarry with uncanny accuracy at formidable distances and describing her daring riding, where she had leapt her horse over walls, ditches and streams. Howison and Dalry, after pretending to be duly impressed, replied with their own stories of hunting boar, landing huge fish, and of camping out on high mountain tops in screeching gales.

Their little group would alternately either completely neglect or obsessively indulge in the boardgame that sat between them. The game was played on black, white, red and blue squares. It was one of skill and tactics and involved simultaneously moving pieces on the outside perimeter of the playing board and around the inside squares. Howison and Dalry, familiar with a version of the game played in London, were faring slightly worse against the queen that either of them was happy to admit.

Dalry kept a careful scrutiny on the queen and an even more careful scrutiny on Howison. Looking at him at every opportunity that presented itself – congratulating him on a good move or commiserating when he lost one of his pieces – Dalry was vigilant for any hint or sign of how the poisoning of the Queen of the West was progressing. He had no doubt that she had taken the poison, but was unsure exactly how it would work on her.

From his demeanour, Howison seemed to be perfectly happy with the situation. At one point, the queen blinked and screwed up her eyes for a moment, seeming to be abruptly fatigued. Then, she recovered herself and continued speaking and playing with no adverse effects.

Dalry looked at the jug of wine, then at the queen's cup, then back and forth between his own and Howison's cups. These receptacles had been moved aside and then returned to their positions several times, both by the queen and by her closest 'servant', as the board game had been unpacked from its box. This didn't seem to sit well with him. Howison could tell that Dalry was confused and this prompted a flicker of a smile on his lips. The queen presumed that this fleeting expression related to a cunning move he was contemplating and paid it no heed.

All of a sudden, Dalry felt himself fall forward for an instant. It was as if he had blacked out, but only for a fraction of a second. He had easily caught himself, but it made him feel uneasy. Howison looked concerned.

"Are you unwell?" asked Howison.

"No, no, I am fine," Dalry lied, a little too quickly, "I think it is just the heat from the fire."

The queen looked from one man to the other, her face utterly placid. The blankness and detachment she conveyed made Dalry nervous. Howison looked at the queen a moment too long, causing her to raise an eyebrow at him. It was plain to her that something was on his mind. She absentmindedly licked the corner of her lip, tasting a droplet of wine. It was more tart than it ought to have been, she decided. She dismissed this as the grapes having possibly been picked a week too early and not having been given time to ripen to perfection. Howison saw her do it and caught the glimmer of her thought. She did not fail to notice the concern in his eyes. Dalry picked up on this silent exchange and worried some more. He saw the queen look from one to the other of them, again, just as she had done before. Her face was the absolute replica of what it had been before: utter placidity.

Abruptly, Howison caught his breath. The queen ignored him. Dalry shot him a glance. Howison fought back the urge to swallow and cleared his throat.

"Are you well?" asked the queen, softly.

Dalry didn't like the way she had said it. There was something about how she spoke the words. An odd emphasis on one of the syllables? No, perhaps there hadn't. He may not have been listening properly, he told himself. It was his mind playing tricks. Or was it?

Howison waved a hand, fending off the queen's question, seeming the slightest bit irritated by it.

"I am good," he assured her, "It is nothing."

She gave him a long, steady look. This unnerved Dalry. It had the same effect on Howison before he caught himself. Dalry looked nervously between the cups of wine, again. He felt his head swim.

"You're wondering, aren't you?" the queen asked.

"What?" said Dalry, alarmed.

"You're wondering if you acted unwisely."

Dalry flinched at her words and looked alarmed. What did she know? Did she suspect something?

"The game," said the queen, a hint of mockery in her voice, "You were questioning the wisdom of your last move."

Dalry felt reassured, but couldn't manage to fully convince himself of it. The queen smiled. The smile was ever so slightly sly. Or was it? Dalry wasn't certain. He watched her lick the corner of her mouth, again, but not with one tongue, this time, but with two. Dalry jolted. What was this? She seemed to be becoming a serpent, then the transformation stopped and retreated? Did she still have a forked tongue? Abruptly, he began to see two her, sat side by side. He felt a sudden wave of nausea.

"Or," she asked, "Are you wondering which cup you have? Am I right? Was it the one you had to begin with, or is it not?"

While Dalry swayed in his seat, Howison looked at her cooly and grimly. He knew that he had the upper hand. He was proud of himself. His tactic had not, in fact, been to poison the queen, but to poison them *all*. The queen would soon die. He and Dalry, meanwhile, had already taken the antidote. Dalry had taken it without his knowledge and, apparently, had not received quite enough of it. Rather than merely feeling queasy for a while, he was starting to display seriously ill effects.

Dalry had turned pale and was struggling to breathe. Without warning, he pulled out a long dagger and thrust it towards the queen, aiming for her heart. His aim was awry. Groggy and suffering grievously, he had been unable to make up his mind which one of her to assassinate and had guessed wrong. The queen, who had swiftly moved out of range, stood up and stepped back from the table. As she did so, her 'servant' raced at Dalry, reaching him in three strides. Whirling, Dalry aimed his blade at the third head of the four-headed servant that assailed him. It was a lucky guess. His dagger glanced off the man's jaw, pierced his throat and came out of the back of his neck. The lunge had been a powerful one. It had been the final frantic effort of a man in the last throes of life. They both slumped to the floor, writhing slower and slower, until they stopped and didn't move again.

Howison was on his feet in flash, quickly drawing out from inside his jacket a strangely limp blade that flopped like the tongue of an ox. Lifting it up, then snapping down, as if cracking a whip, it made a sharp metallic *thwack* before becoming perfectly straight and rigid.

Howison thanked his luck that the queen's second 'servant' had chanced to step out on some errand. Howison was conscious that he would likely return at any moment. Now, he knew, he must clash steel with the woman who was famed and feared as one of the fastest and most deadly blades ever known.

As he stepped towards her, she had already mysteriously lofted a sword. It must have been hidden close at hand for her use, he observed. She was extremely quick on her feet and, almost effortlessly, had nimbly positioned herself to put two of the huge armchairs between them.

"A woman with a sword!" Howison gasped in mock surprise, "Such a pathetic sight. Everyone knows that the female wrist is too weak to wield one to any good effect."

She did not reply, but he saw the merest hint of nervousness in her eye. Perhaps this Queen of the West was not as sure of her skills as she pretended to be? Perhaps, as he had always assumed, the stories about her had been exaggerated. He decided to be cautious. He needed to be fully alert. He did not want to let himself be drawn into a trap.

He circled a couple of steps to his left. She mirrored his move, stepping to her right. He needed to rid himself of the two armchairs between them. He glanced down. It was a fleeting moment, but he saw her sword rise the slightest bit, as if she had considered making a move. He held her eye, but strenuously concentrated his mind on what was in front and below him. Almost surprising himself, he reached and threw the nearest armchair aside. In a flash, her sword tip flew towards him, forcing him to turn his head aside to avoid being skewered by it.

She was fast, he admitted, but maybe not as fast as he would have expected. Was this still a bluff? Was she inviting him to underestimate her?

Howison danced first to one side, then to the other. She responded perfectly, shifting her weight from her left leg to her right while turning herself to maintain the narrowest of targets.

Howison took a step forward. She took a step backward. Howison took another step forward, followed by a half step. She took a single step backwards and then lifted the point of her sword to be level with his throat, refusing to yield further. Howison's weight was on his forward leg. Her weight was evenly balanced. He stepped back, sensing her lunge rather than predicting it. Her sword came too close for comfort to his cheek, but – he was disappointed to note – she resisted the temptation to overextend.

Howison moved slowly from side to side, trying to get a feel for a moment to attack. To his surprise she took a long step towards him and slashed across his body, turning sideways as she did so, her blade finding only air as he hopped away from her.

Her style of movement, Howison decided, was not classical, nor did it reflect a particular discipline. Instead, he was convinced, she was following a fighting style that came from the battlefield. It was daring and unrestrained. She was every bit as comfortable attacking as she was defending. This made him feel a little wary. It was like fighting a man. He stopped himself. What was that thought? What had he just gone through his mind? He had only *ever* fought men! Why would it be otherwise? What use had a woman with a sword?

She came at him again. This time, she touched him. He managed to dodge away, but he felt her cold steel. It made contact, flat against his ear, as he stepped out of its path.

Howison took a deep breath and steadied himself. He was not going to allow her to gain the upper hand. She was a woman. He was a man. It was ridiculous enough that he was having a sword fight with a mere female, but he was not going to let his outrage at such an imposition impact on his skill and ability.

Recovering himself, he drove her back repeatedly, almost pushing her into a corner before she advanced against him – employing a ferocity he found disturbing – with a perfectly executed sequence of well-rehearsed moves, each flowing seamlessly into the next. If she had been a man, he would have been impressed, but she was less than a man, so he was contemptuous.

With his lip curled, he replied with a splendid display of classic swordcraft, powerfully lunging and cutting, as he regained the lost ground. He was dismayed to find that she let him rush at her with no attempt to counter him. Instead, keeping just out of range, she let him expend his energy to little or no effect.

Howison was puzzled. Was she toying with him? Were her abilities with a blade far beyond what she had permitted him to discover? He started to tire of the cat and mouse situation. With a sudden explosion of aggression, he quickly stepped within close striking distance and subjected her to a blizzard of attacking moves. He was pleased to see that, at one point, she floundered at his onslaught. She was *not* as good as her reputation boasted!

Now breathing heavily, he drove on, interspersing sharp jabs and low cuts with sweeping slashes. Unfortunately, she knew the position of furniture in the room with absolute precision. As he attempted to force her into objects, she would frustrate him by stepping aside and avoiding collision with an almost uncanny ability.

With a sudden surge of satisfaction, he realised that she was tiring. So was he, but not quite so quickly. If he kept up his attack, he knew, she would weaken to the point of vulnerability. Her recoveries and moves to stop or push him back became fewer and fewer.

He could tell from her eyes that she knew that she was doomed and that defeat was now inevitable.

With steel ringing and both now straining and gasping, Howison finally forced her into making a mistake, as her foot slipped he leapt at his chance and kicked her to the ground. As she fell, he pounced forward and managed to deliver a cut to her cheek. As she crumpled, she struck her head on the edge of the table. She tried to get up, but fell back, dazed.

Against his better judgement, Padraic Howison relished the sight of her helpless form.

"Time to die!" he cooed.

CHAPTER 55

Logan Grant's eyes sprang open as she jolted awake and sat up in bed. She had a sense of panic. There was something wrong. In all her twenty years of life, she had never disregarded her instincts. She was not going to disregard them, now.

She took a deep breath. There was something to be done. She knew it.

Beside her, her husband, Collym, grunted and turned over, putting his back to her.

Logan laid back down, her head nestling into the pillow and closed her eyes. As if the mattress were froth and bubbles, she allowed herself to descend, sinking deeper and deeper into the warm embrace of a world that existed in another time.

CHAPTER 56

Padraic Howison blinked in surprise, then froze, his nerves jangling. They were no longer alone in the room.

It was almost as if the man had taken form out of the very air. He was tall. He was athletic. His approach was completely undaunted, with the lithe, powerful movements of a mountain wildcat. His gait was fluid, very nearly feminine, and his feet made no sound.

Howison was immediately taken aback by the man's cool confidence and felt a little uneasy at his piercing golden eyes.

The hairs on Howison's arms sprang up, causing his skin to prickle and twitch.

The newcomer didn't look at the queen on the floor, instead concentrating fully on the assailant who had put her there. Howison felt himself gulp and swallow.

"Who are you?" Howison demanded gruffly, then added, for no reason he could fathom, "*What* are you?"

The man smiled. He was clearly amused.

"What," he replied, "Is the better question of the two."

"I am going to kill you," Howison responded, defiantly.

His opponent smiled, again, even more amused.

"No you're not. You're going to die."

Without a further word, Howison moved to attack. The stranger effortlessly parried his blow. Howison struck harder, aiming for the heart. His blade met empty air as the other, with the grace of a dancer, skipped to the side.

Howison renewed his attempts to connect with his enemy, cutting and slashing and thrusting but his every effort was rewarded with failure.

Howison began to draw back his sword. The man leapt to stand beside him and put his blade against Howison's to restrain it. Howison slid his weapon free and moved to strike again, but – just as before – it was met with the other's blade, holding it back.

Howison snarled with annoyance.

"Give up!" the man implored.

"I will not!" Howison protested, indignantly, "Though I have never met your match before."

The golden eyes narrowed, "On a good day, I could very likely fight the Queen of the West to a draw."

"Her?" scoffed Howison, "You are wine. The queen is piss!"

Her golden eyes twinkled and the Flashing Blade gave a wicked grin, "The Queen of the West marches with her army to Boat of Garten. She left two days ago."

"What?" cried Howison, looking to the girl on the floor.

The girl struggled to her feet and bowed.

"I," she declared, "Am here to fool the foolish."

Howison looked horrified.

His horror stayed on his face.

His horror stayed even as his head was cut from his shoulders.

His horror did not fade until the light of life extinguished from his eyes as his head rolled to a stop on the floor.